LISETTE AUTON

The Stickleback Catchers

Illustrated by
Valentina Toro

PUFFIN

PUFFIN BOOKS

UK | USA | Canada | Ireland | Australia
India | New Zealand | South Africa

Puffin Books is part of the Penguin Random House group of companies
whose addresses can be found at global.penguinrandomhouse.com

www.penguin.co.uk   www.puffin.co.uk   www.ladybird.co.uk

First published 2023

001

Text copyright © Lisette Auton, 2023
Cover illustration copyright © Gillian Gamble, 2023
Interior illustrations copyright © Valentina Toro, 2023

The Secret of Haven Point extract: text copyright © Lisette Auton, 2022; cover illustration
copyright © Gillian Gamble, 2022; illustrations copyright © Valentina Toro, 2022

The moral right of the author and illustrators has been asserted

Set in 12.5/18.5pt Bembo Book MT Std
Typeset by Jouve (UK), Milton Keynes
Printed and bound in Great Britain by Clays Ltd, Elcograf S.p.A.

The authorized representative in the EEA is Penguin Random House Ireland,
Morrison Chambers, 32 Nassau Street, Dublin D02 YH68

A CIP catalogue record for this book is available from the British Library

ISBN: 978–0–241–52205–9

All correspondence to:
Puffin Books
Penguin Random House Children's
One Embassy Gardens, 8 Viaduct Gardens, London SW11 7BW

This book is dedicated to my grandparents:
Iolene & Allan Mill, and Mary & George Grout.
Thank you. I love you. I miss you.

Prologue

Above a river in a small wood in a small town, the sort of place that could be anywhere and nowhere, the sort of place where nothing ever happens, the sky breaks open.

A crack of thunder roars, and the river water is sucked up into a funnel. When it smashes back down, it churns and tumbles like it's been caught in a whirlpool until it finally settles once more.

But now the river is flowing backwards.

It rushes and arches above the riverbed, making a tunnel.

A small girl with plaits and crutches places a green glass bottle by her feet. She looks around, as if waiting for someone to join her. She shrugs. Alone, she walks determinedly down the riverbank, and, with no hesitation, she steps under the mighty arch of water on to the dry riverbed.

The river crashes back down on top of her, flattening out and swallowing her, and confused ducks and debris float in the wrong direction.

A feather tumbles lazily down through the air.

A crow swoops and gathers it in its beak. Then it flies away as if nothing unusual has happened.

Chapter One

A month earlier

'Hello!' I yell, barging through the front door of the bowls club and up the stairs to our flat.

I catch my bright yellow bee-print crutches on the corner of the rug. I lose my balance and tip backwards, scrambling to stay upright, but save myself just in time by leaning to the left to avoid getting my school rucksack jammed in the radiator (which is what happened yesterday – I was stuck like a dangling beetle for seven whole minutes cos Gran wanted to watch the end of *Bargain Hunt*).

There's a loud crash as I collide with the radiator.

I wait for Grandad to yell, 'Enjoy your trip, Mimi?'

Nothing. That's weird. He never misses an opportunity to make a terrible joke.

I wait another moment for Gran to shout at me for shortening the door's lifespan by slamming it. But there's not a bean. Proper mystery.

I smile as I toss my rucksack into the corner of the hallway. I *like* mysteries. I think I'd be very good at solving them. My bag scoots into the antique coat stand – *Oh, I'm in proper bother if I break a precious thing!* I hold my breath and squint as it teeters and wobbles and almost clatters into the dresser with Gran's posh bits on –

– but not quite.

Phew.

The only casualty is a black suit jacket that slides off the coat stand and lands on the floor in a crumpled heap.

Who on earth does that belong to? All our coats are very proudly jumble sale. This one looks shiny, like one a magpie would choose. I hang up my bright red raincoat and make sure the sleeves aren't concertinaed up inside (things have to be right).

No one's even come to check if I'm OK after my crash. Thanks a bunch. It's not like I bash into things on purpose: it's all a matter of hands. When you use crutches like I do, things tend to be a little more thuddy.

We *always* do the routine when I get in from school. It goes like this:

Gran shouts at me about banging the door, and I yell back, 'Crutches!'

She says, 'No excuse,' and tries to stick my fringe down and tidy up my plaits.

Then Grandad comes out and goes, 'Here, Mimi, this'll do it,' and pretends to spit on his hand to slick my hair down. We do the biscuits-on-a-bridge joke routine and noisily bounce into the kitchen for Gran's lemon meringue pie, and they both ask about my day at school.

But . . . no one comes out to greet me. No routine today.

Does that mean that the black suit jacket is *bad news*?

Last time there was a suit jacket in the hall, it was a social worker and a 'we just need to keep an eye on the situation, what with the progressing age of your grandparents, but there's nothing to worry about' chat. Obviously, as soon as someone says that, it makes me do *all* the worries.

I prod the jacket with my crutch and leave a muddy circle on it. I lean my crutches against the radiator cover that was once painted red but is now a faded, scratched pink. I creep towards the Room for Best; that's where the visitor will be. I press my ear up against the closed door.

It's a top-banana idea to check whether a door is properly closed before you start spying.

I do not do that.

The door bursts open, and I tumble through and land in a heap on the swirly, multicoloured carpet.

'Nice of you to join us,' says Grandad. 'You OK? Enjoy your trip?'

Now he says it!

I swipe my hair from my eyes and stick my tongue out at him.

The person who must be the owner of the jacket is sitting on the upright wooden chair, next to Gran and Grandad on the posh settee. Grandad keeps taking his unlit pipe out of his mouth, tapping it on his knee and putting it back in again. He hasn't smoked since 1973! And he only does the pipe-tap routine when he's worried, or someone talks about money. Bert says Grandad has a wallet full of moths.

Then I realize they've taken the plastic cover off the posh settee.

This must be very important.

Is it *worryingly* important?

Gran is dabbing her eyes with a hankie. I peer at her. 'Rheumy,' she says. Which is the word older people use when they have wet eyes.

'Would you like any assistance?' asks Mr Suit, and I realize I'm still in my heap, and I've been doing lots of thinking, which I don't always realize I'm doing, and then I come back to earth and find people staring at me.

I shake my head and crawl over to sit on the floor in front of Gran and Grandad, keeping my eyes on the man. He looks creepy, like if you blinked he'd be able to zip across the room and be right up in your face and staring at you when you open your eyes.

I must not blink until he leaves.

No one introduces him to me. Well then, I'll do it myself.

'Hello,' I say. 'I'm Mimi Evergreen.'

He opens his mouth to speak, and Gran yells out, 'He's an accountant!' just as Grandad yells, 'He's not a social worker!'

Mr Suit goes to say something and then thinks better of it, pursing his lips and folding his hands carefully, then placing them in his lap.

Gran and Grandad both reach for me and each place a hand on my shoulders at exactly the same time.

I know summat is up, and I start to tell them so when suddenly there's a pressure in my ears, like when you go through a tunnel on a train. I slam my hands over them. I squish my eyes tight closed because it makes my tummy feel all woozy, and I think I might be sick. When I open them again, my heart beats faster in my chest, *boom-boom-boom*, faster still – and, as I watch, a crack appears along the wall above the mantelpiece. Like someone has just drawn a jittering line in marker pen.

I can't believe what I'm seeing. Damp cold oozes out of the crack. I do a whole body shudder, and my skin feels like it might crawl off my arms.

'Look!' I whisper, and point. Gran turns round, peers behind the corner lamp with the yellow tassels and says, 'At the ballerina ornament? No need to bring our visitor's attention to the chip in its tutu. What will he think of us!' She giggles and looks coy and nervous and wrong all at the same time.

What? Can't she see the crack?

But when I point to it again, it's gone. *What on earth? Did I imagine it?* But it's left my crawling skin feeling greasy and green, like I need a bath.

Grandad shakes his head at me and rolls his eyes, then

says, 'The *accountant* was just leaving,' and gets up and walks over to hold open the door I fell through.

Mr Suit does not immediately follow but stares at Gran and cocks his head, like he's waiting for her to say something. She doesn't. Mr Suit stands and walks towards me.

Do not blink. Do not blink. Do not blink.

He crouches in front of me. I can still smell the damp in my nostrils, and I can't tell if it's coming off him too.

'It was lovely to meet you, Mimi Evergreen,' says Mr Suit the accountant who isn't a social worker, and he smiles. 'I'm sure I'll see you again.'

'Why?' I ask. 'What if I don't want to see you again?'

'Mimi!' says Gran sternly, and prods me for good measure. 'Don't be so rude.'

'Well, Mimi,' says Mr Suit, 'some things are just . . . inevitable.'

He winks at me, and I can feel the pressure in my ears again. He holds my gaze too long, and I think he's going to say something else, but he doesn't. He puts his hand on Gran's hand, which is still on my shoulder, and I can feel the weight of both of them pressing down on me. I turn to look at her again, and out of the corner of my eye I see another crack appear along the wall. I can actually see it forming, juddering and breaking like a glitchy spiderweb.

Not just breaking, *breathing*.

Suddenly *I* can't breathe.

'Gran, look . . . !'

'Not this again, pet.'

'The —' But when I go to point, it's vanished again. Not even the faintest trace on the wall.

I need to focus on facts, stop my brain looping and spiralling out of control. I turn to Mr Suit, who is heading out of the door. 'Look, are you actually really here about subsidence?' I ask him. He looks very confused (maybe he didn't learn the word in geography) so I explain it to him. 'Subsidence is when the ground shifts and causes damage to buildings.'

He opens his mouth, then closes it. It's still not sinking in for him, so I say, 'Wouldn't they usually send an insurance person? If this is about the cracks?'

At exactly the same time as he's opening his mouth to reply, Gran says, 'Yes,' and Grandad says, 'No,' and then Grandad grins at me and yanks Mr Suit the accountant's arm and hauls him out of the room.

I turn to face Gran and cock my head at her.

'Well, he's a funny one, isn't he?' she says and then giggles.

Her laugh always makes me laugh, even when I don't want to. I try to hold it in and put on my miserable face and say, 'No,' but when I say the word a giggle sneaks out, which I definitely didn't want to happen, but it does. Gran always has that effect on people. Smiles pop out even when you're not expecting them.

'No!' I say again, trying to keep my face all serious, but this time I snort too, which makes Gran laugh more, and then Grandad comes back into the room and asks, 'What's so funny?' which is obviously not a funny question, but for some reason it really is, and Gran and I laugh and laugh until I can't breathe, and I have to waft my hands around to help, and then we all go into the kitchen and lay the table for tea, but I can't help looking over my shoulder to check for cracks.

Chapter Two

Bright sunshine pours through my curtains and wakes me. It warms me up and removes the last of the feeling of green that the cracks left behind.

Are the cracks really real?

The Puzzler would never doubt themself. So I won't either.

The cracks are real.

I put on one of my favourite *Puzzler* episodes for the seventeenth time, one about an old house that had messages in mould growing inside it. I'm properly obsessed with this awesome podcast. The host, the Puzzler, solves mysteries and talks about ancient puzzles. The podcast logo is a jigsaw piece and, inside, it says THE PUZZLER in purple capital letters.

The mystery of the cracks is Puzzler-tastic. Bet if I solve it they'll interview me. Or ask me to be a co-host! *Get in!*

I stretch and bash my toes on the wall. My bedroom is the size of my bed, which is right up against the window, with enough extra width for the door to open. Just. There's a white built-in wardrobe on a sort of hollow shelf because the stairs are underneath. My knick-knacks live in there, like my travelling conker collection (I always keep a different one in my pocket), my Cawlington Bottling Co bottles from the old factory opposite, where Grandad used to work, my four-leaf clover, and a piece of rock that looks like Grandad.

I pop my head under the curtains and have to do a triple blink to get used to the glare outside. I can see our bowling green, a sunken flat rectangle, sharply mowed, not a weed in sight. Jim, Bert and Li Wei's pride and joy.

Then I realize: *Ugh, it's a Saturday.*

Weekends are so *boring*. They used to be fun, full of daydreaming and playing at the river and having adventures. None of us would ring each other, and it wasn't like a 'grown-ups making it happen' sort of thing. We'd just all make our way there and know someone else would be there too. We'd build dens and have battles, using fallen-down branches, and on hot days sit in the dappled shade from the big sycamore tree and stash our drinks in a bucket in the river to keep them cool. Flipping brilliant times!

But when I moved up to secondary school seven months ago, the other kids suddenly stopped doing cool stuff like wanting to search for the hidden entrance to the Cawlington Bottling Co building, or trying to catch sticklebacks in the river, and now they just hang around at Hollywood Bowl.

I think it all went wrong because they call it 'break' instead of playtime. No one *plays* any more. Instead, you just link arms and wander around, complaining about things.

I don't like it. I had to see a therapy person because apparently I 'don't do change very well'. *I* think people don't *explain* change very well, but apparently 'that thinking doesn't get anyone very far'. Grandad said I just had to nod to get it over with, then we'd sort it all out together.

A large, scruffy crow lands on the bowling green. Li Wei will not be happy if it poops. He'll have to bring out a cloth and a bucket of soapy water and wash each blade individually while doing deep sighs as if the bird did it on purpose to upset him.

'Morning!' Gran yells as she bursts in with such force that the door thumps into the end of my bed.

'Fig's back?' she asks me. 'I found another feather.'

'What fig? What feather?'

I pull my head out from under the curtains and, even though my eyes are still sleep-gooey, I can still see that Gran is, well . . .

'What on earth are you wearing?'

'Do you like it?'

'It's an acquired taste,' I say.

That's a helpful phrase Grandad has given me so I don't have to completely tell the truth, and it often goes alongside his helpful cough. He says that sometimes we need to soften my edges a little. Just until people get to know me better.

Gran does a twirl and nearly knocks my calendar off the wall with the brim of her hat. She's head to toe in camouflage, a sleeveless jacket thing that's a grey-beige colour covered in pockets and zips, and, most spectacularly, a pair of waders. She looks like someone who's gone fishing before a job interview at a zoo.

'I thought we could go to town and get you that new jacket you've been harping on about, so I've dressed for the occasion!'

'Dressed as what? A jacket hunter?'

I shake my head at her while laughing at my own joke. I try to work out which is the less awful option: death by boredom hanging out at Hollywood Bowl or being seen in town with David Attenborough here.

Gran starts singing an aria as she waits for me to compute. She knows there's no point in rushing me because it makes me flap, and I'll get stuck in a loop and then won't be able to do anything. Gran will definitely sing while we're out in town together, which makes Hollywood Bowl a slightly better option. I mean, her singing is actually and utterly divine. She travelled the entire world in touring companies as an opera singer. She's incredible! Just not in the middle of my favourite shop when everyone is looking.

'That's ace, Gran. But do you have to wear that?'

'Darling, in for a penny, in for a pound!' She does a twirl and curtseys. 'Once we're done, Grandad can drop you off at The Ten-Pin Bowling Alley.'

Gran always says it in full and like it has capital letters at the beginning of each word.

'You can just call it Hollywood Bowl like everyone else,' I tell her. 'And I don't want to. We don't even play – we just *watch*.'

I roll my eyes and expect Gran to offer unhelpful advice, but she goes a bit blank for a moment, like she's forgotten what we're talking about. I can see in her face that her brain is scrambling like mine sometimes does when there's too much going on. Suddenly I feel that pressure in my ears, and out of the corner of my eye I start to see a crack zigzag across the wall.

Gran yells, 'Breakfast in five, then we're offski!' and disappears from my room – and so does the crack.

Maybe this is a bit much for me solo as my first mystery. I wonder if the Puzzler takes on cases? I'll have to find out. Though I doubt the Puzzler also solves grans – I'm stuck with that one.

★

Grandad is nearly finished frying bacon and eggs, and the smell reminds me to get a wriggle on. It's not using my crutches that makes me late for things. I'm super speedy if a bit wobbly – it's just that my brain gets distracted. One minute I've got loads of time, and then suddenly I haven't. Grandad holds no prisoners when it comes to breakfast, which means if you're not there he'll eat yours too.

Downstairs I make my way over to him, grabbing the kitchen table for support. It's big and rectangular, made from chunky, thick wood. In one corner, you can still read the imprint of a complaint about the vacuum cleaner that Grandad wrote without putting a mat on the table. We always try to cover it because, every time Gran spots it, it's like she sees it for the first time and she tells him off again, and Grandad's had a lot of opportunities to try out different arguments in his defence, but none actually work.

I sit down and check the walls while Grandad dishes up. No cracks. Well, I did say I wanted a mystery.

Grandad pops my plate in front of me with an egg at ten o'clock, an egg at two o'clock and bacon at six o'clock. It's important to keep them separate. He brings over his plate and his cup of tea, milky with four sugars.

'Why are you grumpy, pet lamb?'

'I'm not grumpy. I'm thinking about Gran's outfit,' I say.

'She's wearing it whether you like it or not, and there we go. Your choice as to where your face settles with that.' He pauses to ram bacon, egg, bread and a mouthful of tea in his gob. I can't watch.

'Gran was on about figs and feathers in my room this morning. And she, sort of, keeps, erm . . .'

'Keeps what?'

'Flickering.'

Grandad jolts his head a little.

'You're doing it now!'

'No I'm not,' says Grandad. 'You OK?'

'Are *you* OK?' I ask.

'I asked first,' he says.

'I asked better,' I reply.

Grandad snorts out a piece of bacon. 'That's a new one.'

'OH MY GOD, YOU SHOT FOOD OUT OF YOUR NOSE!'

I don't know whether to give a round of applause and cheer or be actually sick on the table.

Grandad grins. 'I got skillz, me,' he says, then holds up his fingers in V signs, cocks his head and winks. I very nearly snort bacon out of *my* nose.

★

'All aboard!' yells Gran.

She holds the car door open for me. It's an eleven-year-old blue Volvo estate, the same age as me. I toss my crutches in the back and then bundle myself in, and Gran shuts the door. She gets in the front with Grandad, her waders squeaking. Me and Grandad are just wearing average-day clothing – jeans for him, dungarees for me – but Gran makes *us* look like the silly ones.

I look over to the club to wave goodbye to Mrs Marston of the Scarves and Mr Marston of the Hats who are on club duty while we're gone. Grandad is very good at giving people capital-letter names but useless at three-point turns. His manoeuvring gives me time to stare at the roof of the club, which is full of black birds. Crows? I'm going with crows. I shiver. There are hundreds of them, and that's not even an exaggeration. Maybe the roof is really warm, and they're all cold? But they're not jostling for position like birds usually do when they're on a telegraph wire or in a tree. They're not flying or flapping. They're in perfect lines. It looks like they're standing to attention.

Right in front of them, in the middle of the bowling green, is a solitary crow. It's much bigger and tattier than the rest, with more greys and petrol colours in its feathers. It's definitely, one hundred per cent, probably the one that I saw earlier. I watch as it lifts its wing to the side of its head. Is it *saluting* at me? When I look up, all the crows on the rooftop are doing it too. I rub my eyes; maybe they're getting rheumy like Gran's.

Before I can think about what I'm doing, I find myself saluting in return.

'Selfie!' yells Gran, and I have to turn back to do the car routine, poking my head between the two front seats so that all our faces are filling the rear-view mirror.

'Cheese,' says Grandad, and we all grin, but I don't really feel like grinning.

Then I say, 'Snap!' and we're done.

When I turn back, the crows have gone, which makes me feel relieved and sad all at once. Well, every crow except for the one on the bowling green, who drops its salute and flies away.

Chapter Three

'Mimi Evergreen, anyone at home?' Grandad is literally knocking on my forehead. 'Listening to the Puzzler?' he asks.

I nod and grin.

The Puzzler is anonymous, but I've figured out two things.

1. They live near me, because the same mysteries from the podcast turn up in the *Northern Echo*, our local paper, which Grandad gets every day.
2. They're a kid like me. Their voice is distorted, but I can tell from the way they phrase certain

things, the stuff they talk about, the words they
use and the way they say them.

'You getting out some time this century?' asks
Grandad as he holds the door open for me.

I check the time on my phone. 'I suppose so.'

'Cheeky little blighter.'

I slither off my seat, and Grandad reaches in for my
crutches and passes them to me. Gran squeaks her way
over to us. Grandad gives us both a peck on the forehead
and strides off in the opposite direction.

'Where are you going?' I yell after him.

'Away from the fisherwoman!' he yells back with a
wink.

'Pub,' me and Gran say at the same time. And then we
say, 'Jinx!' and link our little fingers together. Grandad
doesn't really drink, apart from a sherry on Christmas
Eve, but he does like the coffee in the Shuttle and Loom
pub, and the buffet they have on for free on a Saturday
if you play dominoes (he doesn't like dominoes, but he
does like free food).

We head down the little snicket beside the bank that
leads us out on to High Row. It should take us four
minutes to get to Guru, my favourite shop in all the

land, where I want to show Gran the jacket. But Gran knows *everybody*. Outside the opticians she talks to Percy, while I pat his sausage dog, Champ, and he tries to lick my face. Champ hangs out in our park with three other dogs, and they all run after a deflated football. Champ never wins, but he doesn't seem to mind.

We say goodbye and make it another twelve steps when we see Helena who does Gran's hair. 'How you getting on, Iolene? I heard –'

'About Champ,' says Gran in an odd squeaky voice, and shoves me out of the way.

I go and sit by myself on the bench that faces the town clock and the undercover market. The outdoor market stalls line the street, and pigeons fight over scraps beneath them, doing their funny head-bobbing walk.

The water rushes down the steps of this modern-art fountain thing, and the noise reminds me of the river. I close my eyes and smile. I swear I can feel the sun on my face in dappled patches, like I did at the river when it filtered through the sycamore tree, before having fun and playing were banned. I can almost smell the moss that entwined with the grass, making the bouncy, barefoot carpet that climbed up the side of the gnarled old tree that leaned over the river. We hung a swing from it on bright blue twisty rope, and we'd leap and yell and zoom out over the river. Breath held, hoping you won't slip, then whoosh, back to the side, and grabbed safe and falling in a laughing heap. The buckets of little silvery fish, sticklebacks, kept carefully in the shade, ready to be put back before the sun started to drop and it was time for home.

It feels like magic is possible and the whole world is about to open up when you lie back with your mates and cloud-spot.

I open my eyes as the town clock does a full rendition of its song to mark noon. Back on my bench.

By myself.

Hanging out is rubbish compared to fishing for stickle-backs at the river. Why did we have to stop playing?

Gran *eventually* comes and sits beside me. She's twirling a feather in her fingers, which she hands to me. It's black and shiny with petrol edges, the same colour as the bird who was on the bowling green this morning.

'Where did you get this?' I ask, and it's her turn to shrug.

'It's yours,' she says.

'Yes, I know, you just gave it to me, but where did you get it?'

Gran does the blank thing. 'Get what?' She begins to hum.

I shake my head. 'Gran, did you always know you were going to be an opera singer?'

'Apparently, I was singing when I came out of the womb!'

'I'm being serious.'

'So am I, pet. It was a house of not much but music, and me mam and me da and me sisters – they all sang to me before I was even born. I think it was inevitable. Nothing else felt as right.'

I shudder like I've just eaten ice cream, and that whole-body cold feeling happens as the paving stone in front of me shears in two. Frozen, I watch a crack ripple out from it and dart through the slabs next to it. I look up at Gran, but she hasn't noticed. It zigzags round a bin and then continues until it's out of sight. It's a Saturday. It's chock-a-block busy, but no one has screamed or leaped out of the way.

Is it only me who can see the cracks?

'You chilly?' Gran sits up. 'I thought it was cardi weather, but maybe we should wrap you up in another layer. Don't want anything getting on your chest.'

'I'm fine, Gran,' I say as I stare at the paving slab. The whole town is falling apart, never mind just our house.

She shoves her head in front of mine and stares at me and then sticks her tongue out.

I giggle. 'Honest. I'm fine.'

But I don't feel fine. Everything is muddled. I put the feather in my pocket.

'I think I'm like Champ,' I say.

Gran looks baffled.

'The dog. The sausage dog. You always knew singing was your thing. I haven't found my thing and neither has he. Except at least he seems happy.'

Gran looks confused but takes my hand. 'Yet – you haven't found your thing *yet*. And why should you? So much to learn and explore and discover! A whole world!'

I snort. 'No one wants to discover it with me. Everyone at school just likes to hang around and *watch* stuff happen.'

'Things change, Mimi. People change. And we can't always hold on to everything the way that we want.'

'I don't like change,' I humph. 'I'll just have to adventure with you!' I say, grinning at her.

She does a little cough, and her eyes go rheumy, then she speaks more quietly. 'You might just need to do some solo adventuring for a little bit.'

'That's rubbish though,' I say. 'It's no fun catching fish by yourself. And who would carry the bucket for me?' I point to my crutches.

She nods, leans forward and picks a dandelion.

'Don't!' I yell. 'You'll wee the bed!'

'Let's see if you like butter.' Gran holds it out under my chin.

'Gran, that's buttercups, not dandelions.'

'Is it? I . . . Of course! Silly me.' She twirls it in her fingers. 'These will all be clocks soon. Tick-tick-ticking.' Gran stares really far off. I look to see what she's focused on, but there's nothing there.

'Gran?' I say. She doesn't reply, but kind of mutters into space.

A crow lands on the bin beside us and distracts me. Is it the crow from this morning? Then a feather, black and sleek with a white tip, floats down and lands on the bench beside Gran. I look up, but there's no bird in the blue sky above us. Just the crow still sitting on the bin. It's creeping me out with its beady little eyes, so I wave *shoo* at it, but it won't fly away.

Gran picks up the feather and strokes it on her cheek and then leans forward and sticks it in the soil, upright like a flag. I take out the feather she gave me and plant it next to hers, and I grin at her, but now Gran doesn't seem like Gran, and it scares me, more than the cracks and the crows. The crow hops down and grabs the feathers in its beak and then hops behind the bin. I wait for it to fly away or reappear, but it's like it's just vanished.

'Mimi, are we getting this jacket or what?' Gran stands up and pulls me to my feet. I look into her eyes: she's back.

But for some reason I can't stop thinking about the crack in the pavement and the eyes of the crow.

★

'Don't step on the cracks!' shouts Gran as we make our way to Guru. It makes my heart soar that she can see them too, but then she leaps, and I realize that she's just talking about the game we always play. Joining in stops my thinking brain from getting all tangled, and anyway I have an advantage cos I can swing on my crutches to get over the bits where the paving slabs are really long. Gran has to take a run-up.

Gran is a bit slapdash at this game and gets herself into a pickle, whereas I like to plan my route. From the corner of High Row, I can see all the way to Guru. If I keep to the left of the planters, and away from the dip where the water runs off, there's a really easy route.

We make it to just outside the door of the tall, skinny old building. The window is full of posters and lanterns. I've got one final jump to make to land on the wide slab in front of the prickly doormat. Gran leaps and makes it and opens the door so all the bells jangle. She holds it open for me. Dead easy. I plant my crutches and swing. My legs leave the ground, and I'm leaping and soaring, and just before I hit the ground –

A crack zigzags across the pristine slab. I land right on top of it.

'You lose!' yells Gran. 'Seven years' bad luck! The Void Collectors are going to get you! Fig's back!'

'I-I didn't . . . it wasn't? What are you still on about figs for? Did you not see that crack just appear?! It wasn't there and then it was! That's not fair!'

'Don't be a bad loser,' says Gran, and goes inside.

★

—— 31 ——

Guru smells of incense, and it's rammed with wooden treasure chests, bright multicoloured rugs, oil burners in hundreds of different shapes and styles, and notebooks wearing padded, embroidered coats. Hung from the ceiling are garlands of stars, prayer flags, mandalas and dreamcatchers. It's a cave of wonder and delight.

I wave to Beryl behind a counter that is filled with silver rings and sparkling nose studs. 'Brought the bank with you this time, I see,' she says, laughing, as I drag Gran over to her. Gran and Beryl have known each other forever. This was my mam's favourite shop too – that's how long it's been here.

'Nice outfit, Iolene. How are you doing?' Beryl asks Gran. 'I was so sorry to hear . . .'

'. . . about Kim,' finishes Gran in that weird squeaky voice. Beryl gives her a look, then glances at me. And then Gran says, 'Me too,' very quietly.

I look from Gran to Beryl. Something is definitely up. 'Who's Kim?'

Beryl nods at Gran. Then smiles at me. 'Never you mind. And how are you, Little Miss Nosy?'

'Fine,' I say, a bit huffy, then I realize it's not Beryl's fault I'm worried about cracks and Gran lying, so I sort my face out. 'Are your foundations OK?' I ask her.

'Erm, yes,' she tells me, looking puzzled. 'Thank you for asking. Are you here for the grand unveiling?'

I grin. The jacket!

Beryl put it away for me after I started visiting it on a weekly basis. It has fourteen pockets and is made of blue patchwork — bits of recycled jeans and some of the material that's used to make the floaty trousers that look like pyjamas that I can't wear because my legs would get in a tangle. It's got a label inside like a jigsaw piece, which makes me love it even more.

Wear local, with love and pride from Telpher Uzz

It's every colour blue that exists, and I don't usually like blue. But this is the right sort of blue. The right sorts of *blues*. It's just right.

But mainly it's all about the pockets. It's multifunctional and probably good for all seasons and, as I heard Gran say to Grandad when she brought home a pair of shoes that made the moths fly out of Grandad's wallet, *it's an investment piece*. Whatever that means. But when I said that, it seemed to do the trick. She laughed so much I thought she was going to keel over and then she said maybe it was time we paid the jacket a visit.

Beryl makes Gran turn round so she can't peek and then helps me put it on. Her long black hair brushes against my shoulders like a waterfall and she guides me towards the mirror. 'You sure this is the one you want?'

I feel calm and my brain unbusies itself. It's like the jacket already belongs to me: the smell is familiar and safe, and I won't need to wear it in little stages to get used to it like I do when I get a new raincoat that makes me feel sick with its plastic fumes. I nod.

'Ready!' says Beryl to Gran, and she turns back to look.

'Oh, pet lamb,' says Gran, 'that could not be more *you* if it tried.'

Over by the handmade card rack, two people with really long hair and dyed purple beards cheer and give me the thumbs up. I can feel my face going red, and I shyly stick my thumb up back at them.

'Though – blue?' says Gran. 'I would never have thought you'd choose that in a million years!'

'Me neither,' I say.

'See?' She winks at me. 'Some changes are good changes.'

I groan. 'Can we stick to the jacket?'

'Everything OK?' asks Beryl.

'Just friend stuff,' I tell her, and she nods like she completely understands.

'Funny age this, pet,' says Beryl. 'All hormones and whatnot spurting out all over the place.'

'What an awful image!' says Gran. 'You keeping it on or are we going to get Beryl to package it up for you?'

'Keeping it on!' I say. Then in very quick succession: 'Please, are you sure?' and 'Thank you!'

'So how much is this going to set me back?' says Gran to Beryl, and Beryl says, 'Ooh, good point!' and gets some scissors to cut the tag off the collar. She gives me the ribbon it's tied with because she knows I save them, and hands the tag to Gran.

I run the purple ribbon back and forth between my fingers. It's smooth and cool.

'You OK there?' asks Beryl, and I'm about to explain how the ribbon could be a little worm, a *silk* worm – *badum tish*, when I realize Beryl is not asking me but Gran, who's raking around in her handbag.

'I just can't seem to find . . .' Gran looks really worried and a bit sweaty.

'Can I help?' asks Beryl, but I'm already beside Gran. It's my job to help her, and I'm good at it.

'Pop it on the counter,' I tell her.

Gran does, and I look inside. Right at the top of the handbag, nestled on top of a pair of gloves, a triangular plastic headscarf in a see-through bag and umpteen packets of hankies, is Gran's bright red purse. 'Here it is,' I say, and hold it out to her. 'How could you not spot that?'

'That's not mine.'

'Yes it is!' I wait for the punchline to the joke, but there doesn't seem to be one.

'Where's my purse gone?' says Gran, frightened.

She won't take it from me, even though I'm holding it out right at her. I feel a bit hot and bothered, and the people by the cards are looking over again, and the room feels like it's shrinking. The smell of incense is getting stronger, and it's catching in my throat.

I open the purse. Nestled in the little plastic compartment is a smaller version of the photo from the paper of the three of us. I show it to Gran. 'See, there's us! Who else would have a photo of us in their purse?'

Gran peers at it and doesn't look any more convinced at all, but she nods and says, 'Ah, yes,' then looks in the bit where you'd keep notes and finds nothing, then unzips the section for change. She tips it upside down on the counter, and a mint falls out. She pushes it across the counter to Beryl and says, 'Will this do?'

I'm still waiting for the punchline – I think maybe it's a grown-up joke – but Beryl doesn't seem to get it, and I'm very confused. I do this little laugh thing in case I'm meant to find it funny, but it gets all caught up in my throat.

'Gran,' I say, 'you always pay by card.' I look over to Beryl, and Beryl is just staring at Gran and being no help whatsoever. 'Grandad always tells her off for having no change.' My words come out all tumbled, and my cheeks burn. 'He says you should always carry an emergency fiver. Don't you think that's a good idea?'

'Yes, definitely,' Beryl answers, but I really don't think she heard the question. 'Mimi, do you know where George – er, your grandad is?'

'Pub,' I say.

'Ah, good, he's in town. Buffet Saturday. Let's get you and your gran sat down with a cuppa, and I'll ring the pub and get them to give him a shout.'

We don't need Grandad, I think. *We can manage just fine. We always come shopping by ourselves, just us!* But then I look at Gran, and she's running her hand back and forth over a little bleb in the glass on the counter, and as I'm watching a little crack splinters out from under her finger. I stare at it and then at Gran. She doesn't look like Gran.

I feel very little and scared, like I did when Grandad used to have to check under my bed for monsters.

Everything was OK today until I stood on that crack.

'I think that would be a very good idea,' I say.

★

We pull up in the Volvo back at our bowls club and Gran keeps looking in the rear-view mirror to tell me she's all right. Just a funny turn. Blood sugar a bit low. The sugary cuppa and the chocolate biscuit Beryl gave her sorted her out just fine. Wasn't the biscuit nice? Did I like my biscuit too? And Grandad is telling me Gran's fine and dandy.

But it feels cold inside me, like my internal heating system has been turned off, and for the first time ever I don't believe them in the slightest.

Chapter Four

I pull off my headphones. Even listening to the latest episode of *The Puzzler* doesn't distract me, and it's one of the best ones yet, about a fire that didn't leave a mark. For the last two weeks, I've watched Gran like a hawk. Or a crow. I don't need *The Puzzler* to hunt out this mystery. I know something is up with Gran, and that Mr Suit must have something to do with it, because he was there when the cracks began.

Bigger question: what is *it*?

Every day, I race home from school to check up on Gran. I don't even go to comedy club on a Thursday. I keep my head down. I do my work. At break (not playtime), I sit in the library. I tell Miss my legs are sore and she lets me, no questions asked.

There's too much to think about.

I'm scared *I* made Gran have the funny turn. If I hadn't stood on the crack outside Guru, would she be OK? I've studied the *Northern Echo*, but there's nothing about subsidence or shifting ground, and *The Puzzler* hasn't covered it either.

Out of my bedroom window, I see someone in a big hoodie with a smiley face on it walk towards the building. They're about my age, which is at least fifty years younger than the average age of the bowls club. No one new for months, and then a Mr Suit and the Hoodie all in the space of a fortnight – very unusual.

I watch as the crow, the scruffy bird that saluted at me and disappeared behind the bin in town, hops along the wall beside the Hoodie. They don't seem to be fazed by it, but why isn't it flying away? Gives me the creeps.

The Hoodie disappears from view, and the sky grows suddenly dark, and when I look up it's like storm clouds are swirling in, but it's not. It's a squawking, cawing, fighting, flying mass of crows.

I shake my head because I must be making this up, but there they are: the crows are in the trees, on the away-visitors' hut roof, on the green, filling the bandstand, more and more of them pouring from the sky, crashing down like the water coming over the dam at the river when there's been a storm.

I rub my fists in my eyes, and they're still there when I take them away, even though I counted to ten and thought about happy things, just like I used to do when I was scared of the monsters under my bed and I needed my mam's jumper to make me safe.

The park is noisy and full of kids running about because it's sunny, even though it's cold, and the bowls club is packed because it's match day, with everyone in their whites, and the crows are *still* perched everywhere. No one else seems to be bothered about them. Well, I certainly am! *What's going on?*

Li Wei is playing bowls, and he'd usually be clapping his hands or firing an umbrella up and down at one bird, never mind hundreds.

No one can see them but me.

This is ridiculous. I am not going to be defeated by some imaginary crows. I try not to think about how weird that sounds in my head, and I leave my bedroom to head downstairs and check it out. *This is the sort of thing the Puzzler would love to get their teeth into*, I think, and I wonder why we say that about teeth because I don't think a mystery is necessarily very tasty.

At the same time, Mrs Marston of the Scarves yells, 'Mimi! You up there?'

'Yes!' I yell back.

'You've got a visitor.'

A visitor? The Hoodie? This day just gets stranger and stranger. I head downstairs and, instead of going along the corridor to leave via our private front door, I head towards the heavy brown fire door that leads to the bar and has a sign saying PIRATE on it because I couldn't say private when I was little, and it stuck. All of a sudden Mrs Marston pops her head round the door before I get to it.

I scream so she screams, and her head disappears.

I'm on edge and all tingly. I walk through into the bar and hope nothing else is about to set me off. I take a conker out of my pocket and hold it tight; the cool and the smooth calms me.

Mrs Marston is sitting at one of the tables and mopping her brow with her bright pink scarf. 'What was that all about? You'll be the death of me one of these days.' She tuts, then waves frantically at the door like she's trying to usher someone closer. 'You've got a visitor. Over there. What did you say your name was, pet?'

'Titch,' says the massively tall person, the Hoodie who I saw from my bedroom window, but who didn't look that tall from above and now looks, well, enormous.

It's rude to stare. And I hate it when people stare at me and my crutches. So I try very hard not to.

I sneak a glance from under my fringe. Titch is, hand on heart, no exaggeration, at least double my size. Upward. But about the same as me in width. Which makes Titch looks like someone who has been stretched up and up.

Gran appears from the kitchen and saves the day because it's gone very silent with me trying not to stare but to look casual, and forgetting how to speak, and Titch saying absolutely nothing else, and Mrs Marston shaking her head and doing more tutting.

'Hello,' says Gran. 'Welcome! Are you one of Mimi's friends?'

'Erm,' says Titch, 'no. Not yet. I'm Titch and my pronouns are they, them.'

'What a glorious answer!' says Gran. 'I'm Iolene, she, her, though I answer to anything that's not rude.'

Titch holds out a copy of the *Northern Echo* and says, 'Is this the right place? I've come about the advert. We don't usually get a paper; the corner shop delivered it by mistake, but my dad saw this and he . . . Well. That's why I'm here.' Titch stands there, holding their arm out with the newspaper in one hand.

It begins to feel *really* awkward, more than I can stand, and Gran isn't hurrying to move, so I walk over and take the paper from them.

It's folded over at the classified section where people sell everything from cars to hamsters. I pop it on one of the tables and look to see if I can work out why Titch is here. The big red-pen circle helps.

> **WANTED**
> STICKLEBACK
> ~ CATCHERS ~
>
> Are you Bored or Lonely?
> My granddaughter is the Queen of Adventure and
> is looking for a Gang to share them with her.
> INTERESTED?
>
> Contact Mimi Evergreen, age 11, care of Iolene
> Evergreen, North Cawl Park Bowls Club.

I look from the advert to Titch and over to Gran, who is smiling sweetly like butter wouldn't melt.

'Gran, could I possibly have a word with you?'

I shuffle backwards, directing a fixed grin towards Titch, and make it to the kitchen door, only knocking over two salt cellars and four menus.

Gran has moved, but not in my direction. Instead, she's bustling round Titch. 'Can I take your jumper? It's way past cardigan weather now. You must be hungry. We're allergy-aware here, thanks to missy reversing over there. Don't be scared! We can cater for you, whatever you want . . .'

'*Gran!*' I do one of those stage-whisper things where it's kind of breathy but still really loud.

Both of them turn and stare at me. I can see now that below the smiley face on Titch's hoodie it says SMILE. Titch is not smiling. I can feel the red rising from my chest, up my neck. It's warm and glaring, and I can't pretend everything is fine while I'm now pulsating like a tomato.

I yell, 'Gran, come here, *now*!'

'Well I never,' says Gran to Titch, and actually does a tut. Mrs Marston does one too, to match. She can never be out-tutted.

'You have a seat, my dear,' says Gran, plonking Titch down at a table whether they like it or not. 'And I'll be back sharpish once I've dealt with buggerlugs back there.'

She tuts once more, and so does Mrs Marston, just to rub it in. Gran adds a shake of the head *and* a sigh for good measure, and then heads towards me without knocking over any salt cellars or menus.

I keep doing the big fixed grin at Titch, all my teeth showing and plastic face, and swipe my fringe out of my eyes. As soon as she's near enough, I grab Gran's arm and yank her inside the kitchen with me. I close the door behind her, doing the grin thing round the door until I have to extract my head awkwardly at the last moment. I nearly lose my balance so I grab on to the tea-towel rail.

'Mind them,' says Gran. 'I've just done a wash.'

'Mind the tea towels? *Mind the tea towels?!* Is that the best you can do? Gran, what on earth have you done?'

'Oooh, I don't know. What *have* I done? I can't remember . . .'

'Gran, that's not funny! I don't know where to start. There's an advert in a paper and a Titch in the bar!'

'Oh, look, it turns out you *did* know where to start.'

'Gran!'

'Oh, pet, you think I haven't noticed you getting

under my feet these past couple of weeks? You need adventures! I know you miss playing rather than all this hanging-about stuff. So there you go – can't whinge about who will hold the bucket now!'

I begin to pace round and round the island in the middle of the kitchen. If I loop, it will stop my brain from exploding.

'I've found you a new friend. Moping is officially over,' says Gran as she calmly folds the tea towels.

'Does Grandad know about this?'

'Of course not! Don't be silly. He would never have let me do it.'

I cannot believe she's done this. She's the Queen of Hare-brained Schemes and Ideas, but before now they've never been aimed at me.

'Stop wittering – you've got someone waiting. And they haven't even got a cup of tea. What on earth must they think of us?'

Gran leaves the kitchen. Just like that. Leaves me standing there like *I'm* the one who's done something wrong.

I can hear her offering Titch a cup of tea, or a juice, or a biscuit, or a cake, or perhaps a doughnut? I'm now stuck in a loop that was meant to get me out of doing a loop, and I have to make myself spin round on the spot to stop me circling the kitchen forever.

I need to get this sorted. If there was ever a reason for *not* having new friends and staying right here to keep an eye on things, well, Gran has just proved it with this ridiculousness.

I take a deep breath before leaving the kitchen. I go back out into the bar and make my way over to Titch.

'I'm Mimi Evergreen. Which I think you already know, thanks to my gran.' I give her dagger eyes, which she pretends not to notice. 'My pronouns are she, her, and you need to come with me.'

I beckon towards the big double doors, back the way Titch came in. Titch looks relieved to have an excuse to stop being harassed by Gran and quickly follows me.

'See you in a bit, Stickleback Catchers!' yells Gran as we go outside.

I don't turn round to check, but I can hear Titch's footsteps behind me. All the crows have gone, so I can't even make use of Titch and ask them if they can see them too. I walk past the edge of the green and all the players, all the spectators, Mr Marston of the Hats with his pot of tea and his Stetson matching his pinny, and Grandad. They all turn and stare. News travels fast here.

Their bodies don't necessarily move that quickly, but their ability to pass on gossip certainly does.

When I reach the gates, I continue through into the park and keep going until we're at the bandstand, and no one from the club can overhear us. I grab hold of a bench. Titch sits on it and stares at me. I have no idea what to say.

Neither does Titch.

There is the kind of silence that you can physically feel, and it makes me wriggle awkwardly on the spot.

'Look at that bird,' says Titch eventually, and points to a scruffy black crow. 'It's like it's watching us.'

'Well,' I say, 'it probably is, because now I appear to be the centre of the crow universe, and they follow me everywhere and keep appearing in huge flocks.' My brain is so overwhelmed I'm worried it might start pouring out of my ears.

Titch looks at me. Opens their mouth, closes it, then opens it again and says, 'Cool. Murder.'

'Pardon?'

'Not a flock. A group of crows is a murder.'

'Sounds about right,' I say, sitting down beside Titch and leaning my crutches next to me. 'I could murder my gran right now.'

Titch laughs. 'She placed the advert without you knowing about it?'

'Yup,' I say, and get the conker out of my pocket.

'Cool,' Titch says again, and gets a pebble out of theirs. 'You collect stuff too?'

'I always have a conker in my pocket. If there's ever an issue where there is an evil baddie clone of me, that's how people will be able to tell us apart; the real me will have at least one conker in their pocket. And a pebble too.'

Titch holds their pebble out to me. 'This is from the river near my house.'

I take it and hand them the conker. 'You live near the river? Wish we did. This is from that tree just over there.'

'Cool.' Titch puts it in their pocket, and I think, *I wasn't actually giving it to you – it was just for a little hold*, and then I feel the river pebble, and it's smooth and cool instead of smooth and warm, and it seems like a good swap.

'If your gran hadn't put that advert in the paper, I think maybe my dad might have done something like it.'

I cock my head at them.

'Says I'm spending too much time in my bedroom. Which is stupid because he spends the same time in his.

It's just rubbish going to the river by myself or, even worse, with him.'

Titch does what I do when people stare, and changes the subject. 'Nice collection of pockets.'

I put the pebble in my new jacket, and I think maybe they're being mean, but when I look at their face I don't think they are, and I don't really know what to say.

The skateboarder is over the road, by the path that leads to the car park behind the Cawlington Bottling Co building, with its beautiful purple brick arches and white walls. I point him out to Titch and say he's there every day, with his notebook, tallying how many times he makes a flip.

Titch waves at him, and he waves his skateboard back. 'Do you know him?' I ask.

'Nope, but it's nice to be nice, isn't it?'

I smile. It's something Gran would say. I tell Titch how it's the stuff of legend around here that Gran came hurtling through the park doing kick-turns and ollies, after Grandad once gave her skateboarding lessons as an anniversary present.

'Younger kids still come up and whisper to me, *Is your gran the one who did the boardslide on the bandstand rail?* I can tell you for nowt she did *not* do one of those, but I'm not going to be the one that crushes the myth.'

Titch laughs, and their eyes crinkle up. 'Your gran is mint.'

'Yeah. She is, isn't she?'

We sit in silence for a bit, watching the skateboarder. 'So the advert says "Stickleback Catchers", and I'm well up for that,' says Titch, breaking the silence.

'You are?' I say, but then I pretend that my crutches need cleaning and rub them with my sleeve cos I'm embarrassed at how eager I sounded.

'Duh, yeah! But did you have any other adventures in mind?' asks Titch.

'Do I?' I yell.

'I don't know, do you?'

I stare at them, and they stare back, and I'm really confused, and then Titch sticks out their tongue. I giggle and stick mine out too.

'We could try and get in there,' I say, and point to the Cawlington Bottling Co building. 'It was built in 1900. Look, it says so at the top of the wall.'

Titch puts their hand over their eyes to shield them from the sun and stares intently at the factory's name and date:

'And look what's missing . . .'

Titch keeps on staring and then drops their hand and looks right at me. 'A door!'

'Yup. No entrance round the back either. I've done loads of research, and I can't find out who or maybe more importantly *why* someone sealed it off. I bet the Puzzler would work it out in seconds.'

'Aw, no way! Do you listen to *The Puzzler* too?'

'Do I listen?!' I say excitedly.

'I don't know. Do you?' asks Titch, and we laugh. 'Did you hear the latest episode?'

'The one about the fire that didn't leave a mark?'

'Yes!' yells Titch.

'Best one yet,' I say. I stare back over at the purple arches, squished between two modern glass-and-breeze-block buildings. 'There's definitely something inside it, something someone wants to stay hidden. Maybe treasure? Or a hidden dragon? Definitely something both creepy *and* exciting. Sometimes I swear it looks like it's breathing.'

Titch stares at me, and I know I've blown it and gone too far, just like Grandad warns me. I need to remember to just trickle me out in small doses. I babble on about how Grandad used to work there, and how Gran and him were born just over the road, and their mams were best friends, and that makes us the Triangle Trio, and Grandad doesn't know when the door got blocked up even though he worked there and lives opposite; it's like it magically disappeared overnight, and I've thought about asking the Puzzler but I want to solve the mystery myself, but I sort of thought maybe someone would help me because that would be more fun, but everyone just hangs out these days, and they don't even go to the river any more.

Titch carries on staring at me, and I don't know how to make my mouth stop, and everything about Mr Suit and the cracks and Gran being weird and the crows and me standing on a crack and all that being my fault blurts out, and maybe they're just like the others who stopped playing with me at the river, and maybe they don't really want to do adventures, and they're going to tell everyone, and they'll laugh at me, and this is all going wrong, and I finally run out of words, and there's a big pause, and I want to curl up and die. And then –

'Mimi Evergreen, you don't half talk a lot,' says Titch, grinning. 'I'm in.'

Chapter Five

Next day, true to their word, Titch is in, and we're in my room so we can do some research before we begin our first Official Adventure as the Stickleback Catchers. We have old episodes of *The Puzzler* playing in the background as inspiration. There have been no more cracks and no more visits from Mr Suit, so we've decided we're doing Mission Find the Entrance and Get Inside Cawlington Bottling Co first and then, after that, Mission Solve the Cracks and Crows.

'Ooh, or maybe both simultaneously if it turns out they're linked,' says Titch.

'But how will we know?' I ask. Titch shrugs.

They look at my knick-knacks and say, 'Nice.' Then

they pick up one of the old Cawlington Bottling Co green glass bottles from my shelf and hold it up to the light, then they look out of my window at the mystery building. Usually, I don't like people touching my stuff, but Titch puts the bottle down gently and says, 'Good find. Maybe it's a clue to how we find a way in?'

I shrug. I've thought that too and got nowhere. But maybe now there are two of us we'll be more likely to finally get inside.

We sit on my bed and play a game on my tablet where you have to solve puzzles to be able to move on, and Titch and I are ten-out-of-ten rubbish at it. I want to be good, and it's really interesting, but we spend a lot of time searching for walk-throughs on our phones and doing what they tell us to do and then going, 'Oh yes, of course!' My faith in us solving the Mystery of the Cawlington Bottling Co is fading fast.

'I bet the Puzzler could figure out how to get into the CBC in minutes,' says Titch.

I nod. 'Nice abbreviation.' Titch grins.

We both stare out of my window across to the CBC building. I jump when Titch breaks the silence and asks, 'Mimi, why sticklebacks?'

'Me and Gran and Grandad used to catch them all the

time when I was little. I love going to the river. Sticklebacks are dead good. They change colour when it's mating time, and it's the dad that builds an underwater nest and looks after the baby sticklebacks. The mam doesn't bother once she's had them.'

'Pretty much like mine,' says Titch.

'You don't have a mam?' I ask.

I take a big gulp of the hot chocolate and marshmallows Grandad made us. It's a bit too hot so I scrape my teeth along my tongue to try to stop the burn taking hold. Titch plucks a fresh tissue out of their pocket and hands it to me, miming for me to wipe my nose.

'Nope,' they say. 'She left when I was seven, haven't seen her since, just me and Dad. He had a girlfriend for a bit. She was OK, but it didn't last.'

Titch picks up a paperweight from my knick-knacks and passes it back and forth between their hands. I worry because it's beautiful, filled with tiny feathers, and I'm scared they'll drop it and it will smash.

'Do you live with just your grandparents?' they ask me as they put down the paperweight.

'Yeah,' I say.

'Cool,' says Titch. And it's a bit awkward so I tell Titch I don't have a mam either, except mine is dead, which is technically sad, but it's fine because I don't remember her so I can't miss her, and it's always just been me and Gran and Grandad.

There isn't much conversation at all then, so I go into babble mode about the rules for lawn bowls as advocated by Bowls England and then a glossary of bowling terms. I fiddle with the conker I gave to Titch, which they've brought back with them today, and the pebble that Titch gave me, rotating them in and out of my fourteen jacket pockets. I'm telling Titch that the green is the playing area, like the pitch, and usually, like at our club, it's divided into six sections called rinks. I'm about to move on to a jack being the white ball, rather than the name of the player, and woods being the other balls, when there's a sudden crash downstairs followed by a thud.

We look at each other, then Titch races out of the door, and I head after them.

★

Gran is in a heap on the kitchen floor and there's crockery all around her. Grandad runs in just after us.

'The crockery was the crash,' says Titch, grabbing a brush from the cupboard and beginning to sweep up.

'And you were the thud,' I say to Gran. 'Who needs *The Puzzler*?'

Grandad brings a chair over, and together we help her up.

'Are you OK?' I ask Gran. I'm worried she might disappear like before. She looks sweaty again.

'Yes, yes, I'm fine. Don't need to fuss. I just . . .'

'Yes . . . ?' I say, trying to make her finish her sentence.

'Yes, what?' says Gran. 'Don't just stand there – pop the kettle on. And who made all that mess? Does that have to come out of your pocket money, Mimi Evergreen?' She looks at me in the way she does when I've fallen over or broken something.

'I . . .' I absolutely don't know what to say, and I look over at Titch, who just shrugs.

'Right, you two,' Grandad says, shoving me and Titch out of the kitchen, 'I've got it sorted here. Go and ask Subeera for a Coke float. Tell her I said you could have one.'

★

Titch and I sit at a table in the far corner of the bar. Subeera, who works at the club and has been Gran's best friend for years and years, has sorted us out with Coke floats. Served with an extra scoop, one of her massive smiles and a hand squeeze. I'm blowing bubbles in my float with my paper straw, and Titch is using their straw to try to submerge the ice cream in their glass. We haven't really said anything because *that was weird*, and I don't think Titch wants to make it any more awkward, and I don't know how to make it *un*-awkward.

I hear yelling from the kitchen that sounds like my gran and, as I do, above the door, a long crack appears, trailing from one side of the bar right over to the other.

'Titch,' I say slowly and quietly, trying to keep calm as I point. 'Can you see that?'

'Whoa,' says Titch.

We watch as it keeps on crackling round the room, like a firework spidering out and leaving a trail, until it joins back up with where it started.

Suddenly it feels like a living, breathing thing. I get goosebumps, as if someone's watching me, and I turn to look over my shoulder, and a feather falls down from the ceiling out of nowhere, and I catch it.

'What are you?' I whisper to the crack.

Titch stares wide-eyed at me.

'Can you actually see it?'

They slowly nod.

I don't know whether to be relieved or terrified.

'I can *feel* it,' Titch says.

We both stare.

The cold that I felt before is all over my body. Titch pulls up their hood and tightens the strings until only their eyes are peering out.

Then I hear a scurrying, a pitter-patter scratching, and I look at Titch and I know that they can hear it too, but it's like we've both been frozen because neither of us moves and neither of us says anything.

The noise stops.

And then there's a pressure, and I can feel something, a weight on my lap that wasn't there before and now is there and shouldn't be.

Adrenaline fizzes, makes my teeth chomp, then grit tight closed.

I am terrified.

What is in my lap?

I hold my breath. I daren't look. Then I take a deep breath. Didn't I want an adventure?

Dare to take a look, Mimi! Dare!

I look down.

In my lap is a tatty crow. It is collecting the feather in my hand in its beak.

I yell and let go in fright, then suddenly the crow's jumping from my lap to the floor and hopping away with the feather. It is most definitely, ten-out-of-ten the bin crow, the bowling-green crow, the one that followed Titch along the wall.

Titch and I watch it jump across the sticky bar carpet. We watch as the crack unwinds and disappears backwards round the wall until it's gone.

And, as the crow tippy-taps away from us towards the double doors, we hear it say, 'Well then, oh my stars, oh dear, oh dear, that wasn't meant to happen.'

Me and Titch stare at the crow, open-mouthed, as it steps through the double doors, spreads its wings and flies off.

Chapter Six

'Whoa,' says Titch, staring at where the crow was. 'That really, *actually* happened?'

'Yes,' I choke out. 'I think it actually did.'

'It's not that I didn't believe you about the cracks, cos I obviously did, but . . .' Titch frantically stirs their drink until there's more liquid on the table than inside the glass. 'Mystery-solving swap required immediately. Mission Solve the Cracks majorly trumps Mission CBC!'

'That crow spoke!' I splutter. And then it appears I can't say anything else for a minute.

Titch dashes to the bar, grabs Grandad's copy of the *Northern Echo* and dashes back. They toss it to me.

'Is reading about someone's fight over planning permission for their bungalow meant to calm me down right now? DID YOU NOT HEAR THE CROW . . . ?'

Titch slams their hand over my mouth and waits until I stop talking. When I finally do, they wipe it on my dungarees.

'Yes, I did. So we need a new plan. Because I'm sorry, Mimi, but we're rubbish at solving mysteries.'

'Why do we need the paper?'

'Let's catch us a Puzzler.' Titch grins as they turn to the classified section, where Gran placed her advert.

★

By the time Grandad comes out of the kitchen, we've got it written down. It's a bit crossed out with lots of arrows and asterisks, but Titch says they can make sense of it and they'll email it to the *Northern Echo* tonight.

THE STICKLEBACK CATCHERS SEEK THE PUZZLER
We have THE BEST MYSTERY IN THE WORLD
EVER and it will make you famous(er) if you
solve it. Contact Mimi & Titch, age 11, care of
North Cawl Park Bowls Club.

'Haven't you seen the time?' says Grandad, glancing back to the kitchen. 'Coat on, Titch. Your dad will be here any moment. Can't have him waiting.' And he bundles Titch out of the bar.

★

The next day school drags and drags, and I get told off in science for not concentrating, but science and its rules seem kind of pointless now that I know crows talk and that cracks are alive.

I'm walking out of the school gates when I turn my phone on to see a message from Grandad: Yes.

Which makes no sense until I read the messages from Titch:

> WE'RE PICKING YOU UP FROM
> YOUR SCHOOL.
>
> YOUR GRANDAD SAYS IT'S OK.
>
> MEET US BY THE CUT. BLACK
> VOLVO.

No wonder Grandad likes Titch's dad. They're car twins. I spot the car parked up and hurry towards it and open the back door and climb inside. Titch grabs my crutches.

'Oh hecky thump,' I say. 'Have you been able to stop thinking about –' Then I see Titch's wide eyes and them gesturing to their dad in the driving seat.

'– going fishing!' Titch's dad says as he turns round towards me.

That wasn't what I was expecting at all, but I nod and smile. Titch's dad has brown hair like theirs, except his is all crinkly and comes down to his shoulders while Titch's is really short and straight.

We do a three-point turn, and I compliment Mr Season on his ability to do it in three, not like Grandad who takes ninety-seven goes.

I lean over to Titch and whisper, 'What about the advert?'

'Done. It'll be in the paper today. Now shush!'

We pass the tide of pupils filtering out from the school gates and the horde waiting by the ice-cream van. We go over all the speed bumps, and Titch's dad says 'WHOA!' every time we do, and Titch rolls their eyes. When we reach the end of the street, we turn right where the posh houses are, set back from the road. I know where we're going now. I used to come here with Grandad and Gran when I was little, and with my mates before they got all boring – it's a prime stickleback spot!

When we're halfway there, heading out of town, Mr Season turns left along a really bumpy road that's now more hole than tarmac. He doesn't say 'WHOA!' this time because I think he's concentrating on trying to hold the car in one piece, but Titch and I both make an *argggghhhhh* noise, and our voices bounce up and down. We get to a little car park at the bottom that is overhung with trees whose branches are about to burst into little leaf buds. Mr Season jumps out and opens the door for me, and Titch gets out by themself.

I haven't been here for so long.

Mr Season opens the boot, and it's hard to hear what he's saying with his voice all muffled, but when he reappears he's holding two buckets, one yellow and one orange, and two sticks with bright green nets on the end.

'The official commencement of the Stickleback Catchers!' he says, and hands them to us. Titch looks mortified, which makes a change from it being me cos of Gran.

He goes back to the boot and pulls out two glass tanks and hides them in some shrubbery by the car. 'Thought you two could catch some of these infamous sticklebacks and bring them home. Watch their life cycles and then we can release them. How's about it? Vaguely educational, and every gang needs mascots!'

Titch pretends it's not actually happening, but I beam. 'Thanks, Mr Season!'

'Happy fishing! Be back up here in two hours. I'll check with your gran, Mimi, but I'm sure you can come to ours for tea. Maybe not fish and chips!'

Titch groans, and their dad tries to give them a hug, but they sort of wriggle out of it. He gets back in the car and drives away.

We're alone.

'Clever,' I say. 'And top-quality nets and tanks!'

I'm about to blurt out all the questions fizzing inside my head. I've got someone who can actually see the cracks and is helping me investigate them! I open my mouth, but Titch shushes me. 'Anyone could be listening.'

I turn to stare over my shoulder, but Titch grabs my face and rolls their eyes at me. 'Act natural. We'll talk when we get to the bottom.'

I forget how to walk naturally and act out an over-the-top nothing-whatsoever-unusual-in-the-slightest-is-going-on-here-style bouncy crutch-shuffle down the steep path, until the feel of being back by the river takes over and I remember how it makes me breathe deep and slow.

Huge trees form a canopy over our heads, and it's damp and cool in their shade. I've missed this. My tummy flutters with excitement. Ivy snakes up the tree trunks, covering them all in green leafy jumpers. There's a rustling in the undergrowth, and a squirrel pops out in front of me and scurries up a fence.

When we get halfway down the bank, we have to zigzag through some metal barriers. 'These are new,' I tell Titch.

'The council added them after Danny Filo in my school's Year Nine decided it would be a good idea to zoom from top to bottom on his BMX that didn't have any brakes,' says Titch. 'He faceplanted and bust his arm in seven places.'

The ground is uneven and crumbly, with daisies and forget-me-nots poking out where the ground splits. I can still manage fine – I'm a bit slower than usual because I don't want to bust my arm in one place, never mind seven. Two fluffy pigeons land in a tree, the branch springing down and back up again like a trampoline, which sets off a squawking retreat as loads of little spuggies and blue tits fly away.

The trees get bigger as we walk further into the woods. Huge, they tower overhead, completely blocking out the light. The carpet of wild garlic with its little white flowers just beginning to poke through makes it smell like someone has used a mild onion air freshener. The path splits in two, and I follow Titch down the left fork. I haven't been this way before. With Gran and Grandad, we always used to go to the right, towards the bench under the apple and pear trees where we once spotted a kingfisher, its blue flashes darting along the river. And with the kids from school we would get to the river from the other entrance by the adventure playground and the big car park with the ice-cream van, where it's all noisy and bustly.

No one else is here.

We pass a sign that says **FISHING PERMIT HOLDERS ONLY**, the capital letters shouting at me.

'Erm, Titch, you sure it's this way?'

I can hear the river before I see it. The magic of the steady rumble flutters inside my tummy. It's like a current is burbling through me and I let out a little giggle, and a thrush hops away in fright. The path bends slightly to the right, and all of a sudden we come to a huge gap in the trees, and there it is. The mighty River Cawl.

I go whooping towards it, and watch it hurtle through the massive stones, a twig caught up in it zooming round the rapids. There is foam churned up and splooshing out on to the pebble bank and up on to the tufty grass at the edge before it drops off to the river. I dip the end of my crutch in the foam until it disappears into rainbow bubbles.

'We're only about fifteen minutes away from the town centre,' says Titch as they come over and stand beside me. 'But out here it's like nothing else exists but the river.'

I know exactly what they mean.

'It's a hundred and thirty-seven kilometres long,' says Titch. 'Which my dad says is eighty-five miles in old money. It begins as a tiny little burble at Cross Fell up in the North Pennines. I've never seen it, and I can't imagine how something so big and roaring and determined can start from what Dad says is barely a drip. He led a Duke of Edinburgh expedition up there once – that's how he met my mam – and he says it's bleak. Bleached-out scrubland for miles, nothing to get your bearings from, and it's always cold and misty, and nearly always horizontal rain.'

Titch sets off again and, as we carry on walking along the bank, I'm careful not to trip over the uneven stones and grassy tufts. It takes up my concentration and stops my brain whizzing so much.

'The tiny burble becomes a mighty river that plunges over waterfalls and carves out valleys, sends streams out to be nosy all over the shop and finally ends up popping out at the sea at the Gares at Hartlepool and Redcar. Ever been?'

I shake my head.

'What? That's shocking. Best thing about visiting? Going for a lemon top. First time we went on holiday to Wales in the caravan, I asked for a lemon top, and the woman in the ice-cream van looked at me funny. Apparently, Redcar is the only place that do them, and I've got no clue why! It's squirty, whippy ice cream, but with squirty, whippy lemon sorbet on top. Tart and creamy all at once. It's heavenly.'

I look blank. Titch stops walking and stands right in front of me so I have to stop too.

'You've never had a lemon top?'

I shake my head.

'Mission one: work out WHAT ON EARTH with the cracks and the crow. Mission two: enter the CBC building,' Titch whispers and looks over their shoulder suddenly in case anyone is around to overhear. They drop their voice even further just to be on the safe side. 'Then mission three: celebrate with lemon tops.'

'Plan!' I say. 'So what do you think –'

'Shh, not yet!' Titch looks around again. 'We need to get off the path. Can you keep a secret?'

I use my finger to cross my chest and mime sticking something sharp in my eye and then choke like I'm dying, which makes me actually choke. When I stop, Titch says, 'That'll do,' and takes a left off the path.

If we shouldn't have gone down the last bit, we definitely shouldn't be going through here. Titch lifts up a rusty bit of fence, and I duck under.

We walk through cow-parsley stalks and try to avoid massive patches of nettles. 'Have you seen how big the giant hogweed is getting?' asks Titch. 'They'll need to torch it again soon. Be careful when you come through.'

I nod. Tall dinosaur-era plants with seed heads as huge as umbrellas tower over us. I've heard about this stuff. If you break a stalk and the sap gets on you, you don't realize at first. Until the sunlight hits and it burns.

It's like it has the power to turn you into a vampire, without the taste for blood.

'All the warning signs work brilliantly to keep my den away from prying eyes.'

My legs get excited quicker than the rest of me does, and they stop walking with surprised shock. 'Whoa. You have a *den*?'

★

Two mallards fly overhead. It sounds like they're laughing. Three seagulls swoop down and land on the water. They look too big to float. They keep drifting downstream and then flapping wildly to get back up.

'They haven't quite worked out rivers yet,' I say to Titch, and they laugh.

We walk a little further along the river, a section that I didn't know existed, and then Titch stops and points into the shrubbery. 'What do you think?'

I've always wanted a den, but I never, ever imagined one as awesome as this. It's got two floors with two rectangular windows downstairs, and a triangular one upstairs in the eaves. There are higgledy-piggledy sand-coloured bricks for its walls, and a corrugated-iron roof. It's got a big wooden door to enter, but it doesn't fit too well, and there are more nails and new bits of wood than actual door. A piece of white plastic is screwed to the front, with black handwritten letters that say KEEP OUT DANGER, which I'm not sure means it is dangerous, or danger should stay away.

Titch gives my arm a tug, and I follow them inside. On the ground floor are little shelves with loads of found objects, a stove and cups and things on hooks. There's a little wonky cupboard with tea bags, sugar and biscuits. It takes a bit of figuring out to get me up the rickety stepladder to the top floor, but with Titch doing some shoving and me doing some pulling up with my arms we manage it.

I gaze round the space in awe.

'Welcome to the penthouse suite,' says Titch as their head pops up behind me.

Paper stars and chains hang from the ceiling, and the floor is strewn with brightly coloured cushions. There are gaps in the planks for windows at just the right height to be able to sit cross-legged in front of them and peer out.

'Did you make the stars?' Some are made from shiny paper, and they catch the light and make rainbows on the wall.

'I made them with my mam.'

Titch goes really quiet, like they shrink, and they sit on one of the cushions. I choose a flowery purple one and plonk down next to them. We peer out at the river flowing lazily by, from right to left.

I want to cheer Titch up.

'What do you call a man with a seagull on his head?' I ask them.

'Cliff,' says Titch.

'Oh,' I say.

I'm bursting with crows and cracks. I can barely contain myself, and my toes wriggle in my shoes, but I feel like I need to just leave Titch be and look out instead. Swarms of midges gather in clouds above the River Cawl. I watch them floating and try to make *myself* more floaty and less wound up. It doesn't really work.

I concentrate on the view instead, trying to figure out where this bit of the river fits in with the sections I know. The Gran and Grandad bit is narrow and opens on to fields. The bit where the kids used to play is wide, and the concrete dam dominates it, with little wire-mesh-enclosed spits sticking out from the sides that you can fish from. Here it's rugged and raw. The riverbank opposite is steep and tall – it meets the sky. It's so epic that whole trees grow out of the side of the cliff face. It's like being in another country. It could be an American river travelling along in front of me. Somewhere out West. A laid-back town with a saloon just over the way where people in Stetsons and overalls gather to drink and listen to music. The river has carved this chasm out. I wonder how many thousands of years it took. I definitely do not have the patience of a river, and I'm just about to try and talk to Titch again when they do the job for me.

'Let's fish,' they say.

★

When we first saw the river at the bottom of the steep bank with the metal barriers, it rushed by, sounding like a motorway, a dull roar. But here whole little worlds live in pools with flowing weeds and trickles of water steadily filtering through.

'At other times of the year, sticklebacks are muddy-coloured,' I tell Titch, hoping this will cheer them up as we splosh into the water with our nets. 'Now – for spring – the males have got their glad rags on!'

I sneak a look from under my fringe to see if the cheering-up bit is working, and then maybe we can talk about the magic.

Whoa. It can't be, can it? Is it really magic?

'Here,' I whisper to Titch, trying to keep the tremor from my voice as my brain scrambles. They hold out their hand to steady me. They follow my finger as I point. 'Be careful not to place your shadow over the pool and frighten it away.'

'I can see it!'

For once, I'm the one that gets to shush Titch. 'Sticklebacks don't have scales,' I say. 'How cool is that? This one has three spines along his back. I know he's a him because it's spawning season so he's got a bright red tummy and throat, and sparkly bluey-green eyes and silvery sides. The females get even more silvery and chubby. See, glad rags. Oh no, am I doing a Mimi and telling you loads of details about stuff you already know?'

'Nope. Crack on! There's loads I don't know.'

I grin shyly, then it's a bit much so we stare at the fish. Sticklebacks really are spectacular. I love it here. In Titch's spot. With my fish. Teaching them. I don't say I love it out loud, but Titch smiles at me, and I think they feel it too.

'Go for it,' I say.

They gently lower their net into the water, not in the weedy bit where it would get crumpled and caught, but on the opposite side that is clear, and they slowly move it towards the stickleback. As I watch, my wobbles disappear. And my worries. The world fades. I focus. It's just me and Titch and the fish. We catch one and pop it in the orange bucket placed in the shade.

Then another. 'Gotcha!' I grab the yellow bucket and help Titch gently turn the net inside out so Mr Stickleback plops inside. 'Nice work,' I say, and they give me a thumbs up. I beam.

But then I remember that the last time I got a thumbs up was in Guru just before Gran went all weird, and Grandad had to collect us, and all of a sudden everything feels a bit much and I begin to cry.

★

We sit on great flat stones and watch the river amble along. I love how it just knows exactly what it has to do and does it, from right to left, flowing on. I wish I knew what we were meant to do. I've finally stopped crying and I feel a bit silly, but Titch doesn't seem to think any less of me. They have their arm round me, and we sit in silence. It's easy.

'Want to talk about the cracks?' asks Titch.

'Finally! Do I?!'

'Don't start that again,' they say, and I laugh and wipe my face.

'Let's go over it again in case we're missing something.'

I sigh. I really don't think this is going to help. Titch gives me a look as they say, 'We might as well try until the Puzzler gets in touch.'

'Do you think they will, though?' I ask.

'They *have* to. So, when did you first see a crack?'

For the umpteenth time, I tell Titch about Mr Suit and how creepy he was. Titch nods, then says, 'You're right. It's something to do with him – he's the baddie. Simple as that. Do you think he planted the cracks in your house?'

'What, like spies or something? To steal Gran's lemon meringue pie recipe?'

Titch snorts.

We go back and forth, forward and back, round and round, over and over, and we decide Mr Suit is definitely part of it, but that it's definitely something to do with Gran too.

'They only appear when she has a moment, don't they?' says Titch. 'So it has to be.'

'You think Gran's *causing* them?'

'Yes,' says Titch. When they see me looking shocked, they say, 'No.'

But then I say, 'Maybe,' and we don't get much further than that. Except that cracks can't just magically appear and disappear, and neither can crows talk, but it turns out that they do, so anything's possible.

'Stand up,' says Titch, and I wobble to my feet. 'Skimming will help us think.'

I look down at the riverbed, properly this time, and I realize that there are *really* good skimming stones here. It's like the ground is made of slate, slice upon slice layered on top of each other. If you take a sliver, you can prise others away too, just like slicing a loaf of bread. I begin to gather and so does Titch. Once we each have a stash, we start to skim.

I'm rubbish at it, and my stones just plop in the water, whereas Titch's leap almost to the other side, zigzagging to the left as the current urges them on.

'It's all in the wrist,' says Titch. 'You don't need loads of power. It's a little flick at the end, a little *oomph*, and instead of going *plop* the stone dances across the top of the water.'

I watch Titch's throw – six big jumps and too many little plips at the end to count. I aim for a sticking-out rock right over at the far riverbank and skim. I pull my arm back and then flick my wrist and let go.

'Ow!' says Titch.

'I am so sorry!'

'Maybe you want to do a little bit of gathering instead?' And they lick their finger and rub the bit where I walloped them on the shin.

I don't think that's actually a question, so I move away to gather up some more stones.

There's a rustling noise in the treeline, sounds bigger than a bird, and I quickly glance behind me. No one there.

I go to collect more skimmers, but I can't shake off the watching feeling. Then there's the sound of a branch snapping, and I jerk round towards the noise.

'Who's there?' I yell. Titch whizzes round to look at me.

I check for movement. Can't see anything. 'Nothing,' I tell them. 'Just hearing things.' The crow and the cracks have made me super jumpy.

I move well away from Titch to try to skim more stones without thwacking them, but I can't get beyond one plop. I look slowly over my right shoulder, hoping to catch whatever made the noise. Nothing.

Suddenly there's a clatter to my left, and a handful of little stones land on the ground. I look up. Do stones fall from the sky these days as well? All the rules that keep my head safe have vanished.

'Titch, did you see that?'

'See what?'

'Nothing. I think it was nothing.' I look at the pebbles, and one of them catches my eye.

'Titch, I lied. I don't think it was nothing. What's this?'

Titch comes over to take a look. 'Pyrite,' they say as they pick it up.

I squish my face up, trying to remember where I've heard this before.

'Fool's gold,' says Titch. 'People thought that they'd be rich when they found some. I did too the first time! Just look at all the sparkles. But it's worth precisely zip.'

'Cool,' I say as I take it off them and turn it round so it sparkles in the sun. Then I pop it in one of my pockets, and a clatter makes me realize I already have a pebble in there.

Titch's face scrunches into a frown. 'You don't normally find pyrite around here. Yet another ruddy mystery!' they call as they go back to skimming.

Next to where the sparkly pyrite stone landed, there's a really tall sticking-out piece of rock. All the edges are corrugated as it's made up of so many layers. Now *that* would make an excellent skimmer for Titch, biggest one yet, if I can get a piece off intact. I try slicing, but it crumbles before I can extract anything bigger than playing-card size.

I need something harder. I pick up a piece of light grey rock. The edge is really sharp. *Perfect*.

The first sliver I try crumbles immediately. I gouge out all the left-behind bits and try again. Same thing happens. 'Oh, for goodness' sake,' I mutter, and lob the rock on the ground. I'm about as good at this as I am at skimming.

Third time lucky? I throw back my shoulders and huffily pick up the rock at my feet. I start again, really concentrating. I can feel my head beginning to ache from clamping my jaw so tight. This time the rock I'm using continues to slide along the layer, like a hot knife through butter. I put the rock down and gently begin to prise the layer of slate away with my fingers. *Careful now. Careful . . .*

'Ha! Gotcha! I have the world's largest skimming stone ever! Titch, come and look at this!'

There are sprinkles of pyrite in this sliver too, really unusual. I turn it over to see if it's even more sparkly on the other side.

When I do, I nearly drop it. Luckily, Titch comes up behind me and grabs hold just in time.

There's a message on it written in purple chalk.

On a slice of slate that was, a moment ago, part of a rock that's been there forever. And it's addressed to me.

HEY, MIMI, NO TIME (OR SPACE!)
TO EXPLAIN. YOU'LL NEED THIS:

Underneath the message are five stars in squares. They're numbered, but in the wrong order:

☆ ☆ ☆ ☆ ☆
4   3   2   5   1

Titch stares wide-eyed at me, and I look around. 'Did you see anyone do this?'

Titch shakes their head. 'What, draw inside a million-year-old rock? In all the time I've been coming here, no one has ever found my den. I'd be able to *tell* if anyone else had been here. And no one has.'

We stare and stare, keep turning the slate over and over, but it doesn't give us any more clues.

I grasp the message tightly and then hold it to my chest. I just *know* this is important and the clue we need to solve the cracks and help Gran.

'We need the Puzzler,' I say. My forehead is all creased up and my fringe won't stay out of my eyes.

Titch puts their arm round me and looks to see if anyone's watching, then whispers urgently, 'We need the Puzzler *now*.'

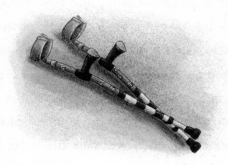

Chapter Seven

Titch and I have checked on my tank to make sure Phillip the Stickleback is OK, and now we're lying in wait under the letterbox. Thanks to their dad, we now have matching miniature rivers. We can watch the life cycle of our very own sticklebacks, keeping them safe for a little while before we return them back to their home. Having a mini-habitat in my bedroom gives me the calm of the river when I'm not there. It slows my thinking and my whirry brain, makes me less distracted, less needing to loop.

'Nearly time,' says Titch, putting their phone back in their pocket.

It's been a week, and both of us are starting to lose

hope that the Puzzler will get in touch. Though we're not saying that to each other. There's been no more talking crows, which we're exceedingly disappointed by, but lots and lots of cracks.

I lift my head up when I hear a noise in the hall.

'Your grandad will ground us forever if he knows we placed an advert in the paper,' says Titch.

'He won't have seen it,' I say. 'He never reads the classified section.'

'How come?' asks Titch as they stretch their legs out towards the radiator cover. Mine don't reach anywhere near.

'Cos he once bought half a Mini that didn't go, as well as fifteen parakeets and a dishwasher that was in bits. Gran's given him a lifetime ban.'

Titch nods. 'Makes sense. Though this doesn't. I can't keep getting here before school. I can barely keep my eyes open by two o'clock.'

There's a clank, and the postie's fingers pop through the box, and the letters fall on our heads. Titch grabs them, and we both sit up with our backs to the door. 'Bill. Bill. Charity bag. "Do you want to sell your house?" flyer. Bowls club weekly newsletter.' They toss them to one side. 'That's it. Nowt. Again.'

They sigh and stand up, and as they do they kick the flyer and something pokes out of it. I reach over and pull it out. It's an old postcard of Cawlington town centre with Guru, my favourite shop, circled in blue. I flip it over and nearly expire immediately.

I can't formulate words: my brain has popped off to Excitement Land. I shove the postcard up towards Titch and let out a shriek, my fingertips dancing in patterns. Titch kneels back down next to me and takes it out of my hands.

They read out loud: '*Pleasure to meet you, Stickleback Catchers! I'm not giving away my identity that easily. Show me you're worthy! To find my address, untangle this riddle: Blue fourteen is your jigsaw puzzle.*'

Titch grabs my hands, and we scream and laugh, bouncing up and down on our knees. 'I can't believe it!' I yell. 'The Puzzler replied!'

'This is the coolest thing ever!' screams Titch.

Titch gives me a massive hug, and we do a dance thing on our knees and laugh and whoop until Grandad arrives.

'You excited about my newsletter?' he asks, picking it up off the floor.

'Are we?' replies Titch, eyes bright.

'I don't know, are you?' asks Grandad, and Titch and I both fall about laughing in a heap, and I can't breathe, and Grandad shakes his head at us and wanders off.

★

'I cannot believe my grandparents are making me come to this,' I say as we walk into the bowling hall. Titch came round straight after school to work on the Puzzler's riddle, but Grandad caught us sneaking up to my room and made us come downstairs. The hall is decorated in reds and greens for our annual bowling awards.

'If you're being made to, what's my excuse?' asks Titch.

'Stickleback Catchers in it together!' I say cheesily, and hold up both thumbs, then offer a high five, but they ignore it and whack me on the head with the postcard.

We keep to the left-hand side as we make our way through the hall. Sometimes this space is used for a grandchild's birthday party, or quite often these days for a wake.

'The wakes are sad,' I say. 'But, with the average age of our club members being three hundred and fifty-six, it's also kind of inevitable.'

As soon as the last word pops out of my mouth, I get the cold pressure feeling. I look around, but no cracks.

My palms are sweaty, and I need to wipe them on my dungarees or they'll blister on my crutches.

We're aiming for the table in the corner where no one can interrupt us. The tables and chairs are set out with room between them, but the seating plan soon goes awry with the hard-of-hearing older folk needing to budge up a bit, and others wanting to be in groups of six instead of four, or else keeping away from the ones they owe money to. Sometimes I want to yell at them all to just flippin' keep the space clear so I don't have to wobble and please and squeeze and . . . well, it's knackering, finding alternative routes *and* keeping the yell inside.

We go past Jim and Bert's table. My forehead is all sweaty and when I try to wipe it I nearly take Bert's cap off with the end of my crutch. 'Eee, you young 'uns sitting with us? Make our day, that would.'

I go to protest, but Jim smiles sweetly, and I look at Titch. They roll their eyes, but pull out a chair.

'As soon as we get a chance, we'll move,' I whisper to Titch.

Bert slides his pint of beer over to me, and Jim slides his to Titch. Titch looks puzzled. 'I don't think I'm meant to be drinking.'

Jim laughs. 'Not drinking, drawing!' which doesn't seem to help Titch's confusion.

'The froth is really good for doing doodles in,' I tell them. 'I mainly do shamrocks, but you can do what you want.'

'See this as your initiation into the North Cawl Park Bowls Club family,' says Jim.

Titch drops their head down to try and hide the blush that's spreading over their cheeks.

Bert notices it and says quietly, 'You are so very welcome here.'

I wipe my hand on a napkin, and I'm about to stick my index finger into the froth when the room suddenly darkens, like there are storm clouds outside, and the next moment there are hundreds of thuds like giant hailstones against the window, and everyone in the room begins to scream.

Chapter Eight

There's the sound of glass shattering and chairs scraping. It's dark for a moment longer and then light again. The strange thudding noise has stopped, but now Grandad is at the microphone, shouting at everyone to 'Calm down!' which isn't working at all.

Bert has his arm round Titch, and Jim, who hadn't heard the bangs but has seen the absolute mayhem, is looking completely bewildered. I stand up to try to see what's going on, but so many people are moving about that it's impossible to tell.

Titch grabs my hand and pulls me back down. Their face is pale, and their eyes are massive. 'Look!'

They yank my head round to the windows, which are

covered in weird grey greasy smears, and I don't understand because they're always clean, especially before we have a do.

'What is that?' I whisper to Titch.

'Bird prints,' says Titch, and it takes me a minute to work out what they mean.

It's like I have to do one of those magic-eye puzzles and squint at it, then all of a sudden I can see. There are hundreds, *hundreds*, of bird marks on the windows. I can see their wings stretched in flight and the shape of their bodies at the moment they went *boom* into the window.

'Wait here,' says Titch, and barges through the crowd. I could barely get through before, but I don't stand a chance now.

'Well, that's one way to get a party started!' says Grandad over the microphone, and people do little laughs. 'Get yourself seated and, to calm us all down, we'll pop a bottle of wine on your tables – how's about that?'

Everyone cheers.

'Though it is coming out of the party fund, just so you know.'

'MOLLET WATH!' yells Bert.

'He means WALLET MOTH!' yells Jim, and the room descends into chats and laughter, and all is forgotten.

Titch sits back down at the table and whispers to me. 'I went outside, and there's not a single bird on the ground or in the sky. None to be seen.'

'What the heck is happening?' I ask.

'I don't know, but it doesn't feel good, does it? It has to be all linked together. The crows, the cracks, now this. We need to find the Puzzler and get them to solve the slate with the stars from the river.'

'Branching out from shamrocks?' Bert asks me.

I'd forgotten we were about to draw in their beer froth before all the commotion. 'Of course not,' I say. 'Shamrocks are my speciality.'

'This is definitely not a shamrock, love, even with your dubious drawing skills.' He looks very puzzled and slides his pint glass over to me, and Jim slides his over to Titch.

'What the . . . ?' says Titch.

In one glass is the outline of something that looks sort of like a star, but also sort of like a pebble.

And in the other is a jacket.

They are intricately drawn, like someone used a matchstick.

Who drew these symbols?

'Did you do this?' I ask Jim.

'With these eyes?'

Titch grabs my arm to pull me over to the spare table, but just then the lights go down. This time no one in the hall screams and everyone goes '*OOOOOOOH!*' like it's a surprise, when in actual fact this happens every year. We're trapped. We don't have time for this!

'Drum roll, please!' Grandad calls from offstage, and everyone starts clapping slowly on their knees, tapping their walking sticks, rapping on the tables. The beat rises, gets louder and louder, faster and faster. I don't like this bit, so I put my hands over my ears to muffle it, and just when it reaches its peak, and no one can keep up with their own hands any longer, the lights burst on, and there is Gran in the middle of the stage.

She has her arms held high. Her smile is a huge beam lighting up her face.

Gran drops her arms and begins to sing. Quietly at first. I have to strain to catch the music before it gets snatched away.

Everyone in the room leans towards her, and we become one, Gran bewitching each of us.

'Wow,' says Titch. 'Just. Wow.'

Gran holds the final note of the aria and raises her arms once more, and on the finish drops them suddenly and falls forward into a deep bow. The audience are slow to their feet, and most of them take about half an hour to get up, but the whooping, cheering and clapping starts immediately. I hold on to this moment as long as I can, with a still head with no crows fluttering in it, and Gran basking in the limelight.

Bert wolf-whistles with his fingers in his mouth, and Jim waves his hankie and shouts, 'Encore! Encore!'

Titch just says, 'Wow!' again.

Gran stands back up, and her silver bob catches the light.

Gran and Grandad are a perfect match. He comes onstage, and the yellow of his waistcoat exactly matches the satin of her dress. Grandad takes her hand, bows and kisses it. He then presents her to the rapturous audience once more before grabbing the microphone.

'Good evening, North Cawl Park Bowls Club!' he yells. The crowd goes wild. 'We are here to celebrate the bowling season and award our trophies. As you know, these trophies are in-house rather than external.'

The crowd boos and catcalls.

'But what do we care?' asks Grandad.

'Nowt!' yells the audience back at him.

'Every year, we have an award ceremony with fake awards because every year we come last in the official league,' I tell Titch. 'Once they begin the raffle, we'll be able to move.'

The audience carry on answering the jokes they know by heart, and pints are drunk and dropped, the noise rises and falls, but I'm not concentrating on any of that. I'm back to thinking about cracks and crows because Gran is being . . . well, odd. She's making my tummy feel funny.

She has moved towards the edge of the stage. She's still smiling, but it's a fake smile. She's reaching up and touching her bob, patting it in place, then smoothing down her dress and reaching up to her hair again. She's in a loop. Like the kind that I get stuck in when I'm in a flap, like when Titch first arrived. But Gran doesn't do loops. They're *my* thing.

She starts looking to the side and, at the same time as the first crack begins to jut-jut-jut across the floor towards her, I suddenly realize *she can't work out how to get off the stage.*

I stand and push my chair back and grab my crutches. Panic builds inside, and I fumble while I try to grab them. I'm only three rows back, but everyone has put handbags on the floor and moved their chairs. The cracks are getting closer, and I can't get to her! I wobble and please and squeeze and try to keep my eyes on Gran the whole time. There's something else happening, something dark, something with a smell of deep-buried-underground that is leaking out from the cracks. I pull my sleeve over my nose.

The hair-touch-dress-touch has intensified, and now I can see she's looking around frantically. The cracks are splintering through the floor, getting nearer and nearer, and no one is going to her. Why is no one helping her?

Coming out of the cracks, it looks like –

It can't be . . .

It looks like there are faces, hungry mouths opening wide.

A man I don't recognize pushes his chair back without looking, right into my side, and I teeter and crash down, bashing my cheek on the table as I fall. It jars so hard my ears ring, and it's like the lights flash on and off. One minute I was standing, next minute I'm not.

'Oh God! I'm so sorry – I didn't see you there! I wasn't looking!'

'No, you weren't,' I mutter.

I can feel the prickly carpet squares through my sleeves and see that under the tables it really could have done with a better clean. My left cheek throbs and pulses. I touch it and look at my fingers – no blood – but it's burning up, and I can feel it swelling already.

'Let me help you,' the man says. There's no question mark at the end of his sentence, and he grabs my arm, yanking it in its socket and moving me out of reach of my crutches.

'No thank you!' I growl.

More people are starting to look over. Subeera scootches off her seat and moves towards me. Subeera knows I don't like a fuss, and I do not like 'help' that isn't help.

The man is sweating now and blabbering and grabbing. I'm saying 'No thank you' repeatedly, trying to spot Gran, desperate to know if she's OK. What were those *things*? More and more people are looking.

Subeera wedges herself between me and the man and gives him her dog-trainer stare. Once she's made eye contact with him, she points to his chair and says simply, 'Sit.'

He does.

'Stop staring,' she says. He does. So does everyone else. Then to me: 'That looks sore. Want me to get you some ice?'

I can't see Gran from down here. I can't see the cracks, but I can *feel* them, feel whatever is coming out of them. I need to move. I can't keep still. I'm all fidgety.

'No thanks.'

Subeera nods. She looks at the man. 'I will train him.' She passes my crutches to me and moves back to her seat, leaving me to it.

By the time I reach the side of the stage, Gran is humming. It's a bad sign. I recognize it in me. It's like she's pulled her drawbridge up. And the cracks are making their way to the stage, across and up the front of it, running along the back wall. That stagnant smell leaks out, and I let out a little moan. There are blurry, open-mouthed faces, with jaws that have so many teeth – and the smell from their mouths!

I can't get up on to the stage from here as the steps are at the other side, so all I can do is call her over, try to get her away from them. 'Gran!' I yell. Nothing. 'Gran,' I try to say again, and it comes out in a whisper. There's a dank mist coming out of those mouths, and it's winding up her legs –

No response.

'Iolene Mill!' I manage to shout.

I don't know why I use her maiden name, the name she had when she sang all round the world, long before I came along. But it works. Her head whizzes towards me, and she stops humming, her performance smile leaps back on to her face, and she sidesteps towards me.

'Highly unprofessional,' she says to me in her posh voice. 'Leaving me up here like that. I will be speaking to the stage manager about this. Where is he?'

'Who?' I whisper. 'Gran, you're scaring me. Can you see them too?'

'Cannot get the staff!' Gran yells at me.

'Oh, OK, he's over here,' I say. Playing along seems to be the only way to get her to move.

Mr Marston of the Hats and Mrs Marston of the Scarves are hurrying over. 'Let's get you sorted,' says Mr Marston.

'I need a word with you!' says Gran to him.

'What have you done to your face?' Mrs Marston asks me, and then they both help Gran off the stage and bundle her away through the PIRATE door. The mouths jitter backwards into the cracks like a jerky rewind button has been pressed, and they disappear in front of my eyes. The smell stays in my nostrils. I snort, but it won't go.

I'm left standing in a room full of people and noise and laughter. People I know and love. People I've known and loved all my life.

And I have never felt so alone.

Chapter Nine

I'm meant to be staying over at Titch's house after the party, but I don't feel like going after what happened at the awards ceremony, with whatever they were that were after Gran.

The mouths were trying to take my gran!

I tell Titch I'm not feeling well because of falling and my face. Also mainly because I can't find the words to explain everything that just happened. Bert will make sure they get home safely. Before they can say anything, I come upstairs, sneak my mam's jumper out of Gran's bedside drawer and get under the bedcovers with my clothes still on. I hug the jumper tight. It's my safety blanket, what Grandad used to give me to protect me from the monsters under my bed, but it must have lost its magic because it doesn't work any more.

Because now I know that monsters are real.

Much later, Grandad comes in, but I pretend to be asleep.

★

I didn't think I would ever get to sleep, but I must have done because I wake up with bright light streaming into my room. My clock says 1 p.m. How did I sleep that long? I'm hot, sweaty and thirsty. I groggily shove the covers off and slowly make my way to our kitchen.

Mr Suit's black jacket is in the hall. My heart yammers in my chest, but I ignore the fear. I'm going to confront him and find out what's going on.

I sneak towards the Room for Best, and this time I check the door is closed before I lean up against it to listen.

'But it's a Special Guardianship order,' I hear Gran say. Though she doesn't sound like my gran; she sounds scared. Little.

'It's my responsibility to inform social services of anything that could get in the way of you both providing safe and full care for Mimi.'

'We are!' shouts Grandad, and I can hear him thumping his fist on the coffee table.

Gran tells him to keep it down or he might wake me up.

'She's asleep. I just checked,' Grandad says. That must have been what woke me up.

'Dr Teller,' says Gran, 'I am still in the early stages, George has reams of support, and Mimi is loved and cared for. This is her home.'

Of course this is my home! I think. *And Dr Teller? You were all lying to me about that . . . ? What's secret about a doctor?*

Dr Teller's voice comes at me through the door like I'm underwater. I only catch a few words, popping like bubbles, as if he's far away.

Or am I the one that's far away?

Dementia.

Accelerated pace.

Alzheimer's – memory loss – unsafe – nursing home – decline – sudden onset . . .

Inevitable.

And suddenly I understand what's happening to Gran.

I know what this means. I've seen it happen to my friends here at the club, to my fake great-aunties and uncles. This can't be happening to Gran! My world crumbles.

Could they take me away?

Is he actually saying that I'd have to leave my home?

I step away from the door and stumble back to my bedroom. As I move, cracks appear in the wall, splintering and spreading out. I pick up speed, and they follow me, moving through doors, across the ceiling, along the floor. In my room, the cracks tear up the shelves, judder through the window.

It's so cold.

The pressure in my ears makes me think my head will explode. It feels *inevitable*.

I grab my phone, my jacket and my crutches, make my way downstairs, and burst outside. The cracks follow me. I'm terrified. I gasp for breath, try to move faster, but I can't outrun them.

I'm looking behind me to see how close the cracks are getting, can't speed up any more, my hands sweaty on my crutches. I turn back round as I approach the corner, and that's when I see it staring at me. The scruffy crow that talked to us is there, sitting on the patio table, cracks threading their way from where I'm standing, up the table legs, across the tabletop.

'Go away!' I scream at it. 'Go away!'

The crow stays still, watching me.

I move towards it, flinging my arms about, trying to make it budge. 'This is all your fault! You brought the monsters here!'

The crow stands its ground. Why isn't it flying away? It watches me, staring with its beady eyes.

I stop still. The cracks aren't following me any more. They're wrapping themselves round the table the bird's sitting on, bashing into each other, making teenier and teenier cracks like veins.

The crow keeps its eyes on me the whole time, then it drops something from its beak. As soon as it does, it's like all the cracks do a high-speed rewind, and they retreat back round the corner, leaving the patio table like they were never there. I stop shivering.

'Impossible to speak with something in my beak!' says the crow, then does a tut to match Mrs Marston's and flies away.

I wipe tears from my face, my head reeling.

What just happened?

I walk over to see what it dropped. At first, I think it's a dried-up, shrivelled worm – it's the right sort of colour and size. But it's too straight. And too grey. I pick it up.

It's light and delicate and feels cool, like a tiny stone tube. When I look at it closely, I can see that at the end of the tube there is a perfect five-pointed star. I run my little fingernail up and down the grooves between the point of the star. It's like the tube has been made of teeny tiny stone stars all glued together, one on top of another in a long stack, about three centimetres in length. It's beautiful. I've never seen anything like it before. And I have absolutely no clue what it is, except that it looks exactly like the symbol that appeared in the froth on top of one of the pints last night.

I text Titch.

Can you come get me? Now!

Chapter Ten

I guess Gran and Grandad think I'm still in bed. I don't really care. As soon as I clambered in the back of their dad's car, and Titch saw my snot- and tear-streaked face all sticking out and swollen with the bruise from the fall for good measure, they told Mr Season to take us to the den.

We didn't speak the whole way, and that was OK. Titch doesn't need to fill the space with words and fluff. And I don't know how to say it all anyway. If I speak it out loud, then it will become real.

Outside the den, there's a new sign. Below KEEP OUT DANGER, it now says

THE STICKLEBACK CATCHERS

I look at Titch, and they smile. 'We needed a headquarters.'

I follow them inside, where I see that something else has changed. The space downstairs is smaller. At the back, there are planks of wood and MDF zigzagging up to the next floor.

'You built me a ramp?' I gasp. My hands flap with shock.

'Dad did most of it. I advised and hammered in some nails. Careful though, because I'm not sure I did a very good job.'

'You did a *brilliant* job,' I say. 'Thank you.'

'What are friends for?' says Titch. 'I'll get some water and put the kettle on, and you can tell me what's happened.'

★

There's something calming about a mug of hot, sugary tea in your hand and the rush of water outside. The way the river always goes the same way, in the same direction, the same route. It knows exactly what it's meant to do and doesn't have any nasty surprises in it. A twig catches round a stone and almost pauses, held back by invisible currents until it scoots and drops and ripples and joins

the rest of the flow. A leaf follows the exact same pattern. I like patterns. I peer up out of the window. The sky is blue with faint clouds that are all bobbly like bubble wrap.

I can breathe here.

As I speak, Titch listens. Not many people do that. Titch has the postcard from the Puzzler in their hands and spins it round and round, stroking the edges with their index finger. They let me go round and round in circles too, until the capital letters and exclamation marks in my brain become softer, rounder letters, slower, less spiky. I tell them everything. About seeing the monsters coming out of the cracks and wrapping themselves round Gran, how I'm sure they were trying to steal her and take her back through the cracks. How I overheard those terrible words Mr Suit (who is in fact Dr Teller) said about my gran. About the cracks that followed me, and the talking crow giving me the star tube.

'Whoa,' says Titch eventually. 'I don't know anyone who's had dementia, but from what I've seen on TV it doesn't look like fun.' They hold their hand out and sort of pat my knee.

'It explains why Gran's been a bit snappy and doing those flickering things,' I tell Titch as I blow on my tea to cool it. 'Why couldn't I tell? It's not like I haven't watched it happen before to our bowls club family.'

Titch twiddles their finger along the knots in the wood. 'When you're with someone all the time, I guess it's harder to see the signs. And, well, maybe you didn't want to?'

I nod.

'What happens next?' asks Titch.

I shrug. 'Who knows? Gran could stay the way she is for ages and be fine, or it might all tumble down fast with the forgetting stuff, meaning she's not safe at home. Titch,' I say, so quietly I'm not sure they can hear beneath the plaits I've wrapped round my face. 'What if Dr Teller takes her away? What if the *monsters* take her away? What if they take *me* away?'

Titch grabs my hand. 'The Stickleback Catchers are not going to let that happen!'

I peer out from behind my plaits. 'Promise?'

'Pinkie promise,' says Titch, and holds out their little finger, which reminds me of doing jinx with Gran, so I smile and laugh and cry all at the same time while I shake their little finger with mine.

'Excellent "smry",' says Titch. I look baffled. 'A smile-cry.'

I grin.

'So how do you feel now?' they ask.

Through the window, I watch the river flow. You can depend on it to do its job, to be going in the right direction. You can rely on it. Why can't people be like that?

'That question is too big,' I say.

It's too much to hold in my head. I'm angry that Gran and Grandad lied. I know it's because they want to protect me, but understanding that doesn't make me less angry. But most of all I'm scared.

'I'm scangry,' I tell Titch. 'Scared and angry.'

'Fair dos,' they say. 'So what are the cracks? They're definitely linked to your gran. And those mouth things – how do we stop them?'

'You think if we stop them we can maybe . . . ?' My lips crumple up tight round my teeth, too scared to hope out loud.

'Save her?' Titch gives me a little smile, and I feel less silly. I feel stronger. Titch *gets* it!

'We know it began with your gran,' says Titch. 'You first saw the crack when they all lied to you. And, whenever she has a blip, a crack appears.'

I nod.

'That crow has something to do with it. Crows are always evil in fairy stories. D'you think it's working with Mr Suit – I mean Dr Teller? Because . . .'

I drift off as Titch works through their theories. I'm exhausted from all the crying.

Titch pauses, which makes me notice the silence and come back to the present, then they quietly say, 'Follow the river.'

'What?'

'My mam used to say it. Before she left.'

It's the first time Titch has said anything voluntarily about their mam, so I keep as still as I can so I don't break the spell.

'When I was confused or in a mess, which was often and a lot, and I wonder if maybe that was the reason she . . .' Titch twiddles with their lace, and I don't even breathe. 'Well, when I was in a mess, she'd say that. *We've got no choice, things move on, they flow. Pick up the pieces, work it out. Whatever happens, follow the river.*'

I sit back down next to Titch. 'That's good advice, that is.'

'Yup. And you know what?' Titch looks me direct in the eyes, and a tear runs down their face, and they don't wipe it away. 'I can't work out whether when she left she was following her own advice. Was she following the river? I wish I could go back and find out. I wish I could change what happened.'

I don't know what to say to that. Gran is going to be taken away from – never mind me – from *herself* if we don't do something. She'll forget me and everything she knows and loves. But she's not *choosing* to leave. She'd do everything possible to stay. So I need to do that too.

The Stickleback Catchers need to do everything possible to keep her here.

I'm scared of saying the wrong thing, so I just hope that Titch knows that I know how they feel, sort of, and I get it but don't get it, but I'm here for them now. They need a friend too, and I'm all in.

I look through my pockets to give them a conker to hold, and instead find the star tube that the crow left on the table. For me. It left it on the table for *me*. The day after we got the postcard from the Puzzler.

'You're wrong!' I yell.

'What?' says Titch, taken aback, as I leap from half asleep to standing bolt upright and thwack my head on the den roof.

'The crow. It's not evil. It's trying to *help* us!'

'What? Why do you think that?'

'Because it works for the Puzzler! Don't you see? It's all part of their riddle! You have to believe me. The clues are joined together!'

'Clues for *what*? To find the Puzzler?'

'Yes!'

Then it hits me, *whump*, and I didn't know I believed it when Titch said it, but now it's the most obvious thing in the world.

'To save Gran.'

I grab at Titch's arm. 'We need to hurry. If Dr Teller decides Gran and Grandad can't look after me any more . . .' I can't finish that thought, so I just shake my head. 'We don't have time! So these are the clues.' I place the star tube next to the postcard from the Puzzler. 'What do they mean?' I try to swipe my fringe out of my eyes, but it won't stay put.

Titch stares at me, then stares at the riddle on the postcard, their lips moving as they say it out loud over and over again: '*To find my address, untangle this riddle: Blue fourteen is your jigsaw puzzle.*'

They shrug and throw their hands up. 'This is too hard! We need a walk-through!'

'Right. Let's be logical. This star was drawn in the top of Bert's pint, and the crow gave me the star thing,' I say.

'And a jacket was drawn in the other pint. Mr Suit's jacket.'

Titch stares at me.

'I know, I mean Dr Teller. Ugh.'

Titch keeps staring.

'What? Have I got food on my face? Tell me! What?'

'We are so stupid.'

'What do you mean?'

Titch points at me, which is really not helping the paranoid food-face feeling. My wobbles sometimes mean I get more food outside my mouth than in, but there's really no need to be rude about it.

Hold on, are they calling *me* stupid?

Then Titch says, 'It's *your* jacket, Mimi! Blue fourteen!'

I look down at it. They're right. How could I be so stupid? Of course it is! All the pockets – how did I not see that?

'What next?' yells Titch, bouncing up and down.

'I don't know!' I yell back.

'Think!'

'What do you think I'm trying to do?' I grab the postcard off Titch.

TO FIND MY ADDRESS, UNTANGLE THIS RIDDLE:
BLUE 14 IS YOUR JIGSAW PUZZLE.

Something niggles. Something is so close.

I take my jacket off and spread it on the floor of the den. *Think!*

'I got it from Guru. But *Beryl* wouldn't do this. She's far too busy smelling incense and persuading people to buy rugs. And nice jackets.'

I twiddle the material in my fingers. The blues are a cascade, all the different colours of different times of day, the depths and the bubbles. I'm wearing my very own river.

I open it out until I can see the label sewn inside.

Wear local, with love and pride from Telpher Uzz

'I just . . .'

I'm so frustrated I grab the jacket and my crutches, can't stay still, need to move. The answer is . . . I go down the ramp and out on to the pebbles. The river does a rubbish job of calming me. I need to help Gran! Why can't I . . . ?

I see the shadows of sticklebacks dancing at the water's edge. I think of our Mr Sticklebacks in our tanks at home.

When it's time to bring them back here, will *I* still have a home?

It's like the whole weight of the river is crushing my lungs, and I want to scream and scream and scream.

I look up to the trees clinging to the cliffside, the green sprouting all around, and I shout, 'IT'S NOT FAIR!'

And then I caw, caw like the crows that lined our rooftop, fill the air with scratchy shrieks, and Titch comes and stands next to me and does the same. Shrieking and cackling into the sky, the noise bouncing back, echoing from the rocks, and it makes my head spacious, room to breathe and think, and it stops my brain tumbling and jumbling.

Jigsaw-puzzle piece

Tumble

Untangle

The jigsaw-puzzle piece symbol on the label in the jacket!

Tumble

Jumble

Jumble up brain
Jumble up letters in my brain
TELPHER UZZ!

I say it over and over in my head as I close my eyes, and I can see the letters darting back and forth round the jigsaw-puzzle piece as I unscramble the anagram.

Unjumbling.

Unscrambling.

TELPHER UZZ

TEL HER PUZZ

TEL PUZZ HER

THE PUZZLER!

I open my eyes with a start and then turn to Titch and whisper, 'We need to catch another stickleback. As a pleased-to-meet-you present. Cos I know how to find the Puzzler!'

Chapter Eleven

'Right, let's go over the plan one more time before we go in,' says Titch as we walk from the bus stop along High Row.

We come to a stop outside Guru, under its canopy of brightly coloured handbags, prayer flags and bunting. Last time I was here with Gran, I stood on the crack. I shiver.

I look at the old picture on the postcard, then up at the real-life version.

Titch is hopping from foot to foot, and I can't stop my fingers tracing letters and making loops.

'We could just ask Beryl for the contact details; say you want to send a thank-you email to the person who made your jacket,' says Titch.

'We've gone over this! If she mentions it to Gran or Grandad, we're scuppered . . . I don't want to lie, but I'm so *scangry* with them right now that I can't be sure I won't end up yelling in their faces.'

'So we stick to the plan!' says Titch, and their worried face does not match the pretend excitement in their voice.

'You distract; I get Beryl's order book and find the address.'

'And I distract her how exactly?'

'You'll work it out,' I tell Titch, and open the door and go inside. All the bells jangle. There are no other customers, and Beryl is at the counter having a cuppa.

'Hey!' She waves. 'Who's this?'

'This is my friend Titch,' I say. 'They're very interested in incense.'

'I am?' asks Titch, and I give them a stage wink with my mouth all open and everything exaggerated. 'I am! Could you, erm, show me some smells?'

Beryl laughs and walks round the counter and through the little archway to the next room. 'Follow me.'

Titch turns back to me before they walk through, and they give me a massive thumbs up. This time the gesture doesn't tug at my heart quite so much, because once we solve this I know we can save Gran.

Action stations! I squeeze behind the counter, leaning my crutches against it. It's full of bags and boxes and pieces of paper. It always looks proper posh from the other side, and I've always wanted to work here and ding the till, but hidden away out of view from the customers it's a mess. Any one of these hundreds of bits of paper could be the one we need.

I wait for a feather to fall from the ceiling to guide me to the right spot . . .

Nothing.

Thanks for the help, crow.

I can hear Titch saying, 'Mmmmm, that one's even smellier,' which makes me giggle. I dive into the paperwork, scanning sheafs of tatty A4 paper, printouts and scribbled notes. My brain is brilliant at this. I've got speedy, whizzy eyes, and they are tuned in to the words *Telpher Uzz*. I scan, flip, put back, zoom.

Nothing.

Nothing!

'Ah, yes, thanks, Beryl. That was very enlightening. Maybe we could move on to holders now?' I overhear Titch say. I don't have much time if Titch is stalling like that. They sound so fake.

Then I see it, on top of the counter, right by the till.

I've been so hyper-focused on Telpher Uzz, I've missed the notepad in plain sight that says ORDER BOOK. *Brilliant work, brain.*

It's alphabetical, and I try to flick to T for Telpher as I can hear Beryl and Titch moving and footsteps starting to come back towards me. No time! My fingers fumble, and I nearly drop the book. I start moving out from the counter at the same time as I'm trying to look, and I crash into my crutches and trip and land in a heap.

'You OK, pet?' yells Beryl, and I can hear her footsteps get faster.

'Erm, but how do I choose just one!' yells Titch as Beryl appears through the archway.

I wave my crutches at her. 'Oops. Silly me!'

★

Five minutes later, we're walking back along the high street. Titch has a paper bag with a packet of jasmine incense sticks and a holder in the shape of a lily pad.

'So you didn't get it then? What on earth do we do now?'

I grin at Titch. 'Who says I didn't get it!' I take the order book out of a pocket and wave it at them.

Titch wraps their arms round me, and we whoop and cheer and leap up and down in the middle of High Row.

'We've got the Puzzler's address!' Titch yells. 'The mission is on!'

Chapter Twelve

The next morning Gran brings me a cup of tea at the table. I watch the walls, but no cracks. I shudder as I think about those faces oozing out of them. I study Gran, her eyes, but she's there, all there. It's a good day.

I just wish she'd tell me the truth.

'How are the Stickleback Catchers getting on?'

'Good,' I say.

'Forgiven me then?'

I don't say yes, but I don't say no, and Gran smiles as she butters a slice of toast, and I slurp my tea.

'Fancy coming stickleback catching with this old dear today? We used to love doing that together.'

'Can't,' I say. 'Other plans.'

To rescue you.

Gran nods and puts the butter in the microwave. A tiny crack zigzags across the glass front.

★

It is not easy to carry a fish tank full of river water and sticklebacks on your knee in a Volvo estate that is going repeatedly round and round the same roundabout.

'It's an absolute rabbit warren, Mimi! I'm not sure we'll ever make it back out!' cries Grandad. We giggle, even though we've done this routine every time we've picked up Titch since we first tried to leave their house, and it took us an hour of roundabout mayhem to get out of their estate.

'If you don't take the exit soon, I'm going to be sick in the tank.'

'This one it is then!'

★

Forty minutes later, Grandad pulls up outside a tall terraced house in Hartlepool. It has a big bay window at the bottom, and two floors up there's a bit sticking out of the roof that looks like a turret. All the wood is painted black, but it's peeling off, and beneath you can see all the colours it's been before. No wonder, cos even though it's sunny the wind is roaring in from the sea behind us.

There are stone steps that lead up to the front door. It's old and there's pretty glass and tiled mosaics next to it. On the plinth where the steps begin there is a bright green gargoyle. It says ROSLYN underneath. I'm not sure if that's the name of the house or the name of the gargoyle.

I sneak looks at Titch from under my fringe. I know Titch is my friend now, like properly. They shared their den with me, and we both have fish – that's practically married. But I'm still not sure why they're *so* keen to drop everything and come on this adventure with me. What's in it for them?

The cracks and the crows are muddling my head and making me mean.

Grandad looks round. 'I'd love to stay and wait for you until your fishing group . . .'

Fishing group? Titch mouths at me, and I shush them.

'. . . is finished, but I'm needed for, well . . .' Grandad stumbles over his words, and before I know it I'm helping him out, even though he's lying and I'm scangry, because he's my grandad and I love him.

'You're needed for all the stuff, Grandad!' I say while looking at Titch. 'Without Grandad, the whole organization would grind to a halt.'

Grandad gives me a funny look in the rear-view mirror and then smiles. No one makes any move to get out of the car.

'You both got your bus fare to get home?' We nod. 'Look, loves, my bladder is always on a timer. Get out. Now.'

I point to the tank.

'Right,' he says with a sigh. 'I'll help.'

★

Grandad leaves us, and we stand at the bottom of the steps. There's a telescope cemented to the wall, and I peer through. When I get it in focus, I'm looking at a place where the beach hits the sea, on the other side of the river, rickety boats all together in a rundown marina, and some green huts. I know where this is. Titch has shown me photos, and we've done that thing on Google Earth where you can soar over places and zoom in for a closer look.

'Paddy's Hole,' I say.

'We go there to eat our lemon tops,' says Titch. 'I didn't know you could see it from here. I must have looked over at this house a million times! Dad likes to talk to the fishermen. Mimi, can you see their green huts?'

'Yup!'

I spot them, then move my eyes along the shoreline. The tide is out. When I look back at them, Titch is staring up at the front door.

'You think this is really a good idea?' they ask.

'Bringing the fish?' I ask. They nod. 'It's flippin' genius! I know that you're meant to take a present when you go to someone's house, so tick; but there's something about our river – it's a part of it all too. Don't you feel it? And if we bring some to the Puzzler, well, maybe it can give them a head start.'

Titch sighs and shakes their head. 'After you.'

They're carrying the tank, and they have the piece of slate with the five stars drawn on it in a bag slung over their arm. I point to my crutches.

'Really? You're pulling that one on me?'

I grin. Titch sticks their tongue out at me, then climbs the steps. I look up and think I see the curtains move in the turret room. Then I follow on behind.

Titch has already rung the bell by the time I get to the top and is anxiously shifting from foot to foot. I think I see something out of the corner of my eye, but when I glance up there's nothing there. No cracks.

It feels like we've been standing there forever. We're about to leave when the door opens, and it gives me such a fright I scream, which makes Titch scream too.

There's someone standing in the doorway, maybe about nineteen years old (they have a beard). They're wearing tracksuit bottoms, white baggy socks and a turban. They do not scream.

They stare.

'Hi,' I say.

Silence.

'Erm,' says Titch.

So I take back over. 'We're friends of the Puzzler,' I say. 'Are they in?'

Silence.

'Do they live here?'

Silence.

'We brought fish.'

Silence.

'That's a bit weird, isn't it?' I say, feeling less sure of myself. 'I knew it was weird.'

They turn round and shout, 'Mam, there are some really weird people here to see Nusrat. And they've brought fish!' Then they walk away from the door down the hall but don't close the door, so me and Titch step inside and follow them.

Nusrat? Is that the Puzzler's real name?

They go through a door, and I'm not sure if we're meant to follow or if we're currently breaking and entering without the break bit, and I don't want to go to jail, and I can feel myself getting all flappy –

A different door opens into the hallway.

Standing there is someone I assume is Nusrat's mam, wearing a shalwar kameez in peacock colours and with long black hair tied in a ponytail.

'Hello, can I help you?'

'We're friends of Nusrat's,' I say.

She looks puzzled. 'Are you sure?'

'Yes,' I say, though my voice doesn't sound it.

'New friends,' says Titch. Then adds, 'Nearly. We're the Stickleback Catchers.'

I smile. 'We've come a long way.'

'And this is *really* heavy,' adds Titch.

★

We've done the introductions and know the bearded man is Nusrat's grumpy big brother Ranveer, and it's

Nusrat's mam who's currently upstairs seeing if Nusrat is able to accept our visit. It all sounds very formal — and is taking far too long. She's left us in the kitchen with tea and biscuits. I keep picking my mug up and putting it back down. Titch lays their hand on my knee to try to stop it bouncing.

Nusrat is the real name of the Puzzler!

★

'I'm very surprised she's agreed to see you,' says Nusrat's mam as she pops her head back round the kitchen door. 'Please talk quietly, and I'll be in to get you after fifteen minutes. No more.'

My legs won't stop bouncing with excitement. I try to compress everything down in my head to just fifteen minutes. Nusrat must be bombarded with people like us wanting her to solve their puzzles!

We follow her mam up two flights of stairs. I wonder if we were meant to bring money to pay her — maybe she accepts conkers? Brightly coloured sarongs and scarves are hanging on the walls, and they're floating gently as we climb past them.

Nusrat's mam peeks her head round the door. 'They're here,' she says, just above a whisper. 'You sure?' Nusrat must say yes because her mam turns back out to us and says, 'I've put two chairs by the bed.'

She holds the door open for us, and we go through.

Inside, the room is gloomy, the curtains are drawn, and it takes me a moment and a few blinks before my eyes adjust. When they do, I see that there's a shelf on the wall beside the bed and sitting on it is a microphone, the sort you plug into a laptop to record podcasts. This is definitely the Puzzler! My tummy flutters, and I can't stop grinning and flicking my fringe.

Titch is already sitting down on a wooden dining chair placed next to the bed. I take the seat beside them. In the bed, with only her head poking out, resting on pillows, is Nusrat. She's wearing dark sunglasses and ear defenders, and her long black hair pools around her.

'Hi,' she says quietly. 'I'm the Puzzler.' She smiles at us. 'And you're the Stickleback Catchers. You solved my riddle! Beryl's best mates with my mam. She said she was so chuffed you'd bought one of our jackets.'

Titch grins. 'We're your biggest fans.'

'My biggest fans who took bloomin' ages to find me!' She shrinks even lower beneath the covers. 'I bet you're disappointed. I'm not quite what you were expecting, am I?'

'Nusrat,' says Titch. 'Talking crows exist: we no longer have expectations about *anything*.'

'Yeah, how did you train him?' I ask.

'Train who?' says Nusrat.

So we tell her about her speaking crow who helped us, the feathers, the cracks and the mouths, show her the piece of slate, and the star tube, tell her about the drawings in the beer tops. Nusrat winces when I get too excited. Titch nudges me to calm me down, and I give Nusrat a little sorry nod, and she grins.

Then I quietly tell her what I overheard about Gran's dementia diagnosis. And how we need to complete all our missions to save her.

'That's a LOT,' says Nusrat.

We wait expectantly for her to say something else. She doesn't. And what with the sunglasses, and only her head poking out, it's really hard to tell if she's gone to sleep or not.

'Nusrat?' I ask quietly. 'Can you tell us why you sent the crow?'

'You think I did that?' she whispers. 'A *talking* crow? How the heck d'ya think I'd have done that? I haven't been outside for years!'

'So the crow is nothing to do with you?'

'No!' she whispers really loudly. 'But it is *awesome*! We need to set up some tests, do some more investigating, but I really think your gran is the catalyst.'

Titch and I must both look flummoxed by the catalyst bit, so Nusrat explains. 'It began when Dr Teller came – the first time. That must have been when he gave your gran the diagnosis. It's all linked through her. Things appear when something goes wrong or shifts and changes. And the crows . . . Heck, what time is it?'

I press the little button on my watch that makes the face glow. 'Four fifty-four p.m.,' I say.

'We're running out of time!' says Nusrat, and glances at her bedroom door. 'Can you leave the piece of slate with me?' I look at Titch, then nod. 'And the star tube?'

I begrudgingly hand it over. I don't want to let it go. 'You can keep the slate, but you can't keep this; only hold it for a little bit.' I feel mean, but then suddenly something clicks and I blurt out: 'My mam was called Asteria!'

'That's nice,' says Titch, and gives my hand a pat and nods at Nusrat in a 'don't worry about her' sort of way.

'No, I mean . . .' I say at the same time as Nusrat says, 'Of the stars.'

I smile at her.

'What's going on?' Titch asks, and throws their arms up in mock exasperation, and Nusrat giggles.

'My mam was named after a Greek goddess,' I say. 'Gran was into all that sort of thing.'

'Asteria is the goddess of falling stars,' explains Nusrat.

'Oh,' says Titch, finally getting it. 'Those symbols are *really* important then.'

Nusrat nods. 'This is the missing link. Not only does it tie everything to your gran, but it also ties it to *you*.'

Titch and Nusrat stare at me and I don't like it, so I take a coaster off the shelf near Nusrat's bed and study it carefully. *This really is all about me and Gran.*

I knew that already. But now I *know* it.

Nusrat hands back my star tube, and I stash it safely in a jacket pocket. 'I'm going to run some tests on the piece of slate,' she says. 'Solving the stars and numbers is the next step. You must keep your phones on you at all times. We need observations. This is my number.'

Titch types it in their phone and sends it to me.

'I can't do calls unless I instigate them. They take up too much energy when I'm not in control, but send me photos, messages, film, all the evidence you find, and I'll review it and get back to you. What time are we on?'

'Four fifty-seven.'

'We've only got a couple of minutes left. Anything else?'

'We left some fish downstairs for you, Nusrat,' says Titch.

'In a tank, not for eating – that would be weird,' I add.

'Thank you. And please call me Nus. That's what my friends call me. Only my mam and my brother call me Nusrat, and that's usually when I'm in bother.'

Ranveer sticks his head round the door. 'Hurry up! And what do you mean "friends"? You ain't got any!'

'Yes she does,' says Titch.

'Us!' I shout, then slam my hand over my mouth and mouth *sorry* at Nus as her brother shakes his head and disappears back round the door.

'Do you want to be in the Stickleback Catchers?' I whisper, trying to make up for my shout. 'We've got a den, but we don't have a handshake.'

Nus grins, then pulls the duvet over her head and squeaks from underneath, 'With this mystery? I'm in!'

'Me too,' says Titch.

'I know you are,' I say to Titch. 'But also me three.'

Nus's mam pops her head round the door and quietly says, 'Time's up.'

Chapter Thirteen

I am as giddy as a giddy thing that's really blimmin' giddy when the bus drops us back in the town centre. Titch and I don't stop talking for a single second, and our words lap over each other's edges so there isn't a single blank bit that isn't filled with wonderings.

I leave Titch so they can head back to their house, and we do an awkward hug thing. We both agree that the need for a secret handshake is TOP PRIORITY. Titch says they'll work on it. And Nus says she'll have our preliminary report ready in a couple of days. Awesome. She's up for a mega mystery because that's her job, but the way she got all shy and hid under her duvet? I think, like us, she just needs friends.

I walk up the ramp from the market square and on to High Row. The busker outside the bank asks me how Gran is. I smile and say, 'Fine.' Then I wonder if he's just being polite or if he knows about Gran's dementia, and I'm the only one in the whole town who doesn't (even though I do). I feel left out and small.

But then I feel mighty because they don't even know that I *do* know, and I'm going to fix everything.

I stop at Taylor's and pick up three pork pies. Gran's favourite. We can have them for our tea.

'You look happy,' says Betty as she hands me my change. 'Good to see your smile back.'

'Has it been missing?' I ask, and Betty seems a little bit confused like that wasn't the *correct answer*. But it is. It's good to have my smile back.

I say hello, or more like shout it in a sing-song manner, to four people, three dogs and a pigeon by the time I pop out of the underpass and start making my way through the car park towards home.

That's when I first notice them, and my toes curl and my face feels too hot, and I need to run, but I've forgotten how.

Cracks.

Exploding through the ground towards me from the

bowls club, ripping up the grass in the park, exposing tree roots and rushing round the bandstand and then meeting again, a groove gashing closer and closer –

My mouth goes all dry, and I'm frozen to the spot.

Run, Mimi!

But I can't move. Why didn't I stay with Gran this morning when she asked? Something awful has happened, and it's all my fault.

Ripping up the tarmac in the car park, bursting towards me, gravel flying, then suddenly the feel before a storm: black sky, wind swirling.

Hundreds of crows are swooping down, lining all the hedges. They're on top of lamp posts, they're on the steps that lead up to the back of the buffet restaurant, and they're making a barrier between me and the crack. They're stopping the cracks!

The big scruffy crow steps out from the crowd, the murder, and says one single word to me: '*Go.*'

I drop the pork pies, get my crutches set and run towards Gran.

Chapter Fourteen

When I reach the club, the members are all in huddles. The bar is full, but it's silent. That makes me even more worried. Really bloomin' scared. It's *never* quiet here. Subeera walks over to me, and I think she's going to stop me, but she just touches my hand and holds open the PIRATE door for me.

When I get upstairs, the black jacket is hanging on the coat rack. Of course it is. This time I don't listen at the door but burst straight into the Room for Best.

No one's there.

I make my way along the corridor, and as I do a little crack – so small it's like a tiny bolt of electricity, maybe all it has left after the big display outside – follows me along the hall and into the kitchen. A very big bit of me is terrified, and I think about going back to Titch and not telling them about any of this, because pretending seems a very good choice right now.

I take a deep breath. That is not what a Stickleback Catcher would do.

Dr Teller and Grandad are sitting at the table. They have cups of tea, but neither of the teas has been touched. I make my way over and out of habit move a place mat to cover the vacuum-cleaner note.

'Where's Gran?'

Grandad gives me a weak smile. 'She's in bed, having a kip.'

I'm so relieved my head goes *whoosh*, and I have to grab the table to stay upright. Dr Teller leaps up and pulls out a chair for me. 'Here you go,' and I let him help me to sit down. He gently rests my crutches against the table. I like how he takes care of them. They are an extension of me, part of me. You wouldn't crack someone's arm against something, and neither should you do that with crutches.

That doesn't mean I like him though.

'Here about the insurance again?' I ask him. He opens his mouth and closes it again.

'She knows,' says Grandad. 'I don't know how, or how much, but she knows.'

'Knows what?' I ask, and cross my arms. I'm going to make him say it.

'Mimi, I'm really tired. No games.'

'Games? *Games!*'

Grandad tries to shush me.

'Don't you dare! Everyone knows but me — *everyone*. Know what that feels like, when everyone's talking about Gran and then stops when I enter the room and put on all these silly fake smiles? It's not nice. She's *my* gran — I should know before them. You should use the proper words and say them out loud. Dementia. Dementia, dementia! We should be in it together, we're the Triangle Trio, and *you* —' I point to Dr Teller — 'you, Dr Inevitable, you're going to take me away!' and then I burst into tears.

Grandad puts his arms round me, and I slump on to the table, my face pressed hard against its surface. I wrap my arms round my head. My feet are tapping on the floor, and they won't stop. Grandad doesn't say anything, just holds me tight until my feet slow down. When I lift my head up, I'm covered in snot and tears. Dr Inevitable hands me a tissue, and I blow my nose. I look at both of them. 'Well?'

'We had a little bit of a close call,' says the doctor.

'What happened?' I ask. Dr Inevitable looks at Grandad.

'No more secrets,' I say. Grandad nods. 'Promise?'

'I promise.'

The doctor picks up his tea and takes a sip, then winces at the congealed milk skin and places it back down. 'Your gran went missing. She can't always remember how to get home.'

My tummy squishes. How did I not know this? Because I've been too busy having fun.

'All her friends have been helping out wonderfully, making sure they're keeping an eye on her, but that meant that lots of people thought someone else was with her, so for a while nobody noticed she'd gone.'

Grandad hangs his head.

'She was found, fully clothed, trying to have a swim in the river.' My head bobs up at this bit of information. 'She'd got herself into a bit of bother so the police and an ambulance were called. Luckily, someone recognized her, so, once the ambulance crew had checked her out, they were able to bring her home.'

'Gran knows everyone,' I say quietly. The doctor nods like I've just said something important. Which I have. 'But . . . why was she at the river?'

Grandad looks so small and old. 'Oh, pet, she said she was looking for sticklebacks for you. We used to do that together, do you remember?'

I feel a pang of love and loss so hard I think my heart will fall out of my chest right on to the table. Why didn't I go with her when she asked?

I take the star tube out of my pocket, hold it in my right hand and rotate it round and round with my thumb.

'We're just having a little chat about what we do from here,' the doctor tells me.

'What do you mean?' I spin the stars faster.

'We need to think about some ways we can support your grandad in looking after your gran.'

'Well, you could have started by being honest with me! I could have helped!'

I smack the stars down on the table and some shatter from the tube, tumble along the surface. Grandad doesn't even try to defend himself, and he looks so tired I stop shouting at him, and hand him one of the shorn-off sliver-stars instead.

'Where did you get . . . ?' He shakes his head, takes it and gives me a weak smile. 'Never mind. Thanks, pet.'

'There is respite care,' says the doctor. 'Just a little bit of time so your grandad can have a rest, and we can get things set up here.'

'You're not taking her away!' Grandad wraps his big hand round mine. The shaking starts in the hand he's holding and moves through me until my whole body is vibrating.

What if you take me away?

Grandad holds my hand up to his cheek, and I can feel his stubble. 'I'm tired. And I'm scared. It could have ended horrifically today.' A single tear rolls out of his eye, and he wipes it away and gives me a little smile. 'But no one is taking Gran anywhere.'

'I should have been here,' I say quietly.

'No, you shouldn't,' say Grandad and Dr Inevitable at the same time.

And then all three of us say, 'Jinx.' And we smile, but mine is a fake one.

'Go and see if Gran's awake,' says Grandad. 'We've got some working out to do.'

I don't want to leave them, but I don't like the idea of Gran being by herself either. I scrape the sliver-stars back up from the table and drop them in my pocket with the tube. I have so many questions I want to ask, and Grandad would usually give me space and time to work through them all, but he hasn't. I don't think he's thinking right.

★

Gran is sleeping peacefully. She's all snuggled up in her duvet. Her hair must have been wet because it's dried curly. Gran would never let that happen: she's ruthless with a blow-dry. I walk to the window and look out over the green and into the park. All the crows are on top of the Cawlington Bottling Co building.

It's really stuffy in the room, so I open the top window a crack. I can hear Mr Marston of the Hats' voice. I look down, and I can just about see the edge of him. He's talking to Li Wei.

'Have you seen them all? Just standing there, watching. It's creepy,' says Li Wei as he points to the crows on the rooftop.

'Not just creepy,' replies Mr Marston. 'They're a portent.'

'A what?'

'A harbinger, an omen,' explains Mr Marston. 'Crows are the bringers of death.'

It gives me such a shock I close the window quickly with a bang. I hope they know they've been heard. Can't have talk like that around Gran. I look over at her. She's still fast asleep.

I take her hand and sing our song, the one she always sings when I've had a nightmare, to help me get back to sleep.

> *Stars shine, you're mine,*
> *My love, my heart, my life!*
> *Glow bright, keep tight,*
> *My love, my heart, goodnight!*

Gran usually goes up at the end, and I go down, and then we giggle, and everything is OK again. Not a peep out of her. I begin to cry.

A single black feather floats down from the ceiling and lands on her pillow. It has to be a message from the crow. Who is he working for? If it's not for the Puzzler, could it be for the mouth monsters? Or is he trying to help? It's freezing in here, and I have to give myself a hug to stop my teeth chattering.

I can't wait any longer for the crow to find me. Gran could have drowned today, and it would have been all my fault. We've been playing about, not taking things seriously enough.

The crow knows everything, and I need to know too.

I take out my phone and go to the Stickleback Catchers group chat.

> We need to hurry. Time is
> running out.

Chapter Fifteen

Titch and I are sitting on the bank of the river outside our den HQ. Their legs reach across three boulders with plenty of leg to spare, and mine only do one. Nearly two.

The dandelions are all out now, but some are beginning to turn brown. There are a couple of clocks near my feet, and I reach down and pluck one. I blow. Eight times to clear it. The little seeds float away. Gran calls them wishes.

The Stickleback Catchers are on high alert and deep in Mission Solve the Stars, Find the Crows. But we are no nearer to solving anything, and Gran is getting further away. Each day there's a moment when I know she's trying to work out who I am, and it breaks my heart.

Nus has analysed the piece of slate. Basically, it's really old but the chalk is really new, and she has no idea whatsoever how the star message and clue got inside or what it means, or whether it's linked to the crows. That's all we have to go on though, so that's what we're clinging to.

The cracks are everywhere. Gran's bedroom is shattered, and I don't know how long we have until the cracks explode everything apart. It's desperately cold in her room; the chill seeps into everything. Gran's skin is freezing to the touch. I told Dr Teller, and he says it's just her slowing down, but I know it's the mouth monsters and the cracks.

Titch picks another dandelion and hands it to me. 'Do you miss your mam?' they ask.

I think about my answer really carefully because Titch doesn't usually bring this up.

'Not her exactly, just the thought of her being there, I guess. But I don't really know her to miss. And I have Gran and Grandad . . . Do you miss yours?'

'Yup. All. The. Time.' Titch says it like the words are spaced out, and it makes my heart hurt.

'Do you know why she left?'

'Nope.'

'Hasn't your dad told you?'

'I haven't asked.'

'What?'

'Well, I figured, if he wanted to, or knew, he would have, and he hasn't, so . . .'

'Titch, you should just ask!'

'Yeah, I know, but what if I don't want to hear the answer? Maybe that's why he hasn't told me.'

'What, like he's protecting you?' I pick up a leaf and twiddle it.

'Yup, exactly that.'

Titch pokes a stone with a stick, and a woodlouse pops out. I want to tell them that everything will be OK, and there'll be a proper reason, but I can't say that because *I* don't know, do I? Adults make some really strange decisions.

'You've never talked about it, not once?'

'Dad did try, right at the beginning, when she first left. But I was angry, and I wouldn't listen, and then . . . Well, time just goes on, doesn't it? And he stopped trying because it upset me so much. Now I want to know, but I'm not sure how to ask.'

'Just say something! Your dad's great; he does loads of stuff with you.'

'Sometimes I think all the stuff is there to fill up the spaces — the gaps that we don't talk about. We fill it with noise and things, but then when we go to our separate rooms the silence feels really loud. It's never enough.'

'Well, maybe . . .'

Just then, both our pockets buzz. Titch looks like they're going to say something else, but I really need to look at my phone — what if it's about Gran? I hold their eyes a moment longer, and Titch gives me a funny look, then I grab my phone.

'It's Nus!' I say.

Go to the den.

Titch sighs and takes their phone out. They're *waaaay* faster than me so they type:

WE'RE THERE ALREADY. WHY?

We wait for Nus's reply.

Can you see anything that looks
like this?

We wait a moment as the picture downloads. It's an old
black-and-white photograph of the section of river we're
on. There are two ladies in coats with big puffy sleeves and
long, voluminous skirts sitting on deckchairs. The trees on
the opposite bank are much smaller than they are now. A
bright yellow circle has been drawn on the photo in
digital ink. It highlights what looks like a little drain
cover near where the grassy bank meets the pebbles.

Titch studies the photo, then leaps up and races over
to the spot circled in the photo. It's covered in grasses,
like the bank has eaten it up. They frantically tear the
grass away. I scoot over and join them.

Titch discovers the edge of the drain cover and grins
at me, then goes back to ripping away all the plants.
They rock back on their hunkers and let out a slow
whistle. On the newly revealed cover are five sunken
stars in a row, exactly the same as the chalk drawing on
the piece of slate.

Titch leaps up and does a joyful flail, but I kick the
heads off some dandelions.

'More puzzles?' I exclaim. '*More puzzles?* This is taking too long!'

Suddenly there's a loud rustle behind us, and we turn round to look. The scruffy crow lands on a tree trunk.

The *talking* crow.

I storm over to it, waving my crutches, trying to swipe at it. 'It's all your fault, you stupid bird. *You* started this, then left us!'

'Hey!' yells Titch, and comes running after me.

There's a clatter as the crow plops through a small hole in the tree trunk and disappears.

'What the . . . ?' I say, all the shout shocked out of me. 'Did you see that?!'

Titch reaches me, and we peer inside the trunk. Nothing. No bird.

'How the heck?' says Titch. 'Where did it go?'

They get out their phone and message Nus and then start taking photos of the trunk and send them too.

There's a clang inside the trunk. We stop and look at each other. Neither one of us moves. Titch messages.

Our phones buzz. It makes me jump.

> What are you waiting for? Look
> inside! Film it.

'That's easy for her to say from the safety of her bedroom,' I tell Titch.

Titch stares at me. 'I think she'd be here if she could, don't you?'

I have the decency to match my insides with my face and look as rubbish as I feel.

'I'll stream it to Nus,' says Titch. 'You check it out.'

'Something might grab me!' I yell.

Titch shrugs and smiles. 'You should have been quicker to bagsy.' They press record and point to the trunk.

I take a deep breath and, holding my head back as far as it is possible from the opening, I look inside. There *is* something in there now. I poke my arm through the hole. Ugh, it stinks of mouldy leaves and something dark underneath, like that stench from the mouth monsters. I'll need to bleach myself after this.

Our phones buzz again.

'Nus wants to know what it is,' says Titch.

I grin at the camera. 'So do I,' I say, 'but I don't fancy losing an arm. How would I use my crutches then?'

'Get on with it,' says Titch.

I stick my tongue out at them, and then I stick my arm back in the trunk.

Two seconds later, I begin to scream.

I flail around, shouting, and Titch dashes over, horror on their face. I look at them, eyes wide –

And start to laugh.

'Your *face*!' I say, wheezing.

'What?' says Titch furiously. 'Are you . . . ?' Then they're laughing too. 'You are *horrible*! You *proper* had me going!'

I wipe a laughter tear from my eye and grin at them. 'But look though. There is *something* . . .'

I pull my arm out and show the object to Titch and the camera. My arm stinks – pity Nus can't smell that. It's a clear pale-green glass bottle. Embossed on it is the image of a really old-fashioned train and a logo I know well.

'This bottle comes from the Cawlington Bottling Co building,' I tell Titch in awe.

'I know,' says Titch. 'You've got some on your shelf.'

'I got them from the Cawlington Bottling Society. The members go round the town digging up bottles from all the old factories, like a metal detector club but for bottles! Though the ones they find are not usually in as good nick as this, mind.' I turn it round in my hands.

Our phones buzz with another message from Nus. She's sent a link with photos of the building in its heyday.

It would have looked like this
when your grandad worked here.

'See,' I say to Titch. 'Those arches were the main door and windows.'

'But now they're bricked up . . .'

I slap my forehead. 'You don't think that's where the crows are — in the flippin' place I've been trying to get into for years? The place with no door?'

'It's all linked to your gran,' says Titch as they take the bottle from me to have a look. 'It would kind of make sense.'

Titch passes the bottle back to me, and it nearly slips from my hand. I try to catch it and end up batting it instead, and Titch leaps to the side and lands on the ground, just managing to save it in time. The sky explodes with thunder, and it begins to rain, huge droplets splatting against us, and then the sky cracks open with lightning.

'Whoa,' says Titch. 'Someone did *not* want you to drop that.'

Or something, I think.

Titch is holding the bottle by its neck, and its base catches the light.

'Look!' I say.

'What?'

'The base!'

On the glass bottom is a star. A star that looks like it would fit perfectly into the shapes on the drain cover.

We message Nusrat and she quickly replies.

> Press the stars in this order:
> 4-3-2-5-1.

Titch and I kneel next to the stars. Dandelion wishes float away where we brush against their clocks. Titch gives me a thumbs up to say they've started streaming again.

Our phones ping again.

> And make sure you speak clearly.

'Is Nus recording this for her podcast?!'

Titch grins and shrugs.

I take a deep breath – it's more wobbly than I would have liked. I lean forward and press the bottom of the bottle against the fourth star. It fits perfectly. The star on the drain cover sinks as I pull the bottle away and stays down. I turn to Titch, wide-eyed.

'Do the next one!' they say.

I press it against the third star. It sinks again. The second. The fifth. I take a deep breath. The first. It sinks just like the others have done.

I sit back on my feet and watch. I stare at Titch; they shrug. Then there is an almighty bang as the stars pop back out to lie flush with the drain cover.

Wind whips up from nowhere, and pressure builds in my ears. I think they're going to pop. I slam my hands over them, and my tummy slides to one side, like the whole world has shifted, and then there's a roar of water. I fling myself round to stare at the river.

Titch slowly moves closer to me and takes my hand. We watch, barely breathing, as the river funnels up into the air like a tornado, swirling and climbing higher and higher, ducks, sticklebacks, weeds all caught up and churning inside. My stomach drops like on a rollercoaster as the river hangs in the air and then crashes down into a massive tidal wave, spraying and smashing into the trees on the bank.

Ducks pop back to the surface, shaking their heads, bobbing around, trying to work out what just happened as the wave gently subsides.

Something is different. Changed. It's like looking at a spot-the-difference puzzle. Everything seems exactly the same as it was, like nothing happened. But something . . .

Follow the river. The saying Titch's mam told them suddenly pops into my head. Then I see it.

Backwards.

The river is flowing backwards.

Chapter Sixteen

We stand on the riverbank and stare. Somehow Titch manages to keep filming for Nus. The roar stops. The river is definitely running backwards! All the twigs are flowing the wrong way!

I feel really dizzy and like I need to sit down and then *BOOM!* A crash, almost like thunder, and suddenly not only is the river flowing backwards but it's now hovering *above* the riverbed. There's a gap, like it's been lifted up somehow and all the pebbles that are normally hidden beneath the water are now visible and dry.

I peer towards it, my fingers flapping. Straight in front of us, in the now dry riverbed, a hole has appeared. I take a tentative step closer, and I can see a metal staircase inside the hole that winds down and down and down. I square my shoulders and walk towards the edge of the river. Titch tries to hold me back, but I shake off their hand. I peer in and then take a step on to the dry pebbles and look up. I can see the river flowing the wrong way above me, like it's travelling over a transparent motorway bridge. A moorhen floats in the wrong direction, and I can see its bright yellow legs with the red garter at the top, its belly all soggy.

It's incredible.

I try to reach up to touch the water, but it curves round the edge of my finger, like when we use magnets in science to repel each other.

'Check out the staircase!' calls Titch from the safety of the bank. 'Can you see the bottom?'

I lean over the edge and stare down. 'Nope.'

They come over to join me, stepping gingerly on the pebbles, holding their hands above their head to protect them from the river above. Titch peers down too. 'Me neither. It smells damp.'

It's really foisty, like the time I left a swimming cossie in a carrier bag in my wardrobe and we had to wash all the clothes in there to get the smell out. There's that lingering undercurrent too that smells really, *really* bad. Like the mouths.

I put my shoulders back to make me feel taller. 'I'm going in,' I tell Titch.

'You what? You can't!'

'Haven't we been waiting for something like this?'

'Well . . .'

'Oh,' I say as my face falls. 'I get it now. You didn't actually believe there was anything, did you?'

Titch looks sheepish. 'Well, it was a bit far-fetched.'

'You heard the talking crow!'

'But did I though?'

'Yes!'

I stare at Titch, furious. Have they just thought this was a silly kid's make-believe game? It has never been more real. My gran's life, my home, *everything* is on the line. I take a step inside and tell them sharply, 'You can track me on my phone.'

'I'll come with you!'

'No,' I say angrily. 'You need to stay here and guard it. And make sure the river stays the wrong way.' My eyebrow raises involuntarily at the ridiculousness of what I've just said.

Our phones buzz.

Which one of you is going in?
Someone needs to stay and keep
watch.

'See,' I say, pointing to the message self-righteously. 'Nus agrees with me.'

I hand over the bottle to Titch. 'Just in case the river closes, then you can get me back out.'

Titch holds their hand out to me. I don't take it. 'Work on our handshake while I'm gone,' I say. Then I grab my crutches and start making my way down.

★

The metal stairs clang with each step I take. Each time it makes me jump.

It's slippy underfoot, and my crutches are unsteady.

The further I wind down the staircase, the darker it gets until, when I look back up, the entrance is just a pinprick of light with a shadow Titch. I'm not sure I completely thought this through, and my fingers tap and won't keep still.

Who on earth built this? And why?

Who can control rivers?

Mouth monsters?

As the light fades, I begin to see shadows. Or are they mouths? I blink and blink, but the images of them stay painted on the inside of my eyelids. I shudder and look back up. I want to go home.

I shake my head. I need to *save* home. Must concentrate. Must keep descending.

There is constant dripping, and the damp smell gets damper, and the dark gets darker the deeper I go. I try to livestream it to Nus, but my data signal dies.

I'm on my own.

That's OK. I'm OK. I'm an adventurer on an actual adventure!

Who am I kidding? I'm terrified.

I can feel a breeze growing. It has an icy under-current, and I sink down into my jumper, wish I'd brought more layers. It nibbles at my ears, and I keep jumping like something is going to bite me. My heart *boom-boom-booms*, and I try to slow my breathing, but I can't. I'm seeing shadows where there aren't any — and, where there are, I'm seeing . . . Don't think about the mouths.

I turn on the torch on my phone and stick it in my dungarees pocket so that its light is shining ahead of me.

Six spirals later and I take a last step, and it changes underfoot. No longer slippy iron rungs but the thud and splosh of trainer in mud. These are my good ones too. Grandad is going to knack me.

I'm in a tunnel. Water is pouring down the walls, and it's not just mud I'm in but a really silty stream.

I look behind me. The tunnel runs in both directions and keeps going far beyond where my torchlight runs out. Which way?

My fingers clench and flap, and I can't blow my fringe out of my eyes because my forehead is so sweaty. It's deep and dark, and shadows flit at the edges of the torchlight.

'I don't want to do this by myself.' It pops out of my mouth in a low whine even though I think I've only spoken it in my head.

'You don't have to,' says a voice behind me.

I leap back and lash out with my crutches. Titch just manages to duck in time.

'What are you doing here?' I ask, wiping tears from my face.

'I've hidden the bottle, and Nusrat's bribed Ranveer to drive over here if we need him.'

Titch smiles shyly at me, and I smile shyly back. It

feels a little bit awkward after what I think was our first argument.

'Time to do what Stickleback Catchers always do,' I say.

They smile at me, properly this time, and point to the stream flowing ahead of us.

'Even if it's going backwards?' asks Titch.

We follow the river.

We've been walking for what feels like forever, and my arms are tired from wrenching my crutches out of the mud, and I think maybe we just should turn back. I'm lagging behind Titch and I'm beginning to worry about the tunnel above us. A big clod of earth fell just next to me a few steps ago and it's proper given me the collywobbles. What if the roof collapses? The tunnel isn't straight: it curves and meanders, so I can't tell what distance I've actually covered.

I stop. I'm going to turn round. I'm going back. I go to call Titch – but they've stopped still before I've even spoken.

Then I hear it too.

A flapping noise.

I look ahead. Is that . . . a faint light?

I turn off my torch to make sure, and so does Titch. My eyes get used to the dark, and then . . . Yes! There's definitely a glow ahead.

I want to run away, but what if there *is* something here that can help Gran? She's at the heart of this. Would Gran be scared? No way. And even if she was, she'd do it anyway.

I give Titch a nod – I don't trust my voice to actually be able to form words – and we set off in the direction of the light.

When we get closer, I realize the light is leaching round the edges of a huge wooden door. There's a brass handle in the shape of a tiny little fist. For some reason, it makes me think of Grandad, and I give it a little fist bump. Then I take hold, turn it and push.

It's like time has stood still.

I know this place.

I know it from the memories that Grandad has shared

and the pictures in local history books I've pored over in the library.

I'm inside the Cawlington Bottling Co building.

'Whoa,' says Titch in awe.

We walk further in, and the door slams shut behind us, which makes us jump.

We aren't the only ones in here.

Sitting in alcoves of brick arches in the walls, on shelves and shelves of bottles, on tables, on the beams in the ceiling, jumping and fluttering, are hundreds upon hundreds of crows.

'Is it just me, or can you see them too?' I ask Titch, hundreds of beady eyes staring at me.

'Yup,' says Titch. 'They are most definitely real. I'm all in.'

'Me too,' I whisper.

It's damp. Rivulets of water course down the walls and seep into the edges around the stone floor. Everything is mossy and burbling.

It's gloomy.

It's *incredible*. All this time, and I've finally made it inside.

The crows stop shuffling and argy-bargying each other and become still.

Then they begin to caw. It's like rusty springs are stuck in their throats, and they're coughing out the noise. I'm about to clamp my hands over my ears –

Someone says my name.

I turn round and look down towards that familiar voice, and my hands flap with excitement.

'So you finally found us then.'

Chapter Seventeen

I'm talking to a crow.

    'No, you're not. I'm not. What a tight spot.'

    Did I say that out loud?

    'Yes,' says the crow.

    'What?' says Titch.

    'No, I definitely didn't.'

    'Did *what*?' asks a very confused Titch.

    'Well, you did that time. And I am not,' says the crow.

    'Not?'

    'Not what?'

    '*What is going on?*' yells Titch.

    'You said it, not me,' I say.

    'Ah, yes. I'm not.'

'Not what?'

'A crow,' says the crow.

'I think I need a lie-down.'

And then it all goes very blurry, and I feel really hot, and the mossy, gloomy green smell is just too strong and overpowering – it's so damp, and I feel sweaty, and all the crows' croak-cawing is now too loud for my head, and then I slump in a heap on a chair by a big wooden table. A crow hops up and shuffle-slides and nudges a green glass bottle towards me. I know I should be worried about poison and stuff, but I'm really thirsty so I drink it anyway. Titch is given one too and stares at me until I've drunk mine, then they drink theirs.

Dandelion and burdock is my third least favourite drink, but it's the first time I've been served it by a crow. It does a little bow and hops back up and perches in an alcove, the other birds around it huffing and puffing and fluttering, trying to keep their perches. They've all got little rectangular grey things beside them, but I can't quite work out what they are.

I realize that the scruffy crow has been standing in the far corner, watching us. It jumps forward and stands at the head of the table, in front of me and Titch.

'Please would you and your friends stop calling me the *scruffy crow*. It's most offensive.'

'Sorry,' I say. 'What are you then, if you're not a crow?'

'Firstly, I am Fig – Fig Archimedes, if you would care to use that instead?'

We nod. Then my brain pings. Is this what Gran has been going on about? *Does she know Fig?*

'And secondly I am not a scruffy crow because I am a raven.' The scruffy raven ruffles up its feathers and preens. 'Can you not tell the difference?'

Now that I look closely at Fig, I can. It is so much bigger than the other birds and has shinier feathers. It has a much thicker, deeper beak and a shaggy neck. Comparing Fig with the other birds, they look nothing alike.

'Sorry, Fig,' I say. Titch nods.

Fig, I think, smiles. 'As for the scruff, well, it's a busy time at the moment, and that does not leave a lot of spare tick-tocks on the clocks for preening. Especially with the havoc you lot have been causing.'

Fig curves its wings to point at both of us and hops along the table and then leaps off.

'Havoc *we've* been causing? We haven't done anything apart from try to find *you*!'

— 177 —

Fig doesn't answer, just stares at us, then says, 'After all this, you're just going to sit at that table and sip at drinksies? Oh my word, get a jiggle and a wriggle on!'

Fig hops along the stone floor, and we get up and walk beside it.

'I'm not sure what to call you, Fig. What are your pronouns?' asks Titch.

'Well, I am definitely not an egg layer. Is that helpful in making a decision? It's not something I've ever been asked before. It's usually just, "Oi, bird, get off the grass!"'

Titch grins.

'I will be he, him,' announces Fig.

'Excellent,' says Titch. 'So much nicer to know for sure.'

Fig stops and gives a deep bow. 'I will call you Titch and Mimi and whatever bits you like because they are your names.'

Titch giggles.

'Have I done wrong?' asks Fig. 'I would not want to cause a fence.'

'It's not *a fence*,' explains Titch. 'And no, that's lovely.'

'Phew. Because it's a while since I did some words with hoomans.'

I'm about to ask *How long?* And *Do you mean Gran?* when

Fig speaks again. 'And I will call the other Stickleback Catcher, the one who is snuggly in bed, Nusrat because that is their name, and I will use their bits.'

Nus! How long have we been here? She'll be worried.

'What even *is* here?' I ask Fig. 'I mean, I know *where* we are – I've been trying for years to get in here . . . Hold on, did Grandad know about –'

'This place?' interrupts Fig. 'Of horses for courses not! We finds old buildings, boarded up and forgotten, invisible even on burbling, busying high streets.'

Fig looks incredibly proud of himself and gives a little preening wiggle.

'It's just . . . I wasn't expecting . . .'

'Us?' asks Fig.

'Yes!' I shout, pointing at all the crows on the shelves with bottles and the damp and the green. 'You! I am having a conversation with a crow. No! A raven. I am in the CBC finally! And it's filled with crows and a talking raven.' I calm down as Fig stares at me. 'It's just a little bit unexpected,' I say more quietly.

'Is the shouty bit over?' asks Fig.

I nod. Then he nods, and Titch nods too, so hard I think their head might fall off, and I have to put my hand on their arm to stop them.

'We are working,' says Fig. 'Always working, working, working. And you have got in the way of work, work, work. We are always working since we were a dot in a blink in a planet in a star. We are stars.'

I feel confused. Titch says, 'No, you're birds.'

Fig sighs and actually tuts at us. 'Look!' he says, and points his wing at the ceiling.

On the flat bricked roof appear pinpricks of light. A whole galaxy above us. It's the most beautiful thing I've ever seen, and I have to take in a little gasp.

Fig claps his wings together, and six crows flap off the shelves and fly up towards a patch on the ceiling where they swoop then circle an area of the galaxy, and then each crow begins to circle a different star, like they're drawing a constellation for us. Five of the stars are connected, in the shape of a kite on a string. One lone star is off by itself top left.

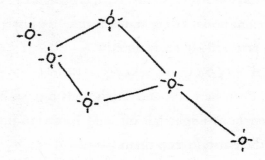

'That is our home. Star points. The constellation Corvus. Southern celestial hemisphere. Ptolemy named us two thousand years ago, but we are older than old. Look! That's me in the constellation in your sky, the raven, sitting on the back of Hydra.'

I look at Titch, and they shrug.

'You don't know Hydra? What do they teach you these days? It's all mobile telephones and flatscreen TVs and doing a google.' Fig gets very shouty and flaps his wings at us, so Titch and I take a step back. 'Hydra is the water snake. You know, *sssssssssssssssssplosh*.'

'I mean, obviously, that was the only bit I was puzzled about . . .' says Titch hurriedly.

'Good, glad that's cleared it up. This way!'

The crows stop circling, but I can't take my eyes off the ceiling. Fragments of light sparkle down like shooting stars.

Fig pecks my leg. 'Asteria, goddess of falling stars, now hurry up. It's time for your training.'

My mouth drops open, and by the time I've realized just what Fig has said he's halfway across the room with Titch. I take one last look up and then dash after them.

Fig uses his beak to pick something up and drop it in Titch's hand. Then he does the same for me. It's one of the tiny grey rectangles that were next to the crows on the shelves. I turn back to stare at them, but they're no longer there, and then there's a sharp scratch on the back of my leg.

'Ow!'

I look down, and the crows from the shelves are all queued up behind me, each of them now holding one of the grey rectangles under its wing, and I realize they're miniature briefcases. The one just behind me pecks me again.

'Stop it!'

It flaps its wings at me, and I realize Fig and Titch have gone on ahead. I hold the briefcase Fig gave me by its minuscule handle and race to catch up. The line of crows follows me.

Fig hops from stone to stone, and it becomes darker, muggier. There are not as many lights over here, and the ceiling gets lower. Just when I think that I'm not going to be able to stay upright and use my crutches any more, there's a gust of air and a cavernous room opens up in front of me.

We gasp.

'Bit big, innit?' says Fig.

Bit big does not cover it.

As far as the eye can see, there are wooden shelves stacked up to the ceiling, higher than I can make out. And lined up on the shelves are green glass bottles, the same as the one we found in the tree trunk.

And inside those bottles are hundreds of thousands – no, *millions* – of feathers.

'Wow,' says Titch.

'Shush,' says Fig. 'You are not meant to be here at training with your briefcases and whatnots. You must stay secretly, cos you are not crows!'

Then the smell hits me. That dark, dank smell that enveloped my gran. And there are *things* floating round the shelves, moving from bottle to bottle.

Ghosts? Not ghosts.

Wraiths.

The mouth monsters.

They look like strands of cobwebs that keep forming and bunching together to create a shape that is vaguely human, then tearing apart. Twist and flow, and the shape is lost. Then they regroup, and they are almost – almost . . . people. People with their mouths open in a silent scream.

I can feel something bubbling inside me: anger. My face grows hot, and I bare my teeth. *Those monsters tried to take my gran.*

And that smell! It's so pungent it makes me want to be sick. I gag and wipe my mouth with the back of my hand. It's like putrid, stagnant river water, burning my eyes and my nostrils.

This is not a good place. These are the things that tried to hurt Gran. Why has Fig brought us here? It felt like we could *trust* him!

Titch holds their arm over their nose. 'Who . . . *what* are they?'

Fig hops and beats his wings, then he is up on my shoulder. 'The Void Collectors. Memory keepers. Librarians of moments.'

I shudder.

I grab Titch's hand. 'We need to get out of here – it's not safe. These are the things that –'

But Titch cuts me off again. 'Hold on,' they say. 'The feathers! The ones that floated down. Are they people's *memories*?'

'Yes,' Fig says very slowly, and rolls his little beady eyes. 'Obviously!' He shakes his head at us, and when he still doesn't see us getting it he says very slowly indeed: 'We give our feathers. Memory writes itself upon the quill. Then we put feather-memories in the correct bottles.'

He sighs at our baffled faces. 'Training will teach you all the bits you need to know! I will do the teaching because I know all the knows.'

He clears his throat, and I try to concentrate on him, but the Void Collectors hold most of my attention. I can't let them out of my sight. Fig's voice tunes out.

A crow pecks my ankle, and I look back down in time to see Fig finishing a sentence I haven't heard, and he's flapping furiously in my direction.

'Did you pay attention to the section on training bottles and feathers, memory-entering protocol, multiple memories mishaps, and duplicates?'

'Erm,' I say, wrinkling up my face.

Fig cocks his head at me and looks cross. 'It was all the important!'

'Yes, definitely!' I say, crossing my fingers behind my back, knowing Titch will fill me in on what I've missed. I look to Titch for reassurance, but their focus is on the Void Collectors too as the wraiths wrap themselves round shelves and bottles and leave a trail of green dust in their wake.

'So the Void Collectors guard memories?' I ask Fig as I rock back and forth on my crutches. Fig nods and rolls his eyes like I'm being particularly slow in getting my head round this concept. 'It's a lot, Fig! And you can *enter* these memories?'

'Only when you are proper polished-up trained. Trainees need training bottles like wobbly bikers need stabilizers. Get it?'

'Well, er, no,' I say.

'I knew you wouldn't,' Fig mutters, flapping. 'I told her you wouldn't. No one listens to me, and I am full of all the knows. Training, as a barter-promise-thank-you, is like gloves to snakes.'

My brain scrambles to try to unravel what Fig has just said. *Her. Does he mean Gran?*

'Your face is smooshed up in tryings!' Fig shakes his briefcase at me. 'For giddiness' sakes! I will do the song! You like songs? Maybe more attention-eyes on me!'

Fig starts to do this weird little dance where he waggles his feathers and bum. All the crows round our feet begin to join in, banging their briefcases on the floor to the beat. Then Fig quietly begins to sing:

> *Feathers are memories of times and of places:*
> *Treat them with care, tread light in their spaces.*
> *You can't interact; you can only watch closely,*
> *Quietly observing the ones you love mostly.*

A warning to heed, or you will leave never;
Smash a bottle, you're stuck there forever!
Smasher beware, the Collectors will chase you;
They'll never stop till they have erased you . . .

Fig bows deeply, and all the crows bash their briefcases on the ground in applause.

'Well, that's, erm . . .' says Titch.

'Charming? Terrifying?' I ask.

'Educational?' asks Fig.

'. . . weird,' says Titch.

I try to count all the memory bottles with feathers in and give up. I look out over all the shelves, at the thousands – hundreds of thousands – of them.

I don't take my eyes off the Void Collectors for long though. They make my head pound with their reek.

'Yes. And each bottle is one hooman. We keep hoomans safe. It is our job, as old as stars. Every town, in every country in all the lands, we have a spot, we corvids, all bundled up together keeping the memories safe.'

'These are everywhere? Hidden away?' asks Titch. 'You mean, these memories are all from people in our town, but that we could find other libraries too?'

'We would rather you didn't,' says Fig all huffily.

I think back to something Fig just said. 'Who is *we*?' I ask. 'Keeping the hoomans, I mean humans, safe. Does that include *them*?' I point at the Void Collectors and a trickle of electricity runs up my spine. It feels like they can sense I'm here.

Fig doesn't answer. He picks up a briefcase that one of the crows has dropped and tuts.

We watch as the Void Collectors move up and down the aisles. I can't fathom how big the space is. I try to count them in one spot and then multiply to get the total, but the way they mesh and change into one another makes it impossible. Their faces and bodies squish together and move apart, blending, tearing and re-forming. But the care with which they tend the bottles and feathers, checking, stroking, carefully adjusting, is completely at odds with the things that appeared out of the cracks at home with Gran.

Gran! I need to get back to her. But they're mesmerizing, and I can't stop watching.

'Why are they so . . . ?'

'Frightening?' Fig asks Titch, and shudders. Is he scared too? 'Because memories are precious, and they need defending.'

'What are the cracks?' asks Titch.

I'm so grateful Titch is here. I'm not thinking straight or asking any of the right sort of questions.

'No time,' says Fig, and begins to flap and hop up and down. 'We've been too long – they know you're here.'

I can feel what Fig feels then. It's like something has rippled through the Void Collectors. They're moving together, blending into one big whirlpool.

They start to spin, arms appearing and legs, and mouths opening . . . The mass rises up, and one giant mouth begins to open. Titch grabs me, and I cover my eyes. They bury their head on my shoulder, and I can feel them shaking . . . or is it me?

The Void Collectors begin to screech, and Titch moans, then all the crows hurtle up into the air. I have to let go of Titch and try to protect myself as they begin cawing and dive-bombing us, mouths open like the Void Collectors, ready to attack.

Chapter Eighteen

Titch folds their body over the top of mine, protecting me.

Their bravery makes me brave. I stand up and, although my heart is pounding and I'm light-headed, I swing my crutches back and forth, smacking into the crows.

Titch joins me, grabs my crutch from my weaker left hand and starts thwacking the crows too.

Fig cries out at us, 'No, don't! They're just following orders!'

I scream back, 'I thought you were their boss!'

He flies up in front of us and opens his mouth like them, and I think he's going to screech, but instead begins to sing at them, singing the star song me and Gran sing together.

Stars shine, you're mine,
My love, my heart, my life . . .

Why would he sing that?

The stench of the Void Collectors is making me woozy, and I don't think I can stay upright much longer. I stumble, and Titch puts their arm round me, and a crow pecks the side of their head, drawing blood. Titch is stunned. Touches their head, looks at their fingers and stares at me.

The whirlpool of mouths pauses, then begins to shrink back, and the crows stop diving.

Fig carries on singing, and I don't know what to do but join in. Titch doesn't know the words, but does la-la-las along with us.

As the birds back away, we retreat behind Fig. There's more screeching and the wind against our faces as the crows still beat the air with their wings. The smell is too much. I'm too hot. I can't work out which way is up, and I go to grab Titch's hand, but I can't find it.

Everything goes dark.

★

The next thing I know I'm waking up beside Titch on the damp tarmac of the car park, with Nus's brother banging on the wall of the CBC building and yelling for us.

'We're here!' shouts Titch before I can work out how to do words.

He marches over to us. 'What the heck do you think you're playing at? Were you *hiding* from me?'

Titch begins to giggle and, though it's not funny, it really is sort of hilarious.

'No!' I say, trying to keep a straight face. 'We wouldn't do something like that!' Then I burst into laughter. Titch is rolling about on the ground, laughing so hard they're having to hold their tummy.

I stare at Ranveer, desperately trying to rearrange my face into a sensible one.

'Kids!' he yells in my face, and storms off.

Titch looks at me and we both crack up.

★

When we eventually stop, we pick ourselves up and head back into the park towards the bowls club, whooping and cheering. Titch dances in front of me, kicking the heads off dandelions. I spot Champ and his friends running around near the football pitch.

We opened a backwards river! We found Fig! The excitement fizzes through me and I give Titch a high five. We're sensational!

Suddenly my whole body slumps, and all the adrenaline oozes out of me so I feel like a wrinkly old balloon, and I have to quickly sit down on the bandstand steps.

'You OK?' asks Titch. 'You worried about Fig? You think he's OK? I mean, like, physically OK obviously, but do you think he's OK too? Like on our side?' Titch climbs on the railing and shoots down to the bottom and then runs to the top to slide down again. 'I mean, he did that training for us, whatever that was meant to tell us. Did you understand any of it? I certainly didn't. And he protected us! I think he's on our side. What are we meant to do now?'

I shrug as Titch continues burbling on. I don't know the answer to anything. When we worked out the star riddle, we were meant to solve everything and save Gran. Everything was meant to make *more* sense.

Not less.

'How do you think Ranveer found us? Nus said she'd send him to the river, not here. What clue do you think she found?' asks Titch.

It's usually me wanting to talk and Titch telling me to shush, but this time it's the other way round. My head is banging.

Titch is absolutely buzzing, leaping about in full-on 'just had an amazing adventure' mode. They yell, 'Did you see that tower of mouths, and that smell! What do you think it all means?'

'That we're no closer to saving Gran,' I say quietly, and then get up and make my way towards the club.

I don't know if it's even possible to save her any more. I can't remember why I thought we could. I wish Titch wasn't following. I just want to be by myself.

I can barely push open the bar door I'm so exhausted, so Titch gives me a hand.

I groan when we go into the bar. Gran, Grandad and Subeera are all sitting round a table, having what looks like brunch. Gran calls to us. Titch trots over, and I try to drop my shoulders, sigh, then follow. There's no ignoring Gran when she's having a blustery sort of day. She offers us breakfast items that don't really match and keeps getting up and down to fill Titch's plate. Titch eats loads. I know why. My stomach is rumbling after all that, and I'm starving, but I can't bring myself to eat anything.

Of course, it's not *their* family and *their* home that needs saving, is it? It's just a game to Titch and Nus.

Nusrat!

I pull my phone out.

'Not at the table,' says Gran. 'How rude!' and puts more fried chicken and scrambled egg on Titch's plate.

Titch giggles at me. I smile my fake smile and hold my phone under the table so Gran can't see.

> How did Ranveer find us?

Two seconds later, I get a reply.

> Found old map online. River tributary led there. I told him where to go.
>
> You OK?

I'm not sure how to answer that, so I just type: Yes.

Then remember how cross her brother was, so I add:

We're fine. Tell you all soon.
I'd pretend to be asleep if
I was you.

Ranveer incoming and he's
not happy.

Nus sends a thumbs up, and I put my phone away.

'It was beautiful,' Gran is saying. She looks really happy, and it makes me smile, a sad one, but still better than I was feeling a moment ago. 'In this gorgeous white, clean space, with windows at the end, floor to ceiling. You could see everything!'

'What are you talking about, Gran?' I ask.

'Erm . . .'

Her eyes flicker, and a crack darts along the floor towards her. I squirm on my seat. Look what I've done! If only I hadn't asked her! There's no way I can save her if I can't even talk to her right. Titch notices and holds my hand, but I can't bring myself to look at anyone.

'Oh, I don't know. Does it matter?' says Gran all huffily.

'Not in the slightest,' says Subeera, smiling at me, then at Gran. 'But I can remind you, if you'd like?'

I love Subeera.

'Go on then,' says Gran. 'You tell them, then I can learn all the bits I've forgotten!'

There's silence round the table, then Gran laughs, and the worry is punctured, and we all laugh too. Titch gives my hand another squeeze.

'We went to that big art gallery in Centre Square in Middlesbrough. Bert told us about it; he used to take one of his friends, and we thought it would keep Dr Teller happy if we gave your grandad a bit of a rest!' Subeera winks at me. 'And Iolene is right: it's in a beautiful room. We sat in a circle and a lady called Claire taught us silly games and played a kazoo, while a woman in a pink fluffy hat played the ukulele.'

'I remember! I was good at that bit.'

'You ruddy were! I couldn't get the damned thing to make any noise, but you taught *me*.'

'I did,' says Gran, dead chuffed with herself.

'And *then* they taught us some brilliant stuff to help you out,' continues Subeera. 'If you get a bit muddled in your head, lost in time, we don't tell you off or try to tell you you're wrong. Because that's scary.'

Subeera smiles at her old friend and strokes Gran's cheek. Gran beams back at her. Why can't I speak to Gran like that? 'We just meet you wherever or *when*ever you are, don't we? When your brain gets tricky. And we'll all be with you together. Always.'

I don't want to cry at the table. I yank Titch's hand to pull them up, but Gran plonks another bit of chocolate cake on Titch's plate next to their bacon, and says, 'Eat up!'

We're all getting used to eating random food combinations. I wonder whether Titch might think that this is strange, but they carry on eating and use a sausage to stop the bean juice seeping into their cake.

I pick up their plate and stand up.

'We've got to go,' I say.

Titch looks at me, and I stare at them.

'Yeah,' Titch says, standing up too. 'Homework.'

Grandad nods and smiles at us as we head upstairs, Titch picking off a bit of mushroom and nibbling the cake as we go.

'Shall we go back again next week?' I hear Subeera ask Gran. 'Entirely up to you.'

'Ten-out-of-ten right we will!' says Gran, and they all laugh together.

★

I'm fuming. It's making me angry that I can't *stop* being angry. It's not Titch's fault that they don't get it properly.

How could they? I stomp up the stairs, making the photos on the walls rattle.

I shove open my bedroom door so that it cracks on the end of the bed and as usual everything on my windowsill wobbles.

Green glass catches my eye as the bottle of feathers sways precariously, then holds itself upright.

My jaw drops.

Sitting on my windowsill is the Cawlington Bottling Co bottle we found in the tree trunk, its condition so much better than any in my collection, and it now contains three feathers – one brown, speckly and long, one faded grey, and a fluffy white tummy feather.

I dash over to it and haul myself on to the bed. There's a tiny label attached to the neck of the bottle with a scratchy, ink-blobbed drawing of a crow carrying a briefcase. In scrawly writing it says:

Mimi Evergreen's Training Bottle –
Use With Care. Love Fig x

'Fig,' I whisper. 'I knew you wouldn't let me down!'

Chapter Nineteen

'That was quick!' says Subeera as we come hurtling down the stairs and through the bar.

'What was?' I say as Titch says, 'Yup, easy-peasy work!'

Grandad gives us a raised-eyebrow look, but doesn't say anything.

I give Gran a kiss on her head and whisper, 'Don't worry – we've got this,' then we zoom out the door.

'It's all about the river, isn't it?' says Titch as we clamber carefully through the hogweed towards our den.

'Yup. Whatever we have to do, we have to do it here,' I reply.

'We found the message here, the tunnel opening was here – heck, your gran wanted you to catch sticklebacks! Everything keeps coming back here.'

'Yes,' I say. 'But *why*?'

Titch shrugs. 'I wish I'd listened to the training.'

Me too. Because something Fig said when we were inside that incredible vault of memories is niggling at me, and I know it's the key. But I can't quite work out what for.

'The only thing that could make this better, right now,' says Titch as they hold a big thorny branch back for me to step through, 'is a MASSIVE lemon top from Pacitto's. We *have* to go and get one. We could take it to the beach, just along from Paddy's Hole. You know, the place you saw through the telescope at Nus's?'

I nod at them. 'Definitely,' I say.

This is helping. I can feel the thing I need to remember beginning to bubble.

'And there are these pink butterfly shells that you can only find on that beach in all the world.'

'The *whole* world?'

'Well, in Redcar,' they say, and I laugh.

'And if the tide is out we can explore the boat bones. They're from an old ship called the *Seahawk*. Maybe finding out about its owner could be our next mystery. That would make a good episode of *The Puzzler*. Bet Nus would be up for that.'

Whatever it is I'm trying to remember is still just out of reach! It's so close, and I keep trying to grab it too soon.

'You've got to be careful though,' continues Titch as we make it on to the riverbank, 'cos when the tide comes in, it comes in *fast*. Dad had to sacrifice a pair of shoes cos we had to leave everything and run! You have to come with us. Promise you'll come.'

'I promise,' I say.

We start streaming to Nus and put my phone on a tripod so I don't accidentally drop it. We tell her all about the CBC and the crows, and then Titch and I pick a feather each from the bottle and stand facing the river. They choose the grey pigeon feather. I choose brown speckly grouse. The fluffy one that looks like a tummy feather from a baby bird falls to the bottom of the bottle and stays there.

'I swear I can see you breathing,' I whisper to the feather. The air around it shivers.

'So these feathers contain memories,' says Titch slowly, like they're trying to make it real.

'Yup. But why would Fig give them to us? What does he want us to *do* with them?'

'He's definitely not trying to send the Void Collectors after us with them. Is he?' Titch whispers, like they don't want to accidentally summon them by saying the name.

I check over my shoulder, just in case that's possible, and shudder at the memory of them shrieking. And that *smell*. Titch touches the scab on their head.

'Do you think Fig is OK?' I ask.

Titch shrugs. 'I hope so.'

My phone pings.

> So the feathers contain memories.
> If so, we need to work out how to
> access them.

'Well, obviously. But I don't know how to open feathers,' I say to Titch. 'Do you?'

'Yes,' says Titch. 'Ten-out-of-ten definitely.'

They do some elaborate dance thing that ends in a pirouette and them slicing the air with the tip of the feather. I give a standing ovation. But nothing happens. Titch tries again.

'I'm hot,' they say, and strip off down to their pants and vest.

'Going in?' I ask them. 'It's freezing in there!'

'Do you dare me?' Titch grins.

'Dare you? I *double* dare you!' Titch's phone pings, and I look. 'Nus *triple* dares you!' I yell.

'Can't ignore a triple dare,' says Titch, and I point my phone towards them as they go running and shrieking right into the river. They gasp and pause for a moment when the water hits their tummy, and then they take a big breath, hold their nose and plunge under. Seconds later, they burst out with a shriek. 'It's flippin' freezing!'

I laugh. Titch's phone pings again.

> Get the bottles and fill them with
> river water. No time to play.
> Experiment time.

I groan and put the phone down and get three bottles off the windowsill in the den and take them to the river's edge.

'What are you doing?' asks Titch, bobbing up and down and trying not to shiver.

'Your lips are going blue,' I tell them. 'We've got another task from Nus.'

Titch groans.

'I just did that too!' I say. Then: 'Oi!' as Titch splashes me.

They dive under the water and when they surface they call quietly: 'You have to come in. It's full of sticklebacks.' They peer down through the surface of the water. 'They're all round my feet!'

'Still not coming in,' I say.

Titch laughs as I try to fill the bottles with river water, but it's too shallow, so I take off my dungarees and lay them over a rock so the dinosaurs on them can watch. I go in deeper, the freezing water up to my knees.

'Give me a hand!' I yell to Titch.

'Nah,' they say. 'No way. This is comedy gold. I bet you –'

I slip on a rock and flail and nearly, not quite but nearly, hold myself up, and then I know I've saved myself, and I let out a giggle too soon as my other foot slips, and I fall in face first.

The cold *bites*.

I pop up, gasping.

'— fall in!' finishes Titch, and swims straight over to me. 'You OK?'

I spit out water, too shocked to speak, and then I start to laugh, and they laugh too. I lie on my back and float, my T-shirt clinging to me, and I stare at the blue of the sky, the green of the trees against them, and I hear Titch cackling, and I can't stop laughing either.

I flip over on to my tummy and swim like a fish. Like a stickleback. My arms and legs are wobbly on land, unpredictable, but in the water I am free and strong.

When I get so cold that I can't stop my teeth chattering, we get out and sit on the bank. Titch fetches us big fluffy towels from the den to snuggle up in.

'Only one way to get warm,' says Titch, and picks up their feather again and starts dancing with it and prodding it at the sky.

I pull on my dungarees, then get a bag of crisps from the den and sit on a rock and watch. Maybe salt and vinegar is the key to solving mysteries.

Nothing is happening from Titch's flailing, but the entertainment value is high. I cheer after a particularly energetic leap.

When I finish eating, I lick my finger and dab it in the corner of the packet to get out the flavour bits, then I fold it in half lengthwise, half again and then into a triangle. I drop it into the snack pocket of my dungarees, where it pops straight out and lands on the ground when I bend forward. I pick it up because littering is ten-out-of-ten rubbish. I giggle at my own joke and then tell Titch, and they groan and go back to leaping. The point of the triangle digs in my finger and makes me yelp.

The point.

That was what I've been trying to remember.

'The points!' I yell at Titch, who just stares at me. 'The *star* points. The stars on the bottles, the drain cover, Bert's pint! Even Gran's song! It's all about the stars!'

I grab my crutches and zoom towards the river's edge, then plonk myself down just where the water touches the pebbles.

'It was an odd way for Fig to phrase it,' I tell them. 'Remember? "That is our home. Star points. The constellation Corvus. Southern celestial hemisphere."' I look at Titch, and they look blank.

Titch sits next to me, all sweaty from their acrobatics. 'You're turning into Fig. You're not making any sense.'

'Grab the phone,' I tell Titch. They do, and they focus the lens on the brown speckly feather in my hand.

'I just need to remember . . .'

I close my eyes and picture the crows circling the ceiling, the galaxy of pinprick-light stars in the roof, the constellation of Corvus that Fig told us was their home. I open my eyes. The river flows in front of me.

I bend forward and use the quill end of the feather to draw the shape of the constellation on top of the flowing water, just like I'd use a pen. Sticklebacks swim over as if they're watching what we're doing from below.

Nothing happens. I try again. 'Star points,' I whisper to myself.

Titch gasps as they realize what I'm doing. I dot the feather in the river to form the shape of the constellation, and each time I do a stickleback swims over and stays in place until we can see the constellation drawn in silver fish under the surface of the water.

'Wow,' I say very quietly. We watch the fish, mesmerized as they sparkle and hold their positions against the current.

'I don't know what to do next,' I say, and I'm about to launch the ruddy feather into the middle of the river.

'Follow the river,' whispers Titch so quietly I can barely hear them.

'What?'

'Follow the flow,' they say, and I quickly draw the pattern again on the surface of the water, this time from right to left so that it flows with the current, the sticklebacks swimming into position.

Follow the river. Draw the constellation, a kite with its tail.

Nothing happens. Not a bean.

I'm about to give up for good when I remember the lone star, top left in the constellation, so I dot the tip of the feather in the river top right of the fish holding their positions. One swims into place.

The air cracks, like thunder.

The river breaks, splits in two, and swirling, bubbling wind is released and blows in our faces, nearly pushes me over. It roars, and then it sucks back and loops, crashing together in an almighty wave, and then begins to flow backwards. I reach for Titch's hand, but I'm flung up into the air with pebbles and grasses –

– and am sucked right under.

Chapter Twenty

One moment I'm on the bank of the River Cawl, and the next I'm dragged in and under and

through?

I'm sitting at a dining table made of thick red wood with high-backed, ornate chairs. A tiny river flows along its surface, and there are miniature trees and bushes on its tiny riverbanks. I touch a tree. It feels real.

Then all the lights go out.

When I blink my eyes open, I am in a place that feels very recognizable though I don't think I've been here before. It's memory and photograph familiar, just like the bottling company was.

The room smells of stale cigarette smoke.

The door opens. I cower backwards, and I accidentally flop back on to a sofa in relief. Two women burst in. They have curlers in their hair and housecoats on. It's like being in a retro episode of *Coronation Street*. In their arms are babies, one slim and elegant-looking with a shock of black hair, the other with a screwed-up bright red face.

The women stand in front of the fireplace and bounce the babies so that they can see themselves in the mirror above it. I'm not reflected in the glass. They haven't seen me. Have I become invisible?

The babies gasp and chuckle. Try to point at themselves. The red-faced baby is having an excellent go at eating its own hand.

There is an ornament of a dancer at one end of the mantelpiece, a ballerina stretched in an arabesque. Gran has one like it on the mantelpiece in our Room for Best. But that one has a chip in the lavender tutu.

The red-faced baby yanks its hand out of its mouth with a force that surprises it and makes it cry, and its hand hits the ballerina, which tumbles to the hearth. Both babies wail. I slam my hands over my ears.

The baby's mam bends down and picks up the ornament.

I gasp when I see the ballerina in her hands. There's a chip out of her tutu, just like the one in the Room for Best.

★

I blink, and the room sways and becomes blurry, like it's gone out of focus, and when I blink again I'm on the riverbank, but not where I left Titch. I expect to be all frightened and goosebumpy, but I'm not. I'm really calm. That sense of familiar is still here. I'm standing beside the church that backs on to North Cawl Park.

Which is not usually beside the river.

Bells peal, the big wooden doors are flung open, and down the steps come lots of people in their Sunday best. They make two rows either side of the path and have blue cardboard boxes in their hands. Confetti.

It's a wedding!

The vicar comes out and steps to one side, and then out come my gran and grandad.

My gran and grandad.

They're wearing the clothes from their photograph album that says OUR WEDDING AY because I picked the D off when I was little.

— 213 —

Holding hands. Laughing. He whispers in her ear, and she kisses his cheek. And then they're running down the steps, and everyone is throwing confetti in the air, and it's a storm of blue, pink and white swirls of paper. Some of the little pieces settle on the river and float towards me. I pick them up.

They are real. Soggy. Paper. I scrape them off the palm of my hand and smile to myself as I put them in my dungarees pocket.

I'm in memories. My gran's memories.

Fig's training feathers work!

★

When I look up, the church has vanished, and I'm in a cloud of mizzle. I can barely see more than a few steps ahead of me. The ground is springy underfoot, damp and mossy. I know where I am. Titch has told me all about this place. This is Cross Fell, high in the North Pennines, where the River Cawl begins.

Hold on, didn't Fig say one memory per feather? I've skipped through two already! Why didn't I pay more attention to what Fig said? Though I'm not sure it would have helped if I had; his training made very little sense. I close my eyes tightly to help me remember. I know he definitely said one memory per feather, but then, when I got told off for not listening, what was it he said? I squeeze my eyes tighter, and suddenly I can picture it again, him all huffy with me and flapping, saying, 'Did you pay attention to the section on training bottles blah-blah something-something' – I can't remember – and then that's it!

Multiple memories mishaps and duplicate feathers?

These are training feathers, the duplicates that contain lots of memories to tumble through, multiple memories mishaps in his words! This is like a game, a driving simulator. This is how the crows learn how to do their job.

I laugh out loud. This is brilliant.

I begin walking. I shiver. It's ruddy freezing. Does that mean the Void Collectors are coming? I quicken my pace.

'Hello!' I call, but my voice doesn't travel far. It's like the weather takes a massive chomp and deadens my cry.

What's that though? I'm sure I can hear voices. Two voices?

I warily place my crutches on the mossy ground ahead, unsure whether it will hold them. I swing. They sink a little, but if I move them quick I should be OK.

I slip and slide in the direction of the voices, and

suddenly there's a lamp burning on a kitchen table in front of me. What the . . . ?

I pinch the skin on the back of my hand. *Ow*. Yes. This is real.

But it just popped out of nowhere. Hold on . . . it's *our* kitchen table, which is now on top of a moor by the dribbly beginning of the River Cawl. A dribbly river beginning that travels through counties until it becomes the mighty Cawl and meets the sea at South Gare where the boat skeleton lies, near to Nus's house.

Where is anyone? What if I get stuck here?

I cling to facts Titch told us to make me safe and stop my hands from flapping and clenching, and I want to spell out words that I know loop back to the beginning because they make sense in my head.

- *Fact* — at low tide, the boat bones, like whale ribs, jut all the way out of the sand.
- *Fact* — it's the only beach where you can find pale pink seashells that look like butterflies.
- *Fact* — Titch has told us the tale of the *Seahawk* and how it met its grisly end there.
- *Fact* — Titch and I keep meaning to go and play, take our binoculars so we can wave at Nusrat, but we don't seem to have time.

I don't seem to have time.

Will we ever *get* time now?

How do I get home? Why didn't I pay attention to Fig's training? Though even if I had, it wouldn't have helped – Fig makes no sense! Panic mounts in my chest, and the facts aren't working any more.

I blink, and Gran and Grandad are sitting at the table with a plate of scones in front of them, and this memory has to be only about six months ago, because Gran got that lime-green shirt for Grandad for his Christmas box, and he only wore it a couple of times before he managed to get marker pen all over it and the stain wouldn't come out.

I walk over and hang around at the edges of the scene. I know Fig's song said I can't change things or interact, but it feels safer to be out of sight.

'Hey!' says Gran. 'Get yourself over here before Grandad eats all of these.' I wait for whoever Gran is talking to. Am I going to see six-months-ago me? But when no one appears Gran calls again. 'Mimi Evergreen, I will not tell you twice! They'll be annihilated by rent-a-gob in seconds.'

'Cheeky,' says Grandad, then he chokes and sprays a trail of crumbs all over the table.

'Oh, you are disgusting! Why did I marry you? Go and get a cloth.'

Grandad walks into the mist where the sink would be and disappears from view.

That's my gran. The real Gran. My gran who has a way with words and tells Grandad off and knows where she is. Not Gran pretending with that half-smile, or being happy playing the kazoo with other people living with dementia.

I've missed you *so much.*

'What do you mean, you silly billy? I'm right here. How was school?'

Gran holds out her hand to me. I check behind me, but there's no one there. She's talking to me. She can see me.

'Me?' I ask her quietly as butterflies begin to dance in my tummy.

'Well, I don't know another Mimi Evergreen. Do you?'

I shake my head as I move over the rocks and the mossy grass towards her. There are tiny little ferns growing in it, like skeletons.

'Cuppa?' she asks.

I lean against the table, and Gran plonks a mug of strong tea in front of me. I know *when* we are. This was the time Gran made scones and forgot to put the sugar in them, when I thought it was just Gran forgetting, before everything went wrong and Dr Inevitable came to visit. Yes, I'm right! I study the table. *There's no vacuum-cleaner letter imprinted on it*.

'No what?' asks Gran. I guess some of my thoughts are leaking out, just like they do with Fig.

'Nothing,' I say. 'Can I have jam and butter? And extra sugar?'

Gran smiles as I sit at the table, and she slices the scone in half. She does it swiftly and cleanly, no wobbles or pauses or forgetting. The butter cuts easily. The scones are still warm. She passes it over, and I take a bite. Oozy, hot, salty butter dribbles down my chin.

'They taste real,' I tell her.

'Well, I would hope so! You don't half come out with some stuff.'

Grandad comes back into the room that isn't quite our kitchen but is on a desolate moor.

'Glad you're back, pet. We've got something we need to tell you.'

I drop the scone in shock, and it lands butter-and-jam-side down.

This isn't what happened.

I was there. He didn't say that.

Nothing is meant to change!

This is meant to be just a memory. *I'm not supposed to be in it*.

Then there's a whooshy feeling, and I watch a feather drop on to the table where a crack appears and races along like a spiderweb that crackles outwards.

Gran is getting up from the kitchen table and leaving the room. It's full of cracks that flare and shudder and breathe. I think I'm in the same memory, but then I realize the scones have gone, and there's a vase of tulips on the table.

She walks along the hall and the cracks follow. I walk behind, trying not to slip on the mossy ground.

Gran goes into the Room for Best. Mr Suit – Dr Teller, Dr Inevitable – and Grandad are in there, waiting for her.

I know when this must be, and a tear slips out of my eye and runs down my cheek. I wish I could stop it happening.

She joins Grandad on the sofa. Dr Inevitable is sitting on the wooden chair. He goes to speak, and Gran places her hands over her ears. '*La, lalalalalala, lala, lah!*'

'Not listening won't change anything, pet,' says Grandad as he tries to take her hands away from her ears.

It might, I think. *It's worth a shot*, and more tears fall.

'But it's not fair,' says Gran. 'I feel fine! You telling me this is not fair.'

'You're right,' says Dr Inevitable. 'It's not fair. But it is what it is. The tests agree. Your brain is working overtime to help you out. That's why you're so tired at the moment, needing all those little naps to catch up.'

Gran begins to sob, and Grandad puts his arm round her. I hear more crying and realize it's me. I can't keep up with wiping my tears away, so I just let them fall.

I'm right. This is when Gran found out, that first day of the first crack, before I came into the room. I must be coming through the front door right now. I turn to look, and there I am, tossing my bag into the corner and knocking the coat stand.

'Stay there!' I call to myself. I look so happy. 'You don't want to find out – it hurts too much.'

'Oh God, George,' Gran says to Grandad, and I turn back to look at them. 'What will happen to Mimi? She can't know. You can't tell her. Not until we can't avoid it. She's happy, isn't she? She *knows* this is her home. This is her home! Promise me, promise me you'll keep her here. You can't let anyone take her away. Not that social worker.' She stares at Dr Inevitable and slams her fist on the table. 'Dr Teller, you must keep it a secret from her.'

'You know I can't do that,' he says.

'You can,' says Gran. 'For a little bit, just until we work out what we're going to do.' Then her strength crumbles, and she turns to Grandad. 'George, I'm really scared.'

I look at me sneaking down the hall, and I understand properly now why they wanted to protect me. The anger I had disappears. I want to protect me too.

'I know, pet,' says Grandad. 'I'm scared too.'

And he holds her and begins to hum the aria where the lover is torn from his beloved, and she starts humming it too, and it gets louder and louder until it is the roar of the river, and I have to place my hands over my ears because I think my brain is going to explode.

Chapter Twenty-one

The roaring is so strong I think my head will get flattened into mush. My hands are clamped tight over my ears, and someone is trying to prise them away from my head. I open my eyes, and Titch's face is up close to mine.

'Titch? Is that you?' I gasp.

'Of course it's me!'

'Is this you *now*?'

'Erm, yes?'

Titch has the towel still wrapped round them. The phone is on a tripod pointing at me. The river is flowing in the right direction.

'I'm definitely now?' I ask Titch again.

'Yes! So . . . you've been to a *not-now*?'

I stare at Titch and don't reply.

'Whoa!' they whisper. 'You need sugary tea, then you have to tell us everything.' Titch dashes towards the den, yelling as they go. 'The river went backwards, and then you flew and got churned up in it, and I thought you'd drowned!'

I watch the river slowly meander along in the right direction like nothing unusual has happened at all.

'Wow,' I say, and then lie back on the pebbles.

I lift up my head and fold my arms behind it, propping it up, watching the river. A seagull's feather rides the rapids near the boulders on the other side. It gets caught in a whirlpool and spins before being spat out the other side. I used to pick feathers up and pop them in my pocket when I was out walking without giving it a second thought. I don't think I'll be able to do that ever again. I'll be scared that if I pick them up I'm stealing someone's memories.

I lift my legs up and untie my trainers and drop them beside me, then I take off my socks, and stretch my legs out until my toes touch cold river water. I plunge my feet in. I start to shiver as the sun drops and the evening cools.

'It's all the adrenaline,' says Titch. 'We'll make a fire.'

I watch them gather wood and try to work out what I'm going to tell them.

I think back to Fig's song when we were in the Library of Memories. Why didn't I pay attention properly! We should only be an observer in memories. I'm sure that's what he sang.

And yet Gran *talked* to me.

Why could I break the rules?

Gran was *Gran* again. It was wonderful seeing her so free, not trapped in a brain that's not playing fair.

Titch and I put marshmallows on sticks that we've dipped in the river so they don't burn, and we hold them over the fire until they're gooey on the inside and scorched and cracked on the outside.

Cracks.

Titch waits for me to speak.

We sit in silence. Silence that isn't silent. There's the steady rush of water. An owl hoots. *Twit-twoo.*

'One owl says the twit and the other the twoo, did you know that? That's two owls out there,' says Titch. Then a pause. 'So what did you see?'

'My gran and my grandad,' I tell them.

'You watched them in a memory?'

'Yes,' I say carefully, stretching the marshmallow goo into strands.

'Like watching TV?'

'Exactly like that,' I say, and I'm lying to them. Just straightforward lying and I don't really know why. I was interacting, not just watching.

If this was only a training bottle, what could I do with a *real* bottle?

I was doing things Fig said we couldn't do. And I don't know why or what to do with that. So I don't say it out loud. Not because I'm being mean, but, until I've processed it, it won't make any sense.

And a little tiny bit of me wants to keep that for myself.

Titch shoves a marshmallow in their mouth so I can barely understand what they're saying. 'If I got a bottle and I could pick, I'd go back and find out why my mam left.' They won't make eye contact with me.

'You just need to talk to your dad,' I say. 'You don't need a memory for that.'

Titch almost growls at me. But it's true, isn't it? My gran is disappearing, and I'm trying to find ways to make her stay, and all Titch needs to do is ask their dad –

here, now – a question! It's dead easy! They don't need cracks or crows for any of that.

Grandad pops into my head and does one of his little coughs, so I decide not to say any of that out loud, but I can't stop myself from thinking it.

'Could you talk to her in there? To your gran?' asks Titch.

'No. Of course not. It was just like watching a film. I was outside it, even though I was there. Why?' I say, too quickly, and Titch lifts their head to look at me, the fire making their face ripple in shadows and flame. After a while, they drop their head and toast another marshmallow.

I don't know what anything means, and I can't explain it yet. Titch begins to talk, but I don't catch the words; there's too much noise inside my head.

'Mimi,' says Titch angrily. 'Are you even listening to me?'

'Yeah,' I say. 'Definitely.' But Titch knows I have no clue what they've just said.

They speak very quietly. 'Sometimes I wonder whether you even realize I'm here with all the Gran stuff. That's awful to say, isn't it? But it's like you've got too much inside to . . . to let me and Nus in too.'

Some things are much easier to say in firelight. 'Have I been a rubbish friend?' I ask.

'Nah,' answers Titch. 'Rubbish jokes, mind.' They laugh, but it doesn't touch their eyes. 'I'm tired,' they say. 'Can we go home now?'

★

Later that night, I lie on my bed fully clothed and reach into my dungarees pocket. I pull out the pieces of confetti I've brought back from the memory that I didn't show Titch.

It takes me ages to fall asleep.

Chapter Twenty-two

The next day I wake early and go and sit on the bandstand in the park and pick the dandelion clocks that are now out. It's a beautiful day, the sun just warm enough to make your skin glow, but no need for sensory-overload sticky suntan lotion. Perfect. A tiny orange-and-white butterfly dances beside me, and then the skateboarder whizzes past and waves. The dogs dash after the ball, and Champ still never gets it, never gives up.

Am I giving up?

I haven't messaged Titch or Nus. I don't know what to say to them. Titch and I didn't really say anything the whole way home. It feels awkward, and I don't know how to put it right. Well, I do know: I should tell them everything. But I *can't do that*.

Not yet anyway. I can explain it all to Titch once we've saved Gran.

Definitely after that.

I think maybe I should message Titch and suggest we go stickleback catching, because that was the point of us after all, but then I realize they might ask questions so I decide I don't really want to.

I run my fingers back and forth through the grass and watch ants scuttle. Gran seems happy, though her bedroom is still shattered by cracks, and little ones follow her around, snaking after her, like they're eating her up, a memory morsel at a time. But no mouths. That has to be a good sign, doesn't it?

Subeera says that's all that matters now, that we give Gran good feelings, because those stick with her long after the words to describe them and the memory of how they happened have faded.

But that's not all that matters, not if I can save her.

Subeera says it's like she's slowed right down and is suspended in time.

Gran sings when I sing with her. We do our star song. We sit, the three of us, me and Gran and Grandad, and sing it over and over and over because that's something we can still do together, like we're all desperately clinging on to the Triangle Trio.

Gran is disappearing, and I can't bear to watch.

I just need time to stop and everything to stay the same. That's not much to ask for, is it? Because I can't lose her. I just can't! And, if she goes away for good, what happens to me?

Who am I kidding? I don't want time to stop here. I want to roll time *back*, to the Gran I found in the memories.

I blow on a dandelion clock, and the wishes scatter.

Can I do that?

Roll back time?

I get up from the bandstand and march towards home.

★

'Hey, Gran!' I say as I find her in the Room for Best. 'What are you doing in here?'

Then I nip myself hard, knowing the cracks will come, knowing I've asked a stupid, hard question yet again.

Gran turns round when she hears me and, instead of the grin I'm expecting, she says in full sentences, like I haven't heard for ages, 'Who are you? And what are you doing in my house?'

She looks terrified. And as she speaks it's not just cracks that race round the room. The whole place shatters into smithereens, and the mouths of the Void Collectors start to leak out from the walls. Their faces make my skin crawl, and I want to grab Gran's hand and run and run and never come back.

I go towards her, to take her hand, to take her out of here.

'Who are you? Get away from me!'

'It's me, Gran – Mimi. We need to go.'

I try to take her hand again, and she wrenches it out of my grasp, and the cracks multiply, and the stench is getting stronger and stronger, and the dark, swirling mist starts coming out of the cracks. The Void Collectors will fill this room soon with their stench and their flickering, hollow faces.

We need to run.

'Don't come any closer. I'll scream. I'll – I'll hit you!' Gran grabs a picture frame from the mantelpiece, the one in a solid, chunky frame, the three of us in the paper when our bowls club got its first Britain in Bloom award, the same one that Gran keeps in her purse.

'There,' I say desperately, anything to try to calm her down and get her to take my hand and get us out of here. 'Just look at the photo – it's you and Grandad and me, Mimi!'

Gran glances at the photo, and she has absolute fear on her face. 'Who is that?'

I watch her stroke the face in the photo, looking confused and scared. Oh, that's it, isn't it? In Gran's head, she's in a different time, much younger than the person in the photo. This must be terrifying for her. I'll help her, I will, but right now we need to get out because those mists, the open, gaping mouths of the Void Collectors, are getting closer to her, fingers trailing towards her, seeking her out –

'Who is that?' She's shrieking now as she looks at the photo, then turns back to me. 'Who are you?!'

I panic and flap, and I just want to hug her, but I know that will make her worse. I want to cry, but that's not fair.

Then I remember what Subeera said. Facts calm me. Facts are good and real. Gran's brain is glitching, and as far as she's concerned she's much younger right now. Anything that doesn't agree with that is terrifying for her.

I just need to meet her exactly where she is.

The mouths open, fold away so their jaws snap back, and then another head appears through the jaws, and they fold back too, hundreds of glitchy heads appearing and folding back. The smell is overwhelming, and I choke.

Concentrate!

It's what Subeera taught us and what Grandad and I have decided to do, never mind what Dr Inevitable says. That's what we do. That's what we will always do. No matter how much it hurts.

Gran comes first.

I take a deep breath, and the smell hits me in the back of my throat, burns my nostrils, nearly makes me retch. 'I'm just here to make lunch,' I tell Gran as I try to hold off the wobble in my voice. 'Your mam sent me to check up on you, make sure you get something warm inside you.'

'Ah, yes,' Gran says.

I'm looking at her, and she doesn't appear convinced, but she's stopped yelling. She seems puzzled rather than scared. The mouths dance up and down her skin, caressing her. It's giving me goosebumps. Can't she feel them on her?

There's a shrieking inside my head. Is it coming from *them*?

I take a chance and walk over to her. 'Here, let me take that from you,' I say, and she hands me the photo.

The mouths open out and nearly touch me, and I try to leap away, and my skin fizzes. I can feel the little hairs on my arms burning; an acrid smell catches my throat; my vision goes blurry and green like everything is getting covered in moss. I try not to jump and scream, and I fake calmness for Gran as I put the frame on the far side of the mantelpiece, right out of her reach, just in case she decides to use it as a weapon. My hands are shaking so much I nearly drop it.

I frantically brush at my arms as Gran points to the photo and in a very small voice says, 'I don't know who they are.' I stop moving and my heart glitches, like it suddenly gets squished.

'Shall we have a little sit-down before I put some soup on?' I give her a smile and hope she can feel the love in it and take her hands and move her towards me. The plastic squeaks on the settee as we sit down next to each other.

The mouths begin to circle us, like we're in a slowly churning whirlpool. I keep hold of her hands. I won't ever let go.

Through the mouths, I can see out of the windows that face the green. Peeking through the treetops is a single star shining in the bright blue daytime sky. 'Look, Gran – I mean, Iolene,' I whisper, and hold up her hand so she follows it and sees.

She beams at me, and I grin back as tears roll down my face, and the mouths whip up faster and faster around us, our hair bristling.

Gran clears her throat, and then she starts singing:

> *Stars shine, you're mine,*
> *My love, my heart, my life . . .*

The mouths slow down, glitch and separate, stop spinning. But as she hesitates with the song, they start to crawl towards her once more. I join in with her. Loud and triumphant.

You are not taking my gran.

> *Glow bright, keep tight,*
> *My love, my heart, goodnight!*

Gran goes up on the last note and I go down, shoving my chin right into my chest. She laughs and squeezes my hand. 'Time for a cuppa, Mimi. Have we got any flapjack left, or has Grandad eaten it all? I'm really tired all of a sudden. Maybe I'll go and have a nap?'

The mist and mouths judder and reverse, begin to retreat, and the cracks undraw themselves. Gran gives me a kiss on the forehead and wanders out of the room like nothing at all has happened.

I lie back on the settee, my sweaty arms sticking and rubbing on the plastic.

I can't do this alone.

I message the Stickleback Catchers.

> Code red. Mouths alert. We
> need to meet now.

★

Subeera stays with Gran when I leave her, squeezes my hand tight. 'Oh, Mimi, I know this is so hard – for you and Grandad. For me too. We're watching someone we love vanish in front of our eyes.' I know how much Subeera loves Gran; they've been best friends forever. 'This is not linear. There are no rules. There is brightness among the dark. Let's grasp it when we can.'

I nod. And don't tell Subeera that I don't think a little bit of brightness is good enough, but I think I know how to fix this, before the cracks come back and we all lose Gran forever.

★

The bus journey takes ages. I don't even enjoy the bit where the sea appears up out of the fields because I spend the whole journey with my brain cycling from being terrified for Gran to the message Titch sent back.

Titch is already at Nus's house.

Editing an episode of *The Puzzler*.

Both of them. By themselves. Without me.

I didn't even realize Nus was still making podcasts. I haven't had time to listen, and I've got more than enough on my plate with my own mysteries to solve.

When I eventually arrive, I join Titch, who is sitting by the side of Nus's bed. We've been given our fifteen minutes. And biscuits. But it's *really* awkward because this is Titch's second lot of fifteen minutes today, and none of us are mentioning it.

'Do you think this will work?' asks Titch quietly.

'I don't see why not,' I reply.

We've got Nus's tank balanced on her bed. Her Mr

Stickleback swims to the side of the glass and looks at us with his big eyes.

'The water comes from the river,' I say. 'And, by holding a feather together, we should all go inside a memory together.'

I sound more confident than I feel. I need Nus's help to work out the logic of the memories.

'I'm scared,' says Nus.

'There's nothing to be scared of. I've done it before, and I'm fine!'

Titch sighs and rolls their eyes.

'What? If you've got something to say, say it!'

'*You* might be fine, but don't you think Nus has every right to be worried about what the effects of doing this might be for her?'

Nus slides further under the bed until only her eyes and forehead appears.

'Oh,' I say.

'Yes, "oh",' says Titch, and rolls their eyes again.

'Nus, I'm sorry, I didn't think. We'll be there for you. You don't have to come, obviously. I just thought . . .'

'That's the point though, isn't it, Mimi? You didn't really think about anyone but yourself,' says Titch, and stares at me.

'I . . .' I drop my eyes and trail off. I don't know what to say. My fingers won't stop fidgeting, and I need to get up and circle the room, loop and loop until I can make sense of it all.

'Stop arguing,' says Nus quietly. 'It's really rather knackering. I'm in, OK? I'm in.'

'You sure?' asks Titch.

Nus wiggles until she's sitting upright with her pillow behind her. 'Action stations! Let's gather as much scientific data as we can. Titch, have you set the stopwatch? You need to press record.'

Titch presses the red dot on the phone and then the button on top of a stopwatch on a string, the kind Mr Todd dangles round his neck when he's timing our laps at school. I've already used the speckly grouse one – I guess it'll be the same memories again, and I don't want them to see those – so I take the grey pigeon feather out of the bottle, and we all grasp it together.

'What if your mam comes up and we're not here?' asks Titch.

'I guess we'll deal with that if it happens,' says Nus. 'Whatever you do, do not let go.' Titch squeezes her hand and smiles.

I go to squeeze it too, but it just feels awkward, and Titch stares at me, so I stop.

I guide our hands to make the constellation pattern. I look up at both of them and grin, really meaning it, the excitement beating in my temples. Nus grins back, and Titch tries not to, but the corner of their mouth wrinkles into a smile.

'Stickleback Catchers, ready?' I ask.

They both nod. With their hands holding on to mine, I lift the feather out of the water, and I sploosh it back in for the final point, the lone star.

Thundercrack.

Water split. Stomach-churning whirlpool. Backwards. Air pull.

Gone.

Chapter Twenty-three

I blink, and we're together, the three of us. Where though? It takes me a moment to get my bearings. At the riverbank, near our den.

We look at each other and giggle.

'I'm at the river!' says Nus. 'For real!'

'Nice clothes for it,' says Titch.

Nus looks down at her dressing gown and plops her sunglasses down so they're over her eyes. We all laugh. It feels good, as if everything will be OK.

'Data-gathering time,' says Nusrat. 'We need facts. We don't know how this works. How we get out, what the boundaries and edges are. It's like playing a board game without rules.'

'And where's the fun in that?' asks Titch, mocking one of Nusrat's favourite phrases.

'Exactly,' she says. 'I'm sitting right here. I don't know what effect this will have on me when I'm back at home, so I'm in charge of bossing you two about. Deal?'

I groan, but say, 'Deal.'

Nusrat has us taking water temperatures and patrolling the edges of the space. It's like it goes gooey about fifty metres from where we landed. The edges begin to ripple and get sticky, and it's not that you can't go any further; it's just that further seems to duplicate itself so it's like walking on a treadmill. No matter how far you go, you're in the same spot.

Titch comes back to Nusrat and reports the same thing. 'It's like we're in a dome,' says Nusrat.

'Or a bubble,' I say.

'A memory bubble,' says Titch.

'I like that,' says Nusrat.

'Smarty-pants,' I say to Titch, and they stick their tongue out at me.

'But whose memory is it? Who does the feather belong to?' asks Nus.

We all turn at once. We can hear footsteps. Someone's coming.

'Hide!' says Nus.

'Why?' I ask.

'I don't know!' Nus looks really scared.

I realize I'm scared too. It was a stupid idea to do this. To risk my friends! I feel the panic rising in my chest, and I clench my fists.

'Can you walk?' Titch asks Nus. I should have asked her that!

'I don't know.' Nus is almost crying now. The footsteps are coming closer. 'We need to go! NOW!'

'We will,' says Titch. 'Am I OK to carry you?'

Nus nods, and Titch swiftly bundles her up in their arms and half runs and half stumbles towards the treeline. I follow closely after. We crouch behind some scrubby bushes and peer out.

And out strolls . . .

Me.

Me!

Mimi Evergreen.

I'm picking up pieces of slate and trying to skim them. This is my memory! This is just before we found the slate slice with the stars. Without that, we couldn't have got this far.

'It's you!' says Titch in astonishment, and I nod, and

the me on the shoreline looks back over her shoulder and towards the bushes.

We scurry and duck to make sure we're hidden. '*Shhhhh!*' I tell them.

'Who's there?' shouts the me by the river.

My eyes widen as I watch myself pull up more pieces of slate to skim. I'm a lot shorter than I imagined. And my plaits are *really* messy – no wonder Gran's always trying to sort them out. I don't get more than one skip across the river. I'm completely rubbish at it.

'There's me,' whispers Titch as past-them appears by the river.

'I know why we're here. We have to help her – *me* – find the star slate! Look for pebbles,' I whisper to Nusrat and Titch.

'What?' says Titch.

'Pebbles. We need to chuck some pebbles. That's how she, I, her, me . . . I don't know!'

We scrabble on the ground, but I can't find anything shiny. Titch suddenly pauses and starts hunting through their pockets. They pull out a sparkling stone.

Titch stares. 'I *knew* I recognized it. It's from my collection!'

'Pyrite,' I say, and smile. 'Fool's gold. Of course! What are you waiting for? Hurry!'

Titch gets up on their hunkers and then peers above the bush. They look down at us both and grin, and then lob the pyrite and some other stones from the ground at the other me.

We watch in awe together as past-Titch and past-me find the pyrite, then discover the message in the slate. Nusrat reaches out and holds both our hands, joining us all together.

Titch grins.

I grin.

The memory begins to crackle and fizzle at the edges, wind rushes, the river explodes and suddenly we're back in Nus's room. One moment by the river, the next moment by her bed.

Titch checks the stopwatch. No time has passed, not a second.

'That was us!' Titch says.

'I know!' says Nus.

They are so giddy, and I join in too.

Then Titch suddenly glares at me. 'So we *can* interact and change things?' they ask.

'No,' says Nus, 'I don't think so . . .'

I stay very quiet.

'But we did!' says Titch.

'*Did* we change anything though?' asks Nusrat. And looks directly at me. 'Or is that just a thing that we'd already done? Because I can remember it now, not just from what we saw in the bottle, but I can remember it, like we actually did it.'

'Me too,' says Titch. 'I see what you mean. We'd already done it; we just didn't *know* we'd done it yet until we did it. Mind. Blown. Huh, Mimi?'

'Yeah,' I say, and mime my hands exploding out from the top of my head. 'Mind blown!'

I don't tell them that I know we *can* change things, that we can make things different, because I've done it.

And I need to keep it secret because I have a plan to roll back time.

It stirs and fizzles inside me. I know what I need to do.

Chapter Twenty-four

We wave goodbye to Nus's mam as we pile into Grandad's car. Titch is nattering away to Grandad, and I keep forgetting to join in.

'You OK?' asks Grandad quietly.

I nod and smile.

I'm not. We're not.

But I know how we will be. I've finally got a plan.

I hope Titch will be knackered by now and want to go home, but when Subeera pops out into the car park to greet us and asks them if they want to stay for Coke floats, they say yes, even though I yawn loudly.

Gran's in the bar, and Subeera helps her plop the vanilla ice cream in our glasses, and the Coke fizzes up and explodes all over the place. Gran finds it so funny that Subeera has to go and help her upstairs for a lie-down.

I yawn again. 'Tiring work, this adventuring stuff, isn't it?' says Titch, and slurps a mouthful of their drink.

Our phones ping. Nusrat has sent us a PDF:

Analysis of Memory Bubbles – A Guidebook

1. Are memories fixed? We threw the stones to help past-you-two discover the slate.
2. There are sticky boundaries approx. 50 metres from the most important point.
3. You can't leave a memory and wander elsewhere.
4. Memory ejection – when and why do they end? Needs further study and data.
5. Holding a training feather together lets you all enter the memory.
6. According to Fig, a training feather can contain multiple memories, but one real feather equals one memory.
7. Question – why were we given these feathers?
8. Action – create an emergency jar of river water.

I sip my float and whack my hand on my forehead to get rid of my ice-cream headache. Titch mutters to themself, going over each of Nus's points and nodding.

They get to point number four. That one really troubles me. That could be the bit that mucks up my plan. *Memory ejection – when and why do they end?* How do I stop us popping back out?

Titch stops muttering and smiles at me. 'Your gran is really class. No matter what's going on with, well, you know.'

'Her dementia,' I say, and I smile. It feels important to say the word out loud; it makes things less frightening when they're not a secret. 'I wish you'd met her when she was skateboarding.'

'Me too,' says Titch quietly.

'It's not that I don't love her now; it's just that things were . . .'

'More fun?'

'Easier. Have you seen how knackered Grandad looks?'

Titch nods.

'I found him by the linen cupboard this morning, where we keep all the tablecloths for when we're having a posh do. He looked like he was wearing them as saris.

They were thrown over his shoulder, piled on the floor, draped from the banister.'

Titch chuckles. The straw slurps as they try to suck up the last of their Coke. 'What was he doing?'

'Folding. Apparently, he'd never done it before.'

'You what? How!'

'He said him and Gran are a team. She does the bits she's good at, he does the bits he's good at, and they meet somewhere in the middle.' Tears roll down my face as I remember how old Grandad suddenly looked, and really young all at the same time. He seemed scared. 'I said to him, "I'm good at folding," which wasn't actually what I wanted to say, but I didn't really know how to put what I meant into words.'

Titch nods and passes me a napkin, and I wipe my face and blow my nose. They take the Cawlington Bottling Co glass bottle from their bag. The feathers nestle inside; the white tummy feather, the only one we haven't used, flutters. They hand it to me.

'You should have this. You need the memories more than us.'

Mrs Marston of the Scarves comes out and begins to polish the bar.

Titch is being kind, but they don't get it, and I daren't

explain. I don't know what to do, so I pick up my crutches and run out of the door, leaving Titch staring after me.

Titch walks two steps behind me all the way to the river. Even though it's hot and sweaty and my hands are rubbing on my crutches until they nearly blister, I don't stop. And neither do they. Our pace slows as we get more tired, but we keep on going. I need to be where I can breathe, where the river flows, where the sky is huge and everything stays the same for centuries.

Or it did, until the river decided to flow backwards.

When we eventually get there, Titch rips off their hoodie and dunks the sleeves in the water, pressing the cool against their brow. They offer me the other sleeve, and I shake my head.

'Sorry,' says Titch, sitting beside me on the riverbank.

'What for?'

'I don't really know. I didn't know what to do – I don't have that many friends.'

I look at them.

'Any other friends at all really,' says Titch. 'I'm not sure how you're meant to do it.'

'Me neither,' I say. 'Think Nus could write us a manual?'

'Nah,' says Titch. 'I don't think she has a clue either.'

We watch as a furry bumblebee buzzes from pink clover to little purple flowers that cover the whole of one rock.

Titch holds the bottle out to me once more. 'We could do it together?' they ask shyly. 'Maybe it will be you and your gran catching sticklebacks?' We stare at the fluffy white feather in the bottom of the bottle. It looks like the type that pokes out of posh pillows.

We can't. I need that feather to save my gran!

But Titch is smiling at me, and I'm the first *real* friend they've ever had, and the last thing I want to do is hurt them. I need to make it right with Titch before I leave them behind.

Point number six.

One real feather equals one memory.

I'll have to make a choice. And break into the Library of Memories.

I tap my fingers in fear and excitement. I'm really going to do it.

I'm going to have to somehow work out which memory bottle is Gran's, and steal it. Then me, Gran and Grandad, we're going to live inside one of her memories from when she was well. We're leaving.

But first me and Titch are going to have one last adventure together.

Titch tips up the bottle and holds out the feather to me.

★

We hold on tight together to the fluffy feather and perform the star-point routine in the river.

'Here we go!' Titch whispers as the river breaks open with a thunderous roar and swirls backwards on itself. Some mallards get caught up inside and burst out, all bewildered and quacking that they're now travelling in the wrong direction, and we grasp tight on to each other as we're sucked up into the air and inside and through.

★

I shake my head; it's quicker to settle now I've done it a few times. Titch is beside me. We're hiding behind a bush in our park. They give me a thumbs up.

'You OK?' they ask.

I grin. 'Yup, you?'

Titch peers over the top of the bush, and I look too. 'When are we?' they wonder.

I can't tell at first, but then realize how shabby the paintwork looks. 'It's the park before the bandstand got repainted,' I whisper to Titch.

It's the end of dusk. That weird light where it's still kind of bright, but it's harder to see than when it goes properly dark. There is no one around. Bats flit overhead, silhouettes against the glowing sky.

Titch grins at me. I grin back. This was the right way to leave things.

'Whose memory do you think we're in?' asks Titch.

I shrug. What is the final surprise Fig has given us? And why?

Titch's face falls, and their eyes grow panicky as they point and whisper, '*Look!*'

Around the side of the Cawlington Bottling Co building appear two figures dressed in black. One has a backpack on. Are they burglars? I begin to shake, and my breath goes short and stuttery.

As one of them reaches into the backpack to pull something out, I feel Titch go tense next to me. They take a breath and hold it, and I do too.

Out of the rucksack the figure pulls two skateboards. I feel Titch release their breath and so do I.

'That's your –'

'Gran,' I answer, my pride in her making me nudge Titch harder than I meant to.

'Ow,' says Titch. 'She's actually skateboarding!'

'This must be one of her lessons.'

'What an amazing gift from Fig,' says Titch. 'Something to treasure when things get, you know . . .' They give my hand a squeeze, but I don't need their pity because I have no intention of letting things with Gran get 'you know . . .'.

The two of them, the skateboarder and my magnificent gran, hold hands and run across the road and then head into the park. As soon as they get through the gates, they drop their boards and leap on. The skateboarder stays by Gran, letting her lead the way, set the speed, beside her just in case.

'Wow!' says Titch.

I turn and beam at them. *This* is my gran. The real Gran before she was stolen. I mean, how can you explain to someone that there was once this person living inside, when they're there and still with you but a bit of them has disappeared in front of your eyes? My eyes get all puddly, and I wipe them hurriedly.

They hurtle round the circumference of the park as a warm-up and then start using the routes that criss-cross the centre by the bandstand, flipping and jumping. Sometimes Gran takes a tumble, but she wipes her hands and gets back up, the skateboarder always checking that she's OK and good to go.

I really want to go up and tell her how amazing she is, but I can't do that. And, if I did, what would Titch say? They don't know that I've talked to my grandparents in my memories. That I've lied to Titch. My fingers tap.

Gran and the skateboarder reach the bandstand. 'You sure you want to give this a go?' the skateboarder says.

I can see Gran, all in black (she'll have ruddy loved the drama of that), and she looks uncertain.

'You don't have to, you know.'

Gran looks at the railing running down by the steps.

'*Nooo*,' whispers Titch. 'She wouldn't!'

'She would,' I whisper back.

And she is. The rumours *were* true – of course they were true! I'm about to watch my gran do a boardslide down the bandstand rail.

I go to move to get a better view, and there's a crunch as I step back on a branch and it breaks. The two of them immediately look over.

'Who's there?' yells Gran.

Titch looks at me, eyes massive.

It was a mistake to come here. I have no clue what we're meant to do now. My hands start to get a bit flappy.

'Someone *is* there!' says Gran to the skateboarder, and she begins to stalk over towards us. 'Come out and show your faces. We'll not have any graffiti on the bandstand on my watch!'

How do we exit the memory? We haven't worked that out yet!

The skateboarder starts walking towards us. Titch is scrabbling to get further inside the bush, so I just go for it and stand up and say, 'Hi, Gran.'

The skateboarder stops and stares at me.

'Mimi?' asks Gran, and I love that she's the Gran who knows who I am.

'Are you following me? Spying on me? Why are you in a bush? How are you taller? And what on earth have you done to your fringe?'

Titch gasps. 'Did you know you can change things? Have you done this before?'

I can't meet Titch's gaze. I pat my hair, trying to make it go behind my ear.

'You have! You lied to us.' I've never seen Titch so furious. Their face goes all red and their hands bunch into fists.

I step back to try and get my balance, to give me a moment to work out what to say, and I kick the bottle that held the feather, and it teeters from its perch wedged into a 'V' of branches, and then, in what feels like slow motion, it begins to fall, and I know that this is very bad, a very bad thing.

The air hums. It grows full of wingbeats and darkness. There's that smell, and tendrils of faces with open mouths leak out of the bushes, across the grass from the bandstand.

I watch the skateboarder fade to nothing – *Not Gran, don't take Gran, she hasn't done the boardslide yet . . . don't take my gran* – and there's a throbbing in my ears and I'm not sure where Titch is

where I am

where the edges of anything are

any more.

★

I whomp down, through time and space, and smack down next to Titch, who is already sitting on a bench inside the Cawlington Bottling Co, in the room where we first met Fig. It is full of crows, not standing to attention, but squabbling and flying and shoving, hitting each other with their briefcases.

Fig is on the table in front of us, pacing back and forth. 'I am stupid, so stupid, so stupid. I am stupid. I shouldn't have ever said a yes! They know about you now; they know what you did; they know what *I* did!'

Fig begins to shake and then ruffles his feathers, and I think he's regained control of himself when he starts to pluck feathers out of his chest.

'What *did* you do?' I ask as I try to get my bearings.

Fig ignores me and scuttles back and forth, then goes back to plucking out his feathers. 'Must make amends . . . Can't let them . . .'

'Fig! Stop! You're hurting yourself!'

'Hurting myself . . . This is nothing compared to . . .'

'Compared to *what*? What's going on?'

'Did you not listen to my rhyming, chiming, riddling rules? The crows said they were clear enough, but what do crows know?'

Fig goes back to plucking out his feathers. The crows flutter and scutter, landing on the table, dive-bombing, screeching. Not one of them can stay still – it's like they're electrified.

'Fig, you're not making any sense. *Please* stop!' I bat one of the crows away from my face. 'Titch, do something!'

Titch won't look at me, just slumps in a chair, no help whatsoever.

'I made a promise,' Fig mutters quietly so I can barely hear. 'But not a hurting, punishing promise. I didn't know I'd have to deal with . . .' Fig stops, then walks to the end of the table and stares straight at me. '*She* understood the rules. Why can't you! You could have been stuck!'

Then he begins to pace again, muttering stuff to himself under his breath that I can't make out and I'm not sure is English. *Who's 'she'?*

I'm about to ask out loud when he stops again. 'I gave you fun! I gave you adventure! But you, you do not take care of things!'

'It's not like we asked for any of this!' I yell at him. 'It's not *my* fault.'

'Did you not?' asks Fig. 'What are wishes if they are not asks?'

'That doesn't make any sense!'

'Stuck,' says Titch finally, sitting forward in their

chair, nudging a crow out of the way. 'What do you mean by "stuck"?'

'How did you not listen to my training song? Oh my stars, I am dealing with fools! You nearly broke a bottle! A precious memory bottle!'

Titch looks blankly at him.

'And,' I say as Fig looks ready to explode, '*remind* us what would happen if we had.'

'*You* had,' says Titch to me.

'Then that is where you stay!' squawks Fig. 'Forever! No forwards in time. No backwards memories. No growth and living. Just stuck. No more feathers for you! What was she thinking? What was *I* thinking? . . . You were not doing *any* thinking at all!' He begins to pace again.

Stuck. We could have been there forever.

That's the missing piece of the puzzle I've been searching for. The niggly thing I couldn't grasp. I don't have to be worried about getting ejected from memories.

If I break the bottle once we're in the memory, we get to stay with Gran forever.

Fig suddenly stops. I have so many questions I need to ask. I go to count them off on my fingers when he looks up and twitches his beak. 'They're coming.'

The crows stop flapping. The room is still and silent.

'Who's coming, Fig?' And I shiver because he's shrunk to half his size and is shaking so hard I think he might fall off the table. I hold out my hands to steady him and he cowers in them. His feathers are beautifully soft, inky petrol, and I want to hold him safe forever.

Forever. That's the key.

'The Void Collectors. They know what I've done.' Then he shuffles round in my hands and peers out from under one wing. 'What *you've* done.'

Fig is too busy muttering and shaking to give me any more information. Titch has gone back to slumping, but I can see their eyes are alert.

The room suddenly goes dark, and the crows stand to attention, then fly up and perch on bottles and shelves and in the arches, and they all place their heads beneath their wings.

I look at Titch for help, but they're too busy staring at all the crows. 'What's happening?' I ask, and I can hear the tremor in my voice.

'Uh of the oh,' says Fig, and then a screeching noise begins.

I slap my hands over my ears and close my eyes.

Chapter Twenty-five

The crows descend and surround each of us, pecking and fluttering until we have no choice but to walk in the direction they push us. I can't see where Titch and Fig are. I can't hear anything above the screeching, the cawing and wing flapping. The crows press down on my head until I'm sitting on the ground, then they scatter and I can see again. We are inside the Library of Memories. The stacks and stacks of shelves tower above us and beyond us. Thousands, millions of bottles stuffed with feathers.

I couldn't see them last time, I wasn't close enough, but beside each bottle is a printed ticket, all catalogued in codewords I don't understand. Now that I've got something to latch on to, I can hold the terror at bay.

I need to think.

I need to crack the code.

I had a training bottle: that's why the memories were all jumbled. But one bottle on *those shelves* equals one person's memories.

There's a bottle here that's just for Gran.

I need to find that bottle!

I want to tell Titch that I've cracked it, what our next mission is, but then I remember that Titch hates me because I lied about being able to change things, and at that moment the Void Collectors come together in one seething mass. I can feel the mossy-green cold blow against me as they begin to whirlpool round us. I suck myself inwards as Titch does the same, scrabbling away from them so our sides press together.

Where's Fig? Where have they taken him?

I remember how the mouths fizzled and burned my arms. The smell.

Titch and I aren't tied together with rope, but we might as well be. We can't move because the Void Collectors circle us. The stench is unbearable, and they glitch in and out of view, like they're here and somewhere else all at the same time. I try not to look at them, but my eyes don't want to pull away, because it feels like I'll fall into their gaping mouths and be lost forever.

We are surrounded by cobwebby wisps like jellyfish tentacles. I try to wriggle, and my hand touches one of them. I yell and watch a streak on my palm fizz, blister, burst, and within seconds the skin is back to how it was, like it didn't even happen. I trace it, and when I do I can feel the echo of pain, like a leftover nettle sting.

Titch is frozen, staring up and straight ahead of us to where Fig dangles inside a cage suspended from the ceiling that is so high I can barely see it.

Then they turn their face to the side and stare at me. 'You knew!' they explode through gritted teeth. 'You *knew* you could talk to people in your memories, that we could change things.'

I shrug.

'You *knew* and you didn't tell us?'

'Is now really the time for this?' I ask.

'I just can't believe you knew! What we could . . . I just can't even . . . With the pyrite, you let us believe that it was something we've always done, but that was a lie!'

'Do you think maybe we could have this argument later, because logically it doesn't make any difference whatsoever if we're stuck here.'

Titch glares at me, but falls quiet.

The cobwebs zap and twirl round Fig too, mouths and limbs coming into view and then fading again. The ones next to Fig are even more terrifying than the Void Collectors that are guarding us. It's like we've got the junior division, and Fig is being guarded by the elite squad. We've lost. I can't work out how we'll get out of this one.

A monstrous moving bubble of gaping mouths and bits of shadowy humans circles Fig. He cowers inside the cage, leaping away from the tendrils that creep through the bars.

Who gave you the right to meddle? The whole swirling pack of Void Collectors speak as one, but with a time delay so that bits of words jut out and echo. Their different faces slide over each other until they form one slipping, sliding face with a single mouth. I recognize it. It's a collaged, messed-up Dr Teller.

Of course it is.

It always was.

Dr Inevitable.

'I am sorry. It won't happen again. I promise!' Fig shrieks and cowers. 'They were only training-feather spares! Duplicates! Crossover duplicate feather memories! No originals.' He grovels and bows, over and over again. 'No more, of course no more. I'm good – I know my place – I'll never do it again. It is my honour to serve you!'

Serve us? Serve us!

I can't take my eyes off his rolling, jumbled, spiralling face – the Void Collectors holding the whirlpool together, and the stench coming off them as they shout as one.

Fig shakes so hard his cage jangles.

You do not serve us – you serve the memories!

'Yes, yes, of course. That's right. It will never happen again!'

We have heard this from you before, Fig Archimedes. We let you in, not even a crow! And this is how you repay us.

'Sorry, so sorry. I am. No harm done.'

This time . . .

The swirls move faster round the cage. Mouths leap out and gape, rows and rows of teeth, jaws and eyeballs where there shouldn't be. The screeching begins again, and it makes my eyes water. I reach over and take Titch's hand. They let me, but when I squeeze it they don't squeeze back.

No harm done. This time . . . the Void Collectors screech, and all the bottles vibrate, sing and rattle on the shelves.

I can't cope — it's too loud and it hurts — and I don't know what's happening, and I just want my gran. I let go of Titch's hand and clamp my hands over my ears and close my eyes.

I think the roar in my ears is going to make them pop, and I open my eyes to see if there's any possible way to escape, and the sound suddenly stops, and Titch and I are back on the riverbank. It flows the right way. We are now.

The wind blows and scuffles the tree branches higher up and then swoops down so it ruffles my fringe.

Titch looks over at me. 'You lied,' they say. Titch tries to hold their face fixed, but their bottom lip wobbles, like they're trying not to cry.

I can't hold their gaze. I drop my eyes and nod.

'Do you think you're the only one that wants to change things?' Titch asks through gritted teeth.

I shrug. I don't know what to say.

'Do you even care what memory Nus would go back to, if she could? Have you even asked? You're so caught up in *you*. She told me I could tell you, but I was so sure you'd ask her yourself. But that's never going to happen, is it?'

'Yes, it is!' I say. Then I shake my head. 'No, it's not,' I say very quietly. Then even quieter still, 'If she's said it's OK to tell me, I really do want to know.'

Titch stares at me for so long that I think they're not going to tell me, and I go to walk away because I don't know what else to do.

'Nus wants to go back to the day of her school photo, with her brother. The last time she went to school. The next day she got sick. She wants to remember what it was like to run around and argue and chase and not be in bed all the time. Do you not think that she deserves to know what you kept from us? That she may want a chance to change things too? You don't ever talk about anything other than *you*!'

'But Gran . . .'

'I know, and it's so sad, but your gran is *still here*. You're so fixated on making things better that you're losing the time you've got left. Do you think *I* would waste that? That Nus would? You've got a chance to change things *now*. You could spend actual, real time with your gran *now*, without messing with memories. We don't have that option, me and Nus. The memories of before: that's all we have. At least, that's what we thought. But you didn't bother to tell us it's possible to *change things*.'

'I didn't know . . .'

'No, because you didn't bother to ask!'

I can't believe how badly wrong things have gone between us. This was all meant to be an adventure. Gran brought me and Titch together so I wouldn't be alone when she . . . I'd have friends, so we'd have fun catching sticklebacks, and going on adventures and solving puzzles!

Gran just didn't realize the puzzle would be her.

I sit back down with a thump as the realization hits me.

Is that why she put the advert in the paper?

Titch is right. I've wasted so much time.

Time.

Ticking. Ticking.

Titch, even though they're hurting, looks at me and reaches up to take my hand. 'Time stops while we're in the memories. But it hasn't stopped *here*.'

I smile a little bit at them, to test it out on my face, and they don't smile back, but they don't take their hand back either, and I think that maybe I can make it OK.

I put on my best bossy Nus voice. 'Have you made your emergency jar of river water yet, as per instruction number eight?'

Titch half smiles, and then their eyes widen and their mouth drops.

I let go of their hand and look up. There are hundreds of crows standing to attention in the trees, more and more descending until the branches creak downwards under their weight. Once they have our attention, they fly back up into the sky and form a huge arrow, pointing away from the river.

Titch goes to speak to me, but I'm already up and grabbing my crutches.

★

I'm so exhausted I can barely breathe. My lungs are burning, and my arms are shuddering, trying to keep swinging my crutches. Titch puts their arm round me to help as we get to the edge of the park. The crow arrow descends and lines up on the roof of our flat.

Our little flat above our bowls club, the centre of my universe. Covering it like tiles so there's not a single empty space.

The ground rips and ruptures, and cracks bigger than we've ever seen before tear the bowling green in two and slash a chasm directly towards us.

I look down at my feet as the ground begins to splinter and shatter, throwing me off balance, like it's had all the moisture sucked out of it. I follow the cracks with my eyes as the ground ripples and bucks, leading towards the growing chasm, and beyond that the bowls club and my gran.

I can smell them before I can see them. The Void Collectors burst up out of the ground, their mouths open and the stench hitting me, their jaws wide open as they shriek towards the club.

Titch crushes and crunches my wrist in their hand, but I shake them off.

This time I don't freeze.

I grab my crutches and run.

Run towards Gran.

Chapter Twenty-six

I burst through the front door, slamming it behind me on a tendril trying to get through. A shriek comes out of it that liquefies my insides as it drops to the floor, burning its imprint on the carpet. I knew it. I knew his black suit jacket would be on the coat stand.

I march over and grab it down, flip it open and find a seam, then rip and rip and rip.

'Your face was in those awful shadows – I knew it was you!' I scream as the lining tears and the sleeves rip off. Every time I blink, I can see Dr Teller's face glitching and morphing as the Void Collectors screamed at Fig in his cage.

I rip and rip until it no longer looks like a jacket, then I drop it on the floor and stomp.

'Everything was fine until you started coming here. We were managing fine!'

It's like I can feel the power of the cracks inside me. They tear up the wall, and my eyes follow them. I stride down the hallway, muttering to myself. 'There were no cracks or crows. I had friends at school, and Gran was singing.'

I watch the cracks explode the wall so that pictures fly off, and I have to duck.

'Singing? Gran was *talking*! I was spending time with Gran, not wasting it on stupid adventures that haven't solved anything!'

Where is Gran?

My body feels cold, and I can't remember when I last ate, and the most important thing in the world is finding my gran. I pick up speed and start yelling for her. 'Gran! Gran, where are you?'

I bash along the corridor and throw open the doors. Not in the Room for Best, not in the kitchen, not at the table, not in her bedroom. I get to the end of the hallway and notice the fire door is open, the one that leads down to the rickety outdoor steps in case we need to escape. I shove open the door.

Dr Inevitable and Grandad are leaning over the rail. Grandad quickly passes a cigarette back to him.

'What are you doing? Gran would murder you if she saw you doing that. You haven't smoked since 1973!'

Grandad has the decency to look a bit sheepish. I study his face. There's not much round left in him. There are deep bags and bruises under his eyes. It's like his skin has lost the elastic, and it just hangs wrinkly in places and is then pulled tight over his cheekbones. His hair is too long and straggly.

'Let's go inside,' says Dr Inevitable.

'Let's not,' I reply. 'Let's not do *anything* you suggest any more, because I know exactly who you are!'

I turn to Grandad. 'We can't trust him – he's *dangerous*.'

'Oh, pet lamb, I'm too knackered for this right now.'

My voice turns to pleading. 'I know! That's his plan – it's all his fault!'

Dr Inevitable reaches out his hand towards me.

'Do not touch me!' I spit at him, remembering how the tendrils of the Void Collectors burned like nettle stings.

I realize I'm crying when I have to sniff, and there are hot tears running down my face. I swipe them away.

'Come on, pet – let's all go inside,' says Grandad.

'No! Are you not listening to me? Not with *him*!'

Grandad and Dr Inevitable exchange looks.

Why won't Grandad trust me? My calm just disappears, poof. I can *feel* my brain igniting.

I hate being ignored.

'Oh, that makes a change.' I don't recognize the sarcasm in my own voice, and I have to squeeze my arms by my side to stop me from wanting to shake Grandad and *make* him listen to me. Words spill out, and I've lost all control:

'Let's just ignore Mimi and crack on with things just the same way, because that's been so successful. Take his side over mine! Or is there anything else you want to fill me in on, as you two are *so* good at keeping secrets?'

Grandad looks baffled, like he's about to cry, and Grandad never cries. I know I'm being all snarky and talking horribly to him, but I can't help it. It's all pouring out of me, and I just want him to hug me so it stops. I wait for him to put his arms around me, but he doesn't. He just stands there, looking so old and ridiculous.

'Where *is* Gran anyway? With Subeera at the gallery? What day is it?' I turn to Dr Inevitable. 'Are we really *now*?'

'Mimi, love, you're not making much sense,' says Grandad. 'Do you need a lie-down?'

'Please do not patronize me,' I say very quietly, and Grandad's face crumples. I know I should stop, but I can't. I need to prod and poke him until he feels as bad as I do.

Why is no one screaming and screaming about how unfair and awful this all is? Why is it wrong to want to make everything better?

Why are they just watching and letting it happen?

I turn to go inside, to find Gran.

'Where are you going?' asks Dr Inevitable.

'None of your business.'

'It is mine though,' says Grandad. 'Poppet, what's going on?'

'I'm going to see my *gran*. Going to stop me?' I direct that last bit at Dr Inevitable as a challenge. I know who he really is.

I grab the door, and Grandad gently places his hand on top of mine.

I watch as the Void Collectors' tendrils coil up on to the balcony and slip and slide round their master's feet. Dr Inevitable pretends he can't see it happening. My whole body feels like it's covered in their stings.

Very quietly, I say to him, 'Where is Gran?'

There's silence, and Grandad looks at the doctor, and the doctor looks back at him.

'No secrets. You promised,' I say.

Grandad goes to speak, but nothing comes out, and he turns away.

I begin to shake, and burning tears roll down my cheeks. I can't let go of the door. It's the only thing stopping me from floating away. 'Where is Gran? Is she . . . ?'

'In the hospital,' says Dr Inevitable. 'She's OK.'

'She's OK? She's in hospital!' All the anger and relief I'm feeling comes rushing out of me, and I spit my words at him like bullets. 'Did you put her there?'

'She had a little fall when she was on her own. They're doing some X-rays and things, but I think it's pretty certain that she's broken her hip.'

'Gran was left alone?'

She was by herself in all that pain and not knowing what was going on. Did she cry for help? Did she call for *me*?

'Where were *you*?' I ask Grandad.

He flusters.

'Playing bowls?' I ask quietly, and there's a laugh in my voice I can't control, which makes this sound even worse. 'Having a great time with your mates? It's your job to look after her, to keep her safe. *Why did you leave her alone?*'

He doesn't say anything. Crows come to roost in the huge hawthorn trees. It's like they've got a prime viewing spot; they are an audience to witness how much he has let her down. Their presence cheers me on, and I can't back down now. The tendrils snake up Dr Inevitable's body until he's wearing them like armour.

'Answer me. Why did you leave her by herself?'

Grandad won't look at me. I wouldn't be able to look at me. I just want this all to stop, and now I've backed myself into a corner, and I can't get out of it, but I am so angry. At him? Yes, but at *everything*.

Titch's head appears over the edge of the balcony. 'I heard shouting,' they say. 'You OK?'

'No! Gran's in hospital, and it's all his fault.' I point at Grandad.

'Now, now,' says Dr Inevitable. 'That's not fair.'

'Shut up!' I yell at him. 'Just shut up!'

'Mimi, that's enough,' says Grandad. 'We did not bring you up to behave like this.'

'No? But I didn't have any choice in that, did I? I didn't choose to have two old people for parents, two old people who are going to *abandon* me. I didn't choose any of this! One who can't speak sense, and the other one who doesn't know how to keep her safe. So I'm going to end up God knows where!'

I don't know where this is all coming from. They can barely hear me over my snotty breathing.

'I just want to be in control . . .'

Grandad looks like I've just thumped him, and I feel as if I have. He tries to take me in his arms, but even though that's all I want I push him away. 'Last time I'm asking you: where were you?'

Grandad looks me straight in the eye and says, 'Looking for you, Mimi. I was worried. No one had seen you. I was just about to call the police.'

There is silence. No one says a thing.

Finally, just when I think the silence is going to eat us all up, Titch – their head popping up into the fire escape from the ladders – smiles gently at me and says, 'Mimi, how about you come for a walk with me maybe . . .' and then they trail off when I stare at them.

'No,' I say quietly, and I can't stop my tears from falling. 'I don't want to. You don't understand!'

'Try me,' says Titch.

'No. I can't!'

'Why not? I'm your friend – you can tell me anything,' and they do their eyebrow-wiggle thing to try and make me smile.

'Because –' I scrunch my face up and do three big breaths through pouty lips – 'you never believed it was real. You came into my life, and you swore you were my friend and you'd help me. But you're not! Because you don't understand what it's like for *me*.'

Titch's face crumples a little bit. 'I do!'

'No! I still had a chance to save my gran, and I would have done if you'd helped me.'

'Mimi!' says Grandad, his face twisted by shock and upset. 'I have no idea what's going on, but you shouldn't be speaking to Titch like that. Apologize immediately.'

'No,' I say. 'It's true. I don't want anything to do with *any* of you.' I stare at Dr Inevitable and then Grandad and then finally Titch. Tears are rolling down their cheeks.

I turn to Dr Inevitable, all my fight gone, and quietly say, 'None of this would have happened if we hadn't met you.'

I pull the door open and step inside, turning my back on everyone.

'Mimi!' tries Titch again.

I turn back to them. 'Go home, Titch. The Stickleback Catchers are done. It was a stupid idea anyway.'

There's a split second before Titch gasps, and then they turn, and I can hear them clanging down the metal steps, and then they're cutting straight over the bowling green and running away through the park. Grandad charges down the steps after them. Dr Inevitable follows behind, the tendrils dissolving as he runs.

Titch reaches the main road and doesn't even check for traffic. They just keep running until I can't see them any more.

The crows jostle in the trees and then flap their wings and fly away, leaving me all alone.

Chapter Twenty-seven

'Hey there,' I say. 'It's me, Mimi.'

I sit beside Gran's hospital bed. Mr Marston of the Hats brought me straight here when Grandad got back from not catching up with Titch. He shook his head and walked straight past me through the PIRATE door.

Mr Marston patted my arm and told me not to worry and then worried me a lot with his driving.

The side room is white and airy, but it's full of buttons and wires, and the bed has rails. There is a tray wheeled over Gran's bed, and on it is an orange beaker. A baby's beaker. I roll the tray out of the way so that I can pull my chair further up the bed and be closer to her.

She is just a little head peering out of a sheet. Her hair is curly on the pillow. She would not be happy with that. It makes me angry that no one here knows her enough to make sure that her hair is straight. She beams at me, but I'm not sure her eyes are focused. She seems very far away.

I'm not sure what to say at first, then I remember it's Gran. I can tell her *anything*.

Well, almost anything.

'It's nearly time to take our Mr Sticklebacks back to the river. They're doing really well, but we need to take them home. We'll go together soon.' I smile at Gran and realize it's a lie. I don't know whether the Stickleback Catchers even exist any more. 'Sorry, Gran. It was a brilliant idea of yours, the advert in the paper, but I've messed it all up.'

She doesn't try to make it better. I mean, she never used to, so it's about right. I smile, and my eyes wrinkle. They match hers.

'Shall we sing?' I ask her. She carries on smiling.

I begin to sing our star song, and she doesn't join in. My heart *thump-thump-thumps*. She *always* joins in. This *always* works.

'You're right,' I say to her, because I don't want her to feel bad about not joining in. 'There isn't a star in the sky – highly inappropriate use of singing. Shocking in fact.'

The machine next to her traces her heart. Little beeps pop out of it. Jagged lines rising and falling on the screen; they look like cracks.

No feathers fall, no help from Fig. No cracks appear along the walls.

'Is that what they were, Gran?' I say, and kiss her hand. 'You can tell me. I promise I'll keep it a secret. Were they your memories crumbling?'

I wonder if Gran can even make memories any more now. Maybe she's just living inside the old ones. 'I hope you're in a good one,' I whisper to her. She doesn't reply.

A nurse bustles into the room. His name tag says JOSH: HE, HIM. He smiles at me. 'That's good. Chat away – she can hear you.'

'How do you know?' I ask.

He stops looking at the chart from the end of the bed. 'Well, her hearing works just fine. True, we're not sure which bits are processed now, but anything in a kind tone, she'll feel that. She may not understand all the words, but she'll know the love in it. She'll know that she's loved and she's safe. That's enough, isn't it?'

And I nod, all grown up because that's what I'm meant to do. Of course that's enough, but then I shake my head because no way is that enough.

No way.

'She likes her hair straight,' I tell him.

'That's good,' he replies. 'Very important information for us. I'll make sure it's written down.'

I can't tell if he's being sarcastic, but he smiles so I don't think he is. 'The more we know about her, the comfier we can make her stay with us.'

I pull my phone out of my dungarees pocket.

'Gran, how about listening to this?'

I go to the music bit on my phone and press play. 'That's you singing.'

'Singing?' asks the nurse.

'She was an opera star,' I tell him.

'That's incredible,' he says. 'Turn it up so I can hear it better.' He comes and stands on the opposite side of the bed and crouches down next to Gran. 'That's beautiful!'

I nod at him.

'I love it when we find out things about our patients. All these long lives and incredible things people have done. The people they've loved.'

'She can skateboard too,' I say proudly.

'What a lady! I wish I could have seen that. It's just so sad,' the nurse says as he stands and moves over to the door. 'If only we knew a way to buy more time.'

He leaves the room. I keep the music playing, and Gran closes her eyes. She looks so peaceful. I start to fidget and look at my watch. Another fifteen minutes until Mr Marston comes to pick me back up and I have to face Grandad. I don't want to think about him now.

I see Dr Inevitable's face seared on to the Void Collectors. I see Titch's face crumple just before they ran away.

I don't want to think about any of them.

I look at my phone. There are still zero notifications from Titch. I mean, I don't want to think about them, but I thought maybe they might have been in touch. None from Nus either.

I open the bedside-cabinet drawer — baby wipes, some butter mints, a packet of tissues and my mam's jumper. Grandad must have packed it up for her. I reach in and take it out of the drawer. It unfurls and keeps its creases so I'll know how to fold it back up, just like I always do. I look at my mam's name on the label in Gran's spidery handwriting — *Asteria*. I don't know why I don't tell Gran I know she has it. Even though Gran probably knows I know. Grandad does; it was my protector from monsters, and I know they don't keep secrets from each other.

Just from me.

Gran shares everything she has with me, just not that. It's hers. 'That's OK,' I say to Gran. 'You needed something just for you.'

I feel bad about unfolding it now, like I'm stealing something from her. I lay it on my knees, so I can neatly fold it back up, and realize there's a tiny breast pocket that I've never noticed before. I'm always in such a rush, looking over my shoulder so I don't get caught, that I've never spotted it. I press my fingers on it, and there's something hard inside. I only manage to get one finger in: it's like the pocket has been designed especially for it. I have to wiggle, and the object keeps slipping out of my finger. *Hands, work properly!*

I take a big breath and shake my fingers out, then I have one more try. I roll it, and it finally pops out of the pocket into the palm of my hand.

A tube of stars. Like the ones Fig dropped on the patio table for me, way back. I take mine out of my pocket and hold them up beside each other. They match.

Why did my mam have them? Or was it Gran? Did she have them and put them in the little pocket?

I want to ask her about them. I want to ask her about so much.

Mr Marston pops his head round the door. He's wearing a trilby with a feather sticking out of it. I wonder if the feather is someone's memory.

I wonder whether Gran will make any more . . . or if she's somewhere else entirely.

Chapter Twenty-eight

Two days later, no contact from Nus or Titch, and what Josh the nurse said about buying more time is bouncing in my head.

Everyone is quiet at the club. Gran was the one who brought the sparkle, and without her it's just dull. Her not being here has stolen everyone's pizazz. I need to get out. It's just an epic reminder that's she's not here, where she should be.

I think I might struggle to make it through the bar and out of the club gates, but no one seems remotely bothered. Mrs Marston of the Scarves gives me a wave from behind the bar. 'Want anything to eat?'

I shake my head.

'At least take these.' She tosses a bag of scampi bites at me. I pop them in my dungarees pocket. 'Snack pocket,' she says, and smiles.

I smile back, but it feels wrong on my face.

Mr and Mrs Marston are in charge while Grandad spends most of his time at the hospital with Gran. I thought the change of place would really unsettle her and make her scared, but I don't think she's even noticed, and that makes me even more sad. I haven't been to see her again. I don't think she even knows who I am any more, and I can't bear to think about that.

The flowers are coming out in their pots. Gran will be so angry she's missed this. I think Grandad is spending all his time with her to make *him* feel better. He's barely spoken to me since I was so horrible on the fire escape. Mainly because I've hidden and not given him the chance. He yells for me each morning before he goes to the hospital, and each morning I pretend to be asleep.

I decide to be a grown-up and *do the right thing*, mainly to stop anything else from bouncing in my head, so I dial Titch's number while I'm walking.

They don't answer their phone.

My head doesn't like it when I've made a decision and then I can't follow it through.

I try calling again and leave a message.

Then I send a text to say hello. Nothing.

I realize I probably need to do a little bit more than that. Even though I'm not sure if everything was *entirely* my fault, I send four messages saying sorry in lots of different ways. No reply. I even count to 300, which is five whole minutes, but still nothing.

I try to ring again, and it just goes straight to answerphone, so they must have turned it off.

They're choosing to ignore me.

Be like that then. I've done my bit.

If I close my eyes, I can still see how devastated Titch looked before they ran away.

I decide to walk to the den. Titch might be there, but it's a bit far on my crutches when I'm this pooped, so I go back into the bar and ask if Mr Marston wouldn't mind dropping me off at the river.

He seems grateful to help, and once we get there he gives my shoulder a squeeze before I get out of his car.

I walk along the path, the sun pouring through the canopy of leaves, new grass springy under my feet. My fingers tap on my crutches, looping, spelling out words and phrases. Even when I tell them to stop inside my head, which usually works, they don't.

I want Titch to be there and I don't want them to be there, all at the same time.

When I arrive and find out they're not, I can't work out if I'm disappointed or relieved.

I sit in our den and can feel the river pounding outside, but it doesn't settle me like it usually does. My brain is too fidgety. There's no point in even trying to fish: the sticklebacks will sense the tension in my net and stay right away.

Gran always says to break it down when I get like this. The problem is too big in one lump, so it has to be broken into chunks and swallowed one piece at a time.

I text Nus:

> Any information about the
> star tubes?

Nus doesn't reply with words, which isn't like her, just sends a link to a web page. Maybe she's resting and tired? Or maybe her and Titch have ganged up against me. I click on the link.

There they are! Images of little stars, grey like mine, but some in all shades of brown too. Some look like flowers. Some are really thin like where I bashed mine and realized it could be split into hundreds of sliver-stars too. I try to read. There are lots of really long words, and not all of it makes much sense. Then I learn their name: crinoids. An ancient group of fossils. Whoa. I can't hold that amount of time in my head: 300 million years *before* the dinosaurs? That's just huge! I remember what Fig told us. *We keep hoomans safe. It is our job, as old as stars.*

I message Nus back to tell her that they match with what Fig says, but there's no reply from her this time.

Yup, I bet Titch is over there right now, and they're both talking about me. They can just hang out together and make podcasts; they can be a duo instead of a trio. I sigh. We never did work out a handshake. Or have a lemon top.

Trios are crumbling everywhere. Must be the season for it.

I kick a clump of grass, and lots of dead dandelion stalks keel over. One remains upright with its full halo of seeds intact. I bend down and pick it, thinking of Gran wanting to use the bright yellow flower to test whether I liked butter, and me telling her off for it being the wrong one.

'That was the beginning,' I whisper gently to the dandelion, careful not to blow on its seeds. 'I didn't have a clue, did I?'

I sit by the side of the river and think how childish I was, racing Gran to Guru and trying to avoid the cracks in the pavement. It feels like a different life, but it's only the length of a dandelion's lifespan.

I hold the clock in front of my mouth and screw my eyes up tight, go to make a wish, but I'm not sure what exactly I should wish for. It's the last dandelion. It's really important that I get this right.

Above the sound of the river I suddenly hear Gran say in my head, 'These will all be clocks soon. Tick-tick-ticking.'

I drop the dandelion without blowing on it. I don't need wishes. Titch and Nus hate me; they won't miss me if I go, and Gran doesn't have much longer. It's time to put my plan into action.

★

I do a little goodbye-and-thank-you smile as I look over my shoulder at our HQ for the last time.

I think back again to what Josh said. There *is* a way to buy more time.

I can't *stop* time – that doesn't work. I can't buy *new* time – that was a waste of precious time.

But I can *buy* time.

Old time.

I don't know what happened to the bottle we nearly smashed. But I bet any Cawlington Bottling Co one will work.

There's a line of them along the windowsill in our den, from the time we moved them from my wardrobe shelf to here.

I take one of the bottles. It's full of river weed, a snail and the different grasses we've collected. I slot it gently into my snack pocket and move carefully back to the water's edge on my crutches. I gently pour out the contents of the bottle, saying goodbye to the little water snail inside, then cross to where the stars are on the drain cover brushed back over with grass. I know no one is here, but it doesn't stop me looking around, just in case. A dragonfly bobs by the pebbles on the bank, its blue iridescent body catching the light. I don't think it will tell on me.

In the correct order, I press the bottom of the bottle into the stars. I pause and stand back up before I activate the final one.

I can't work out why Fig helped us. *Was* he helping us?

I'm sure he was. I know he knows something more, about Gran and my mam; there's the star link with her name, and when he was being interrogated he was talking about a 'she' and a 'punishing promise' he'd made.

I pace round and round in a loop to help me process everything.

Those things, the Void Collectors, ten-out-of-ten terrify me, and I don't ever want to see them or smell them again.

What are they doing to Fig right now?

Without instructing them, my feet stop looping. Then I force myself to stand still.

If I want to save Gran, I have to go back.

Back *there*.

I kneel down and press the bottom of the bottle on the final star. I think for a moment that I know it hasn't worked. Of course it wasn't going to work –

And then there's the huge bang.

The river roars and cracks in two. Whooshes up and drops back down, flowing backwards with the gap above the riverbed, leaving the pebbles dry.

I put the bottle down by my feet, then I look behind, sure that at the last moment Titch will burst through the bushes to join me. They don't. I shrug. This is all down to me.

I walk underneath the rushing water, still astonished that I'm not drowning, then I step into the opening in the ground and begin my descent. When I'm halfway down the spiral staircase, the light disappears, and the river closes over the top of me.

No going back now.

I clatter down the stairs as fast as I can without falling. There's no point trying to be quiet: the Void Collectors will know I'm coming.

★

The tunnel is dank and humid. The backwards-flowing stream is high this time. It goes over the top of my trainers, and I nearly slip as I hurry along it. I'm scared of what I might find when I get inside the CBC, what those *things* have done to Fig, what they could do to a human.

More than that, I'm scared of losing my gran forever.

So I keep on going.

I get to the big wooden door and almost expect it to be barred or something. But there it is ahead of me, with the little fist for a doorknob and the greeny, mossy light soaking through.

I need to be quiet.

No, I don't. They know I'm coming.

I need to be *brave*.

'Of course you can,' I hear my gran say. 'You can be anything you want to be!' I know I'm making her voice up in my head, and I know that it's not real, but it's enough to spur me on, and gently and slowly I push the door open.

The place is deserted. There are no crows anywhere.

It's like their staffroom, the place where the teachers keep all the good biscuits. Training bottles line the walls, like the bottle Fig gave to me. Now I need to steal a real one.

Gran's bottle.

I wish I'd spent time just training with Fig, learning more and listening, instead of chasing hare-brained plans that got us all into trouble.

But why did my mam have a tube of 300-million-year-old stars in her pocket?

There are some stray feathers on the ground. Training feathers? Memories that haven't been catalogued yet? Or just plain crow feathers?

The room feels smaller.

It's just a damp, dusty old room without the crows. But I got here via a stairwell that appeared in the bed of the River Cawl as it ran backwards above me when I slotted a bottle into stars.

This is the most un-ordinary dusty old room ever.

I creep across the floor, careful not to barge into anything. The Void Collectors know I'm coming, but there's no need to make it easy for them.

A cobweb brushes against me and I nearly scream, and then I wonder if it's just a cobweb or one of *them*, and I wait for my skin to burn up and roar.

Nothing.

I make my way towards the library. I can't believe that my legs keep on walking. I'm scared of what I'll see. Terrified of what I'll smell, of the screeching noise they make. My hands are primed to block my ears.

I'm more scared of what I *won't* see. That Fig will be gone, and with him everything I need to know.

The tunnel narrows, and my crutches slip into the grooves on the stone floor. Just when I'm doubled up, and I nearly can't walk any more, the space opens back out, and I can stand up again.

This view still makes me gasp even though I knew what to expect.

The shelves are all there. Football-pitch spaces full of them as far as the eye can see; all those bottles and feathers, all those lives gathered.

I shudder – I can't help it. Those wraiths. Those Void

Collector hell-beasts! Looking after those bottles so tenderly, but then terrorizing Fig. Those mouths. The faces they hold. They're just emptiness – long, long, eternal emptiness.

Is that what Gran has to look forward to? I shiver at the thought.

I look across the room. Fig is still in the cage! He looks bedraggled and he's slumped in a corner. I dart between shelves, careful not to knock over any of the bottles. If I did, there would be a domino effect of them all coming crashing down and shattering. I head round one of the shelf ends and nearly run straight into a Void Collector.

It's facing in the opposite direction, and I don't know how it doesn't see me, but I just manage to stop in time and leap back behind the shelf before it turns round. I cower for a moment and peer under the shelf to make sure it heads in the opposite direction. When I think it's gone, I peer back round. Coast clear! I dash across the end of two aisles and get level with Fig.

'*Fig*,' I hiss. He doesn't move.

I look to see if any of the Void Collectors have made a move towards me yet.

'Fig!' I try it a bit louder, and his beak and then his

beady eyes appear through the bars of the cage. 'Look, down here – hurry!'

Fig does, and his wings begin to flutter. 'What the flap are you doings in here? I did a pleading bow to get a yes to you getting to go. I get trapped no flyings. And you keeps tippy-tappying back!'

I don't have time to think what Fig means by *keeps*, and instead I say, 'I've come to rescue you,' which wasn't the plan. But the plan is to find Gran's bottle, and if I'm to do that without Titch or Nus to help me, well, I'll need him.

'You can't rescue me,' says Fig. 'This is where I belong. Always have, always will.'

I need to ask you about that, I think, but out loud I say, 'In a cage?'

'Well, not in particular exactly like that,' replies Fig.

'Fig! I haven't got time for this. Just tell me how to get you down. You can come home with me if you want. Forever! Or just until this dies down. I'm sure it will. People are very good at forgiving and forgetting.'

Fig shudders. 'But Void Collectors is not peoples.'

We seem to be getting sidetracked. In my head, I just assumed Fig would be really grateful and I'd free him immediately, but it's not working out like that. I want to ask him to tell me how to free him, but instead what pops out is, 'I know they're not peoples, so what are they?'

'The Void Collectors are husks,' Fig explains.

He is constantly hopping round his cage, peering this way and that to see if any are looking his way. It unsettles me and makes me even jumpier, and I find myself mimicking him.

'Stand still! Stop drawing attention to yourself.'

'*You* stand still then,' I hiss back at him. 'Husks?'

'They is empty, rolling, roiling shells of people and things. Lost things. None of the feelings, none of the emotions. One job forever and forever and forever – is keeping memories safe from hurting harm. If anything, any hooman or raven, interferes . . .' Fig shudders.

'Like when we nearly smashed the bottle?'

'Exactlies! If I hadn't got to you in time . . .' Fig places his wing over his face and cowers.

'And if we had smashed the bottle?'

'Too forever late!' Fig peers out from under his wing. 'Lost in a web of memories, flitting flapping in a bottle, stuck forever. Smash crash a bottle; no comings back.'

Fig has unwittingly confirmed exactly what I need. I don't know how he knows my gran, or why there are stars in my mam's pocket, but I'll have all the time in the world to find out.

I just need Fig to show me where Gran's bottle is.

'Come on, Fig. Let me help you.'

He huffs and puffs some more and then stands up straight and crosses his wings and turns his back on me. 'Gets out of here!'

I take a risk. 'What would Gran say if she knew I wasn't helping you?'

'How do you have knows about me and your gran?' Fig turns back round to stare at me.

I shrug, which I hope Fig thinks means that I don't want to say, rather than the truth, which is: *I don't know – I guessed. You tell me.*

He huffs a bit, and I just stare at him, and then he points to a handle on the wall. With his wing, he mimes turning it. 'You are carefuls!'

I check the coast is clear and dart across the floor from shelf to shelf, peering out from behind them. I suck in my breath when I look down a row and a Void Collector is tangled round a stack of bottles. It's like they're breathing in the feathers. Or out, blowing on them? I can't tell, but they're engrossed, and I manage to sneak past. Just one row away now.

I run to the wall – but I can barely reach the handle. Titch would have been so much better at this than me! I swipe at it and manage to flip it round one full circle, and I look behind me, and Fig's cage trundles down a way. Still far too high for me to be able to get him out, but it's working!

I look, but none of the Void Collectors have noticed, still too engrossed in the feathers and bottles. I flip the handle again, and Fig comes down another chunk. Just a couple more and I'll be able to reach him. I jump one more time and manage to give the handle a proper welly.

He's down! I turn to scurry back towards Fig, who's leaping about in the cage, pecking at the door, but my crutch gets caught in a mound of dirt and I totter, and I think I've just about held my balance, and I hold myself up, and then in slow motion my foot slips, and I hold out my arms because I'm going now, and all I can hope is that I land quietly and don't hurt myself.

BOOM!

As I crash to the ground, the shelves reverberate like thunder. There is a mighty clattering and jangling as the bottles on the shelves near me teeter, and I think they're all going to fall, and I know that will be a disaster, so I clench my eyes tight shut and wait.

Nothing. I peek out. They're all still upright.

I breathe out in a big *whoosh*. I'm OK. None of the Void Collectors have noticed.

And then the screeching begins.

Mouths – not mouths, *maws* – open on the cobweb wraiths, and there are eyes and bones and brains and people swirling inside, and then they all move and entangle as one, and the smell hits me, and they begin to collide and writhe and move towards me.

Fig yells one word at me from his cage: '*Run!*'

Chapter Twenty-nine

The raven's voice breaks the spell that has me pinned to the spot. I get myself up and grab my crutches.

What is behind me?

I do not look, and I run towards Fig.

I reach up – and there's a lock on the cage! Of *course* there's a lock on the cage.

But what's the key?

I look closer and realize there's not just one keyhole in the lock, but hundreds and hundreds, all star-shaped; all the exact same size as the tube of stars in my pocket. But my stars are all stuck together! It'll take me forever to prise off enough!

'Use the happy paper to split the stars,' says Fig helpfully.

'What does that mean!' I yell. 'Stop speaking in riddles!'

I can't hear footsteps – Void Collectors don't make that noise – but I can *feel* them moving closer and closer. A chill starts through my whole body, and my teeth begin to chatter.

'The happy paper!' screeches Fig. 'I don't know what its word. Blues, pinks and swirls!'

Suddenly I remember the memory of Gran and Grandad getting married. The confetti that was thrown at them, the kiss Gran gave Grandad on his cheek, how he whispered to her . . .

I reach into my pocket, and crumpled in the corner I can feel it. I pull it out, and it's all wadded and faded from going through the wash. I hold it up to Fig. His eyes widen as he looks over my shoulder, and he takes a step back to the other side of the cage, because he can see what I can't. He gulps his beak open and closed.

Breathe, Mimi. Slow your brain down.

I close my eyes and try not to flap. I think of me and Gran making lemon meringue pie together. The way she picks up the butter and flour and rubs them together through her fingers. My fingers mimic hers. The confetti wad begins to crumble as I do so, and the confetti dust falls over the star tube in my other hand.

The tube immediately separates until I have a palmful of hundreds of tiny sliver-stars. I hold my palm out flat, and I blow them towards the lock.

I watch as the little stars twirl and tumble through the air, and they are sucked towards their outlines. When they all hit their targets, there's a clunk as it unlocks, then the cage sways and falls to the ground as the little door swings open.

Fig is out and flying away.

Something is burning my leg. I look down, and cobwebs are trailing towards me. I don't want to see the Void Collectors because I'm scared I'll see Gran's face in them, that she's one of their husks that has been lost, but I can't help it. I'm turning –

Fig darts above me and dive-bombs whatever lurks behind. I can feel the air from his wings and something else, a rotten smell like rancid meat.

'Do not look back!' calls Fig. 'Run!'

He dive-bombs and squawks, and I don't want to leave him like I left him before. But I have to save Gran.

I need to find her bottle, then me and Gran and Grandad can all go into her memory together and smash it closed behind us.

I'm crying and screaming, and I keep running, and the shelves go on forever, and I can feel breath at my back, can smell that rotten smell. Fig is squawking and flapping.

I stumble, but don't quite fall, and I grab a shelf to steady me.

I'm on my knees, panting, desperate. There are no names on the labels; they're all codewords, and I can't work out which one is Gran's!

All the bottles have different sorts of feathers inside: some brown and stubby, some graceful and long. None of them feels like Gran's sort of feather!

Fig swoops down beside me and bats his wing across my face to make me look at the opposite shelf, then flies off, drawing the Void Collectors back towards him. I turn to where he pointed, and there's a bottle with a lilac tint, filled with peacock feathers, yellow canary feathers and a little printed note beside it that simply says ARIA.

A solo in an opera. It must be Gran's bottle.

I grab it, and as I do cobweb smoke grips my hand,

and it burns until it reaches bone, but I will not let go. 'You're not stealing her from me!' I yell. 'She's mine!'

I wrench my hand away, still burning, bubbling, but I have the bottle in it, and I race for the door with the little fist for a handle.

Chapter Thirty

I'm not sure how long I crawl down the corridor after I slam the door behind me. It becomes a tunnel, and then it's filled with water and muck that I don't even want to think about, and I go further than if I was going to the river, and I think I take a wrong turn, and I keep waiting for them all to appear behind me, and I keep looking, and *what have they done to Fig?*

But at least the mucky water doesn't smell as bad as those *things*. And I have Gran's bottle – that's all that matters.

Finally, when I feel like I've been crawling forever and I can't possibly go any further, I reach a metal grate. I push and shove at it, using one of my crutches to lever it. Eventually, it opens up and I tumble out.

I drag myself along the muddy ground, too exhausted to walk. I prop myself up against a fallen tree by the trickle of stream that is the Wentback where it runs through the Denes. Five parks, split by roads: the Sheddy Dene; the Play Dene; the Bowling Dene that now houses an apiary; the Tennis Dene; and, where I am, the Paddly Dene.

The first memory I have of me and Gran fishing for sticklebacks happened right here! I remember my little bucket had a cloud pattern on it. I got so upset at the thought of returning the stickleback to the river that Gran let me bring him home in the bucket.

I need water.

My eyes keep darting to the drainpipe I crawled out from. I keep expecting the Void Collectors to explode out of it.

I've taken something of theirs.

They will come.

I set the bottle down in front of me. The feathers are beautiful and intact. Not a tiny speck of dirt on any one of them.

I look around: the coast is clear. I hear a roar from one of the nearby pubs. Match day. They won't be chucking out any time soon.

I need to check that the bottle really *is* hers.

I can't decide between a bright yellow canary feather and the triumphant peacock feathers. Then I remember the bright yellow of Gran's dress when she sang at the awards night.

The dandelions that weren't buttercups.

'Good choice,' I hear her say, even though I know it's really just me saying it.

I pluck a canary feather out of the bottle and wriggle further forward on my bottom until the stream trickles in front of me. Follow the flow.

Draw the star map.

Lone star, dot.

The sky turns black and thunders, crackles, then cracks.

The cracks spread out across the sky, jerking and juddering, and I shiver and moan: they're heading towards Gran.

I'm still losing her. Is there time for this?

The muddy stream rips in two, churns and swirls until it's running backwards, and then I'm sucked through.

★

It's dark. I reach out and something wafts. Heavy velvet. A curtain? I run my fingers against the pile and it makes me shudder, but I can't help doing it. Like the Strawberry Shortcake paperweight that belonged to my mam.

The curtain is pulled back, and there's an explosion of light. I can't see anything. I blink and blink. There are lights – spotlights – shining in my eyes, from the ceiling and from the front of the . . . what? Stage?

Beyond the lights, I can begin to make out rows and rows of faces. They flow right to the back of the building, and then there are layers and layers of people going up into the sky. They begin to clap and then cheer, and they are on their feet and, well, heck, why not? Pitted, muddy me is about to take my bow when I hear laughter to my left, and out on to the stage walks my gran.

Her hair is wavy and long, she is dressed in a luxurious rich purple gown and her waist is tiny. She looks about eighteen. There are diamonds studded in her hair, and it sparkles as she walks. Her hair looks like it's full of stars. She moves to the centre of the stage, and the whole auditorium quietens.

She has the power, with her smile, to still them all.

The audience holds its breath.

There is not a single sound.

Then the orchestra in the pit soars at the same time as her mouth opens and pure magic pours out. The audience is rapt.

When she finishes, I watch her take a bow as the audience explodes into applause. Roses and lilies are being thrown on to the stage and they pile at her feet. She picks up one pale pink rose. Breathes in its scent, kisses her fingers and throws the kiss out into the audience and then moves offstage into the wings.

I go to grab her arm, tell her how incredible she is. Does she know me? Does she want to stay here?

Would Gran choose this moment to begin her forever?

A young debonair Grandad appears and swings her into his arms and spins her round. She places the rose behind his ear, laughs, kisses him. He sets her down. 'You won't be able to do that any more soon,' she tells him.

He looks puzzled.

'Soon there'll be too much of me to lift,' and she gently places his hand on her tummy. He looks at her again.

'Really?'

'Really,' she tells him.

★

The world ripples, and my ears pop, and I put my hands over my face because my skin feels flobbly, and when I take them away I am back on the side of the stream in the Paddly Dene. That went too quickly!

How do I get them to come with me?

I can work that out. I'll just say it's something for school. Something for English or drama and, if I need to do it, they'll help. I'll go with Grandad to the hospital and take my emergency jar of river water, pretend it's for a project, for homework. We'll all hold on to a feather together.

But which memory? Which one should I choose to be our forever? Because when I smash that bottle there's no coming back.

It was beautiful seeing them like that. I'll just try one more. One or two more. As an experiment, just to make sure . . .

★

Gran and Grandad dancing round their living room and then sitting in front of a map of the world, sticking pins in all the places they'll visit.

Grandad comforting Gran and telling her they'd done all they could, and Gran crying and saying no they hadn't, it was all her fault, she should have loved her harder, and Grandad saying it's not about that, it's time to let her go. And now they have to love me harder to make up for everything I've lost.

In the small office with too many people squashed in, with the smell of coffee and damp and the social workers, and them saying yes, they'd take me home.

Grandad bringing me home in his blue Volvo estate. How carefully he placed me in the seat. The feel of his breath against my cheek.

Gran and Grandad standing in front of the North Cawl Park Bowls Club for the first time, deciding whether it could be our forever home.

Gran holding my hand as I plodge in water, as Grandad fishes for sticklebacks with a bright green net and tips them into my cloud bucket. Him waiting for me to fall asleep and then sneaking the fish back to the river.

★

I burst out of the memory with a gasp. It takes a moment for me to realize I'm grown up now, that I'm not the child with the bucket any more. The evening is getting dark, damp, dusk. The sounds from the pub begin to spill outside. I need to move. Just one more. Just one more moment.

★

In our kitchen above the club. I have hot chocolate with pink and white marshmallows. Gran and Grandad have coffee. I try a mouthful of Grandad's, and it makes me cough. Gran points out of the window. The sun and a star in the sky together. She begins to sing, and I don't know the song. She sings it over and over until I do know it, and we all sing it together.

★

I'm back by the stream with a thump, and my head pounds. The sky is dark.

They could not have loved me any harder.

They gave up everything for me, all their dreams. I stole their dreams from them.

And who knew that they were going to have so little time?

It's unfair, so unfair – but I can make it right.

I hold the button down to turn on my phone so I can see what time it is: 8.34 p.m.

My phone buzzes. Buzzes. Buzzes! It's exploding with previews of message after message from Nus:

What are you . . .

This is ridicul . . .

Where are you . . .

Answer your ph . . .

I place my phone in my pocket without opening the messages. I pick up Gran's bottle with its canary and peacock feathers and begin to carry it carefully home.

Chapter Thirty-one

Mr Marston of the Hats drops me off at the hospital entrance. It's way beyond visiting hours, but I'll just say I'm here to bring Grandad home.

I pull the rucksack tighter to stop it slipping off my arms as I swing on my crutches, safely carrying Gran's Cawlington Bottling Co bottle with its feathers and a jam jar full of the water I scooped out of the stickleback tank. Nus told us always to have an emergency jar.

Don't think about Titch and Nus.

At the corners of my eyes, I think I can see cracks appearing, but when I look they're not really there. And then there they are again, clawing at the corners of my eyes. It's like the world itself is becoming fragile.

I speed up.

When I'm about to go inside, my phone buzzes again. Another message from Nus that there is no way I'm opening. I turn my phone off.

I go in the main automatic doors, bypass the hustle by A & E, then down the corridor and through the doors to the lift. These ones aren't automatic so I have to turn round and shove them open with my bum. In the stark white lighting and the clinical corridors and the signs for all the different departments, it feels impossible to think that a world of crows and feathers and cracks and memories exists. I feel the water sloshing inside the jar, like it's reminding me what I need to do.

I think I might turn back, but I know those cracks, just out of my sight lines, are there waiting, and the Void Collectors are creeping closer . . . I think I can smell them.

They wouldn't dare come here, somewhere so visible and so bright, would they?

I wonder what Gran would do.

I press the lift call button to take me up to the ward.

★

Once I'm out in the corridor, I have to ring the buzzer for someone to let me in. When I press the bell, cracks tremor out from it along the walls. There is the dark, mouldy, musty green smell of the Void Collectors.

They're coming for Gran.

I ring the buzzer again.

Tendrils begin to pour out of the cracks. They lick my fingers and begin to burn. I grit my teeth.

I press and hold the buzzer until someone comes.

The nurse tells me off, but I say I'm here to see my grandad, George Evergreen, that he's here with my gran, Iolene, and it's an emergency. She shakes her head at me, but takes me along the corridor.

I peer into the rooms as we pass, and there are six beds in each, three on each side with sleeping people in them. I gasp. Beside some of the people are cracks, and feathers begin to fall. I watch as they drop from the ceiling.

Some cracks are small, just glitching on the wall near the patient's head. Others are hurtling round the ward, colliding with others, changing course, but always coming back to their source.

'Howay,' says the nurse, 'I haven't got all night,' and she moves me on.

In the next room, there's chaos.

No feathers falling, but the walls are obliterated by cracks, great chunks missing. Someone is trying to get out of bed and shouting and yelling, and the nurses are trying to help them back in, but they're shoving stuff, and in the corner there's a lady with her nightie pulled up, and she's rocking and crying. I must have stopped walking to watch because the nurse touches my elbow this time to hurry me on.

Gran is still in the little side room, all by herself. I push open the door, and when I get inside the cracks are everywhere: tiny lines like the contours on maps filling in all the spaces on the wall. I watch them as they grow and join and divert. There won't be any wall left soon. The thought makes me shiver. I need to move fast.

Grandad is asleep. He's pulled up a chair beside Gran's bed, and he's bent forward, his chin on his chest.

I take the jar of river water out of my backpack and place it on the tray that's wheeled over Gran's bed.

I reach over and gently stroke Grandad's arm. 'Hey, it's me. Mimi.'

His head bobs up, and he looks a bit lost for a moment, then realizes it's me and smiles. 'Hey there, pet lamb. What the heck are you doing here?'

I just give him a little smile because the answer is too

huge and I don't know where to start, and even if I did I don't think he'd believe me.

'Ten-out-of-ten good to see you,' he says, and stands and pulls me into a massive hug. I disappear into it. He's still so strong, and his arms make me feel like everything might just be OK. When he finally lets go, he gestures for me to get a chair.

I sit next to him. 'Is Gran OK?' I ask him.

'Just sleepy, pet. Having lots of lovely dreams, I bet.' He holds her hand.

I take out the bottle of feathers and place it on the tray next to the jar. Then I run through the story I've concocted in my mind, how it's for drama, and it's about spells and potions, Macbeth and the witches, and this is part of my practical exam.

Then, instead, I just say, 'Grandad, there's something I need to tell you.'

Chapter Thirty-two

Grandad stares at me. 'Well, poppet. That's a lot to take in.' He strokes his beard and touches my hand.

'You have to believe me! If we can escape together into the memories, Gran will be safe!'

Once we smash the bottle, the Triangle Trio will be together again — forever.

'I do believe you,' he says.

'You do?'

'Yes.' He smiles at me. 'I trust you with all my heart. I know that you need it all to be true . . . but, Mimi, that doesn't make it real.'

I stare at him. I'm not sure if I've been bamboozled. I try to work my way through what he's just said.

I don't know which feather to use, but I'll just have to guess and hope because there are tendrils coming under the door now, and the smell starts to fill the room. I frantically take the lid off the jar.

'Can you smell that, Grandad?'

'Smell what?'

I'll have to *make* him come with us. He'll believe me when we're all safe together. I grab his hand and place it on a peacock feather from the bottle. I try to take Gran's hand and make her hold it, but she's asleep and she doesn't grip, so her hand keeps sliding off.

'You'll love it!' I say in desperation. 'I've seen the day you and Grandad got married – it might be that one.'

But what if it isn't? I pick up another feather instead.

'Maybe this is your first date, Gran. Or when we caught the sticklebacks together? I'm so sorry I said no when you wanted to go. Gran, please wake up, please.' I stroke her cheek. 'I need you to tell Grandad that this is all real. I know that you've met Fig, that morning before we went to Guru, and I couldn't work out why you were talking about figs, but you were talking about *the* Fig. And you were right! He's back, and he's trying to help us. I just need you to wake up, Gran!'

She doesn't. Grandad stares at me.

'How about this one? I've seen the day you brought me home from the hospital – maybe this is that one! You *have* to pick one. If you don't, I'm just going to choose it for you because we're running out of time!'

Gran stirs, then falls back to sleep. Grandad lets go of her hand and strokes her hair. It's in a bob, not a curl in sight.

'You don't believe me,' I say to Grandad. The frustration makes my body feel like a coiled spring. 'Well, I can prove it. I can fix it all. Just – just take hold of the feather.'

'I do believe you, pet lamb,' he says again. 'I believe *you* believe it's true.'

'WELL, DO IT THEN!' I yell at him. 'Please,' I say more quietly, more desperately. The cracks, the smell, the tendrils are coming closer.

'No,' he says. 'Mimi, no. Because we – you and I – we are needed *right here*. It's cruel and wrong, and my heart is broken in a million pieces, but we need to go forwards not backwards.'

My lower lip begins to tremble, and he pulls me into a bear hug, and I can smell the tobacco from the pipe he doesn't smoke any more, the scent of washing powder, Gran's perfume.

'We stay here, and we let her go, because that's what Gran wants. She wants you to have adventures and fall in love and see the world and be happy and grow old.'

'I don't want to. I don't want to lose her.'

'It doesn't matter what you want. We have to do this bit *for Gran*.'

'I stole your time together,' I whisper into Grandad's neck, which is damp with tears, and I don't know whether they're his or mine. 'I have to give it back to you.'

He shoves me upright. 'What?'

'You were meant to go and travel, and Gran was meant to sing, and you should have had all these adventures, and then I came along and ruined it.'

'Oh, my darling, *our* darling Mimi. You have been our greatest adventure of all. You still are! We get to live through *your* future. But you need to choose to make that happen. Out there. Not in here with us two.'

I wipe my nose on my sleeve.

'They're all stored up there,' he says, and taps on my forehead. Then taps on his. 'We can go to them any time we want.'

I nod. Then I shake my head. He doesn't get it.

An alarm goes off down the corridor, and I hear footsteps running, and Grandad goes to the door to peer out, and the tendrils shrink back from him, but they are there – I can see them writhing round his feet, reaching for me. It's like he's the only thing strong enough to stop them.

'Give your gran a kiss goodbye,' says Grandad. 'You can come back tomorrow evening. You're not meant to be here so late. Is Mr Marston waiting for you?'

But this isn't the plan, I think as the tendrils try to sneak round his feet towards me. *You and Gran are meant to be coming with me.*

I drag him away from the door and slam it closed. Cobwebby fronds ooze through the gap by the hinges.

I'll sneak in tomorrow and wait until they're both asleep, and I'll do it then. I'll just take them with me and explain afterwards.

A tiny crack fizzles along the headboard, and I know I'm running out of time. Tomorrow may be too late.

The smell and the green seep out of the crack and they drip down on to Gran's pillow. Trying to stay away from the Void Collectors is the least of my worries if Gran –

I'm wedged up in the corner with Grandad, trying to keep him away from the door, but they're crawling over Gran's face now, trying to get to the jar.

'No!' I yell, and grab the jar and bottle tight to me.

'Now, you're not going to do anything silly, are you, Mimi? You're in ever such a funny one. Oh, bless you. I need you to promise me you'll just go home and stay put. Mr and Mrs Marston will be there, and so will Subeera. You can have Titch stop over if you want.'

I drop my head. The tendrils recede slightly now Grandad is between them and me.

'Please tell me you've sorted it out with Titch?' he pleads. 'Mimi, you need your friends more than ever right now. Gran knew that.'

I lie and tell Grandad we've made up because I can't bear him to have anything more to worry about. When I've given Gran a kiss, he walks me down the corridor to the door where the nurse let me into the ward.

The cracks unravel as he passes by. He's like a huge wall that stops the tendrils getting to me. I wave back at him through the window in the door to the ward when it closes behind me. The tendrils stay on his side. They don't pass through to mine.

I have a tiny bit of time. I just don't know how much.

Chapter Thirty-three

I've barely slept, and I've moped round my room all day, counting down the seconds until it's time for evening visiting hours again. I've been trying to make sense of everything with Phillip the Stickleback, but he isn't much help. He just swims back and forth in his tank. It really is time to let him go. I'll leave a note for Subeera to ask her to do it once we're gone.

'Thanks for being my friend,' I tell him.

I plunge the jar into the tank, and he swims into the far corner. 'I'm not trying to catch you,' I tell him. 'Just topping up my emergency jar.'

He looks at me, and his spines wave, then he goes back to swimming around and building his nest. It was much better when I could talk things through with Titch and Nus.

I wonder whether they've made emergency jars too? They're probably drinking hot chocolate together right now. I want to be at the river with Titch, swimming and fishing and falling in, and streaming it all for Nus, and her sending messages that are too clever for me and Titch to understand.

I want to make sure that Titch is OK.

The smell of decay has stopped, and there are no tendrils, no cracks appearing, and I can't work out why. It's not as if I've changed my mind.

Maybe they're lying in wait outside. I peer out of my window, but no crows, no cracks, no Void Collectors.

I take my emergency jar and the bottle of feathers and go downstairs to do some moping in the bar until Mr Marston is ready to take me back to the hospital.

I look at the photos on the walls, at the PIRATE sign on the door, all the memories we've made here, and I can't get what Grandad said out of my head. That Gran would want us to stay here.

But she only wants that because she doesn't know that there's another option!

Then I remember that she knows Fig. That she had a

tube of stars too. Maybe she *does* know. My hands begin to flap, and I can hear the humming from the fridges behind the bar, and it's all too noisy, so I put my hands over my ears and screw my eyes tight shut.

When Mr Marston taps me on the shoulder, I jump so high I think I'm going to plant my head in the ceiling.

'Now, Mimi lass, will you answer that blimmin' phone!'

My phone, plugged in behind the bar, is buzzing. Continually. It's so loud. How did I not hear it? I'd locked myself away where nothing could reach me. It's a while since I've had to do that. Not since I became a Stickleback Catcher.

I go over to the bar and grab my phone, and the notifications are full with missed calls, texts, messages, video calls.

'Someone *really* wants to talk to you,' says Mr Marston.

I don't bother reading them all, just text Nus, seeing as how they all seem to be from her:

I'm here.

Where have you been?!

Long story, wassup?

It's Titch. THEY'RE MISSING.

The next moment there's a banging on the door, and Mr Marston is yelling, 'Can't you read? We're closed! I bet they've forgotten their glasses.' And he's walking over to the door. I race to it, barging him out of the way, turn the lock and wrench it open.

Ranveer is standing there in the rain and the dark. 'Nusrat sent me. You've got to come with us.'

Chapter Thirty-four

I make sure I stuff Gran's bottle of feathers and my emergency jar of river water in my backpack before I rush out of the door with Ranveer.

Where on earth is Titch? What's happened to them?

My panic makes me shouty and too fast with my words, and I yell to Mr Marston that this is Nus's brother, and I'm safe, and I need to go, and I'll call soon, but I have no idea if he actually hears any of it.

I run to the car, and the ground is so soggy that my crutches nearly slip, but I correct myself just in time. I grab for the rear door handle.

'No room,' Ranveer says. He opens the front passenger door and shoves me in so I'm sitting forward, resting on my backpack like it's my turtle shell, and he grabs my crutches from me and races to the boot.

There is a little voice from the back, barely audible, which says, 'Hello, Mimi.'

I turn round. Lying down, huddled inside duvets in a big woolly hat with ear defenders and sunglasses, is Nus. I've never seen her out of her bedroom.

'What are you doing here?' I whisper. 'Won't this break you?'

'Maybe,' she says. 'But the Stickleback Catchers are worth it.'

'I am so sorry,' I say. 'I'm so awful. I got so caught up in . . .' I go to explain, but realize this isn't the time. This bit really isn't about me whatsoever. This bit is about my friends and what they need.

'Tell me what you know.'

★

We hurtle along the A66. The stretch with all the roundabouts takes forever.

'How long have they been missing?' I ask Nus, twisting round in my seat. I can see how much effort it takes her to turn her head to look at me.

'Nearly forty-eight hours,' she says.

I breathe out in a whistle. That's two nights away from home.

'Why is no one else out looking for them?' Nus goes to speak, but I say, 'And how do you know they're actually missing?'

'Because their dad phoned me to find out if Titch wanted their phone they'd left behind. He was sure they'd want it to take photos of High Force.'

'You what?' I say as we go round another roundabout, and I lose my grip on the handle, and my head slams into the window.

Ranveer watches in the rear-view mirror as Nus lowers her head. She's pooped. He takes over. 'Titch told their dad that they were on a camping trip with Felicity, a friend of Nusrat's.'

'Who's Felicity?' I ask Nus.

'Your guess is as good as ours,' answers Ranveer when Nus just shakes her head.

'How come you know all this?' I ask him.

'Because we tell each other everything,' he says. 'I'm Nusrat's location scout, sound engineer, sound man . . .' And I realize he's on board with this because he thinks it's all for an episode of *The Puzzler*. I turn back and stare at Nus, and she shrugs.

We turn left at a street corner with cartoon heads painted on the wall, and it looks like they're laughing at us running out of time. Then we drive along a road through a little industrial estate. I can barely see anything beyond the dark and through the rain that hammers at the windscreen so that the wipers can barely keep up. I see the sea through the gaps between the buildings and fences, wind turbines on the horizon.

'Are you sure this is where they'll be?' I ask.

'If Nusrat says so, they will be.' Ranveer grins at his sister in the rear-view mirror, and I think of the Triangle Trio always taking a selfie before we set off, and my heart booms in my chest. 'She's always right.'

'No one believed me that Felicity doesn't exist.' She says it so quietly I have to stick my face right between the two front seats.

'I told my mam, Titch's dad. I even phoned the police.'

'"An active imagination from spending too long away from the world," that's what the police said,' says Ranveer, and I can see his lip curl in anger.

Nus speaks again. 'And I didn't even tell them everything! Just that Titch would be at South Gare, and the tide is coming in. I'm fed up of everyone thinking

that, just because I need to rest, I'm not a proper person.'
She takes her sunglasses off and rubs her eyes and then
puts them back on again.

I should know this. I should know that Nus feels that
way. I bet Titch does. I make a promise that I will learn
everything about Titch and Nus, listen to everything
they want to tell me, do everything I can to support
them.

Just like everything they've done for me.

'Faster, Ranveer, please!' says Nus.

We slow down for a harsh bump where the railway
line that used to carry the steel cuts through the
dirt track, but not enough because there's a mighty
clang and a scratching. Ranveer groans, turns to me,
and I raise my eyebrow in what I hope looks like a
sympathy ouch and sorry, and then he puts his foot
down again.

The old steelworks rear up in silhouette to our left
against a sky laden with pinks and oranges. To our
right, marshland and wild flowers covering the old slag
heaps, leading to the dunes and the marram grass that
slices your legs. I've seen this from the air on maps. It is
the land of lemon tops. I promised I'd come here with
Titch and wave across the river to Nus. And I never did.

Nus checks her phone. 'The tide's really coming in fast now, hurry!' She leans forward and says to Ranveer, 'They'll be on the beach, just before Paddy's Hole.'

'Where exactly?' asks Ranveer.

I look back at Nus, and she nods. Where Titch has told me about so many times, where the hull of the *Seahawk* lies rotting on the sand, where you can collect pink shells that look like butterflies.

'By the boat bones,' I tell him.

★

We screech to a stop, and I fling myself out of the car before Ranveer has a chance to open the door for me. I don't have time to get my crutches. I lurch and stumble up to the top of the hill so I can peer over. The sand is soft under the stubby grass, and it holds me back.

Through the gloom, I can see Titch.

The beach is hiding in shadows and faintly illuminated by the lights from the chemical works over the water. Titch is lying down, curled up in the boat ribs, a Cawlington Bottling Co bottle clasped tightly in their hands.

There are long feathers in it, the tallest I've ever seen.

The tide is curling round the edges of the boat bones, which stick up and out of the water like a giant seaweed-covered ribcage. The water is sucking at the bones, trying to claim them once more, creeping steadily onwards towards Titch.

'Titch!' I yell, but they don't hear me. Or if they do they don't move.

Something catches my eye, and I look over the River Cawl, over the estuary before it joins the sea, towards the towers and lights of the chemical works climbing the horizon. Like spaceships from a sci-fi film, they dominate the sky.

Creeping round the pylons and pillars, it looks like mist, but I recognize those cobwebs, those tendrils, and they are multiplying and reaching out across the river, moving towards Titch.

I scream again at them and then try to make my way down the bank, but without my crutches I can't stay upright. I pick up speed; I tumble and fall, keep rolling and crashing until I'm a heap on the wet sand. I can feel the damp rising up into me. Then the smell of off meat.

The Void Collectors are coming.

Chapter Thirty-five

The little pink shells that Titch has told me about line the beach, and they cut into my hands as I press on them to stand up.

'Titch!'

Still nothing and the tendrils are getting closer, and then the screeching begins. The sky becomes one giant swirling mouth, made from thousands of mouths, all chomping and biting and shrieking. I am trying to run across the beach towards Titch, falling, tangled up in my own feet. I crawl.

The tendrils left me alone because they were coming after Titch instead. What has my friend done that's worse?

I have to get to them before the Void Collectors do.

I'm exhausted and wet and cold, and all of me is covered in scratches and scrapes, but I keep going and finally reach their side and launch myself spreadeagled into them.

'Wake up!'

Titch opens their eyes.

'They're coming for you! Give me the bottle.' I wrench it out of their hands, but they grab hold of the feathers, leaving me with an empty bottle. I look at the label: HOODIE. This is Titch's bottle!

'Give me the feathers,' I say frantically, grasping for them.

Titch doesn't say anything.

'*Give me the feathers!*' I yell it at them this time.

Titch sits up, shrugs and holds them out over the waves that begin to lap at us.

I see that the tide is coming closer. We'll be cut off soon as the water begins to race up from both sides and swallow the bones of the *Seahawk*.

I can see the grip of their hand loosening on the feathers. 'Don't let go,' I say, horrified. '*Why would you do that to your memories?*'

I look over as the screeching and shrieking tumbles through the sky, and the still-just-not-quite-yet submerged sand tendrils that now look like fingers with claws begin to creep towards us.

'Some of us don't have memories we want to hold on to,' Titch says.

'What?' I say. My face wrinkles up. 'What do you mean? What's wrong with your memories?'

'Until your gran put that advert in the paper, I'd say there's not much I wanted to keep hold of. It's all fake with Dad; he tries to be lovely, but there's this massive thing we don't talk about! You're lucky. I bet your bottle would be full of rainbow colours and brightness. My feathers before I met you and your grandparents and Nus are the colour of mud. I don't want to keep those bright new memories if you're ditching me. I'm not going back to how it was before the Stickleback Catchers. I was so lonely.'

'You went back and stole your bottle?' I ask.

'Not just you who had the idea, or who can solve codewords. And you weren't around to care,' says Titch, scraping the toe of their trainer in the sand.

That's what Fig meant by '*And you keeps tippy-tappying back!*' He didn't mean me – that *I* kept coming back – he meant *Titch*. Titch had already been and stolen their bottle.

'You don't care, do you?' says Titch, and I don't know what to say. 'You're leaving me to go and live in the past. I know you're losing your gran, but at least you have her here! I don't have my mam. I need you now!' Titch lies back down and curls up on their side, the water reaching up their body.

'I'm not going anywhere,' I lie.

The sea laps at me where I'm kneeling behind Titch. It's freezing cold, and with each wave it's getting deeper and deeper. Titch refuses to budge even when I try to drag them; they're too heavy, and I'm too wobbly without my crutches. I'm scared they're going to let go of their feathers and they'll be washed away.

What happens to a person who suddenly has no memories? What would happen to my friend?

I try to hold Titch's head and hand above the water. I can hear Ranveer calling our names. The smell of the Void Collectors is all I can taste, and I want to be sick, and their shrieking pierces my ears, but I can't slam my hands over them. I don't flap. I want to, I need to – but not now, not just yet.

'You're lying! I don't believe you,' Titch says. 'You'll leave me too.'

Cracks are forming in the bones of the boat and they're ripping them open, and inside there's dark and decay. Stinking, creeping mould pouring out of the edges, and it's oozing towards Titch.

'It's all about *you*!' Titch yells at me. '*I* need you. Your grandad needs you! Your gran needs you *now*, not *then*.'

'She doesn't know my name,' I whisper.

'She does! Somewhere. Those memories – they're yours too. And some of them are mine. And Nus's. Don't let everyone lose you. *We* need you.'

'I don't want to say goodbye to Gran,' I say.

Titch pulls me down into a tight hug, and the cold of the rising tide bites into my arms. 'But *we* don't want to say goodbye to *you*!'

The water, the mould, the damp, the smell, the tendrils, the burn – they're all gathering closer.

The sky is squalling thunder, crackle, crows. The air is full of crows. Beating their wings and sending the Void Collectors closer to us with every flap.

And suddenly I know that it's true. I'm not lying any more.

I'm *not* going anywhere.

That's why the Void Collectors left me alone.

They knew, before I did, that I wasn't going to smash Gran's bottle.

I have a choice: being stuck in memories of the past or making my way into a future that bewilders and terrifies me, and I'm not sure I can do it without Gran, but I have to try.

She gave me the Stickleback Catchers to do it with. She knew what she was doing all along. Her and Fig, they knew I'd end up here, now, making this choice.

They know I have the power to choose.

The Void Collectors are just husks. They're doing what they're programmed to do – protecting the memories.

And protecting the humans they belong to.

It is our job, as old as stars.

Well, I can do that too.

'Run!' I yell to Titch. 'I can't make it, but you can!'

'No!' Titch screams at me. 'Stickleback Catchers stick together.' They grip on tight to their feathers with one hand and with the other they take mine.

I can hear Ranveer calling for us, frantic, and Titch lies there in the rising sea, staring at me ferociously, and my phone buzzes, and this is here and now, and this is everything I could still have right here and now.

But, if I don't do something, I could lose them all.

I take the Cawlington Bottling Co bottle out of my bag. Gran's feathers fall. I frantically try to grasp them, but they float away on the tide.

I feel Grandad knocking on my forehead, telling me all our memories together are stored in my head. He's right; Titch is right. I don't need her jar or feathers: we've all got her safe in our memories, in our hearts. She has no use for them any more. It's our job to remember her.

Nothing is inevitable. We have a choice. I can choose to do this.

It's hard, it's heart-breaking, but I can do this.

I stand. 'Here!' I scream to the crows and the Void Collector husks swirling in the sky. 'Take this. I'm staying — we're staying together! *You can have the memories.*'

Chapter Thirty-six

The air howls, and the largest crack there has ever been splits the entire sky in two as the whole of the sea is drawn up from the beach, and the waves roar as they roll backwards.

I'm lifted up and snapped through the dark sky with the crows swirling, through the stench of the Void Collectors, and dropped on to the riverbank. The sky is bright blue, not a cloud to be seen. The sea and the boat bones have vanished. So has Titch.

Is Titch OK?

I look behind me. Our den should be over there, but it isn't. There's a faint smell of onion air freshener again – wild garlic in the air, though that season is long past, way back when Titch first shared the secret of their den with me. But where is it? Something isn't right.

There's a scuffling noise and then a cawing that's like fingernails down a blackboard. I look up into a big horse chestnut tree. Bundles of leaves crash to the ground, and then down plummets a scruffy baby raven.

'What's all this then!'

My gran comes hurrying down the bank of the river, in a summer dress with bare feet. She looks the same age as she was on the stage in the memory when she told Grandad she was going to have a baby.

I'm in a memory.

Gran is carrying a picnic basket. She has a little pregnant tummy, and she holds it as she races towards the bedraggled baby raven on the ground.

Gran kneels beside it and scoops it up in her hands, 'Hey there, little scruffy thing,' she says, then she smiles at it. 'George, hurry up, pet! I think we've just found our practice baby!'

Grandad appears from the edges of the scene, and he sees Gran kneeling and walks over to her. 'What on earth are you holding? Can't leave you alone for a moment without you causing ructions.'

'Come and look! It's so sweet.'

Grandad leans over and peers at the fluffball in her hands.

'Weighs as much as a fig,' says Gran.

★

Gran and Grandad vanish in front of my eyes with the baby Fig in her hands. The leaves in the trees swirl, even though there's no wind, then all the trees are spinning. *I'm* spinning, lifting up. The river is picked up too and dropped back down like a huge waterfall and, when it settles, it's running backwards, and I'm sitting next to it in my muddy, torn dungarees. Beside me is Fig, now a scruffy old raven, leaning all his weight against me.

'Less of the scruffy and old,' he says.

I smile at him and stroke his feathers. They spring back up and out at odd angles.

'Gran saved you,' I say. Fig nods and fluffs up his feathers, shakes me off. 'Are you real?' I ask him.

'You know I am real. Your gran knows I am real. Sticklebacks know I am real. And the Stickleback *Catchers* know I am real. That is all that matters, isn't it?'

I nod. 'Did Dr Teller do this?'

Fig cocks his head at me. 'You already know the answer to that.'

'Then why did I see his face in the Void Collectors?'

'They are the collectors of memories. When something is strong and frightening in your head, they *become* it. He was the face of all your fears.'

A dragonfly dances on top of the water, iridescent blue sparkling in the sun.

'How come I could change things, Fig? I thought I wasn't meant to be able to do that.'

'You blimmin' ruddy well wasn't! Love and wantings are stronger than I thought.'

I look beyond Fig to the mighty River Cawl flowing upstream.

Backwards.

'Now it is time,' says Fig. 'It is time for you to follow *your* river.'

I nod, and I begin to cry. 'Forward,' I whisper to him. I stroke the feathers on the back of his neck, and he wiggles his head. 'Will you look after Gran for me?' I ask him.

'I promise,' says Fig. 'You have hoomans going forward to look after now. I look after the hoomans who go backwards through time.'

'Fig, I wish you'd stop talking in riddles. You know you make absolutely no sense?'

'I know it. Perfect, aren't I?' Then he ruffles his feathers and preens and looks all proud.

I laugh. 'Properly perfect.'

'Are you sure this is your wanting?' asks Fig. 'Once you leave, you can never come back.'

I nod.

'Your gran said you'd make that choice. She was – is – very proud of you. Fit to burst!'

I sob and giggle all at once.

'A soggle,' says Fig. 'Now, less face waterworks. You have one final set of jobs to do,' and he plucks a black feather with petrol colours from his right wing and drops it by my hand.

'What?' I say as I pick it up and stroke it along my cheek. It's soft and cool.

'Who do you think draws symbols in beer, leaves notes in pieces of slate, pops newspapers through doors that do not order them? Who reads papers these days anyway?'

'Me?' I ask.

'No,' says Fig. '*We.*'

★

The sky breaks, and the river roars, and I grab for Fig, but he pecks gently at my hand in a raven kiss goodbye and flies out of reach and up into the churning sky. And then I'm tumbling, falling, and the sky is dark, and I am back on the beach. Ranveer is by my side and so is Titch. The rain has stopped and the clouds have gone.

Starlight.

We are on an island, the only bit of the shore that's not full of seawater, and it is beginning to part. The tide is going out, and our way back up the beach towards the car is opening in front of us.

I grab Titch in the biggest hug I can do and whisper into their hair, 'I'm so sorry. You were right and I was wrong. I will never lie to you again. I promise.'

'Pinkie promise?' asks Titch, and I let them go so we can entwine our little fingers.

Ranveer and Titch help me up the beach, back to the car where our Nus, our Puzzler, lies waiting for us to return.

When I'm by the car I slip and crash to my bum and my head flies up. I've never seen the sky so clear and the stars so bright.

Nus winds her window down to check I'm okay and Titch plonks down next to me, leaning their back against the car.

'Look!' I say to them both and point.

There, shining the brightest in all the sky, is the Corvus constellation. A lone star – a raven not a crow – shines the brightest of them all.

I gasp, and Titch takes my hand and reaches in for Nus's, as a shooting star catapults across the sky.

'It's all over,' says Nus so quietly we can barely hear her.

'Not quite,' I say.

The Stickleback Catchers have one more mission to complete.

Chapter Thirty-seven

A week later, I'm sitting beside Gran's bed, holding her hand, as Grandad goes off to get us both a hot chocolate. She won't be in the hospital for much longer; she'll be back home with us soon. She's just staying in here until she's back on her feet again, then we'll be able to manage together. Subeera and Mrs Marston of the Scarves have made a rota; Grandad said it was too much to ask, but they said nonsense and that was the end of it. That's what friends do: they pull together.

I lean over and whisper in Gran's ear. 'Is Fig with you?'

Nothing. Gran smiles at me and hums. It's like she didn't even hear me.

I try again. 'Tell me he's with you – he promised!'

Nothing. Gran just looks puzzled. And that isn't fair on her. So I smile and say, 'Shall we sing?'

Grandad walks in when I'm reaching the end, and then we are all singing together –

'*My love, my heart, goodnight!*'

I go up at the end, and Grandad goes down, sinking his chin in his chest, and suddenly Gran laughs and laughs, and so do we. When Grandad has wiped his eyes and blown his nose, Gran leans over to me and pulls my face towards hers.

She gives me a kiss on the cheek and beams.

She's there! That's my gran. *I am going to treasure you for as long as we have together.*

She puts her hands up so there is one palm on each of my cheeks; her hands feel soft and warm. She looks at me and smiles, and her eyes crinkle, and when I smile back at her I know my eyes are crinkling too.

Then she gently moves my face so her mouth is right up to my ear, so close her breath tickles it. She whispers to me, 'Mimi, remember this.' I lean closer and put my hands up so they're on her face too. We're a mirror of each other. 'Cracks aren't just darkness,' she whispers. 'They also let in the light.'

★

When we leave the hospital, there is a feather on the doorstep. Grandad picks it up and hands it to me. I rotate it in the sunlight. Each teeny-tiny barb, each frond making up a whole. I stroke it against my cheek. It's soft. Tickles.

It's just a feather.

I let it drift gently to the floor and give Grandad's hand a squeeze as we head to the car.

Chapter Thirty-eight

Grandad drops me off at Nus's house, and when Ranveer opens the door he actually says hello to me rather than just grunting, which is a definite improvement.

I rush up the stairs as fast as my crutches will let me. I know Titch is already here, but that's OK because we all tell each other everything now, and they've been editing the last bit of our *Puzzler* podcast episode while I spend time with Gran.

I burst through the door and immediately trip over Titch's hoodie sleeve and hurtle into my dining chair. I'm trying so hard not to laugh loudly I'm shaking, and Titch is giggling their head off, and Nus is shushing them because otherwise her mam will storm in and tell us off.

'Ha!' I whisper to Titch. 'You got shushed by Nus!'

'Shush!' says Nus to me this time, and I can't help it: a massive laugh explodes out of me before I can choke it down.

'The Stickleback Catchers are together,' I say, and grin at them both. 'And we're on a mission.'

'Last time ever,' says Titch, and their eyes go a bit rheumy. Nus gives their hand a little squeeze.

'How did your session go today?' I ask Titch, and they nod.

Titch and their dad are going to counselling together. It's not a quick fix, learning to talk to each other and ask all the unanswered questions, but we're all in it together, helping them through it, and that's what matters. They don't want to talk about it yet, but when they do, *if* they do, we'll be ready to listen.

Nus's fish tank is in front of her, and together we hold the feather that Fig gave me the last time I saw him a week ago.

Together we swirl the water round, and Nus's Mr Stickleback hides in his nest.

We find and follow the flow.

We draw the star map.

We dot Fig's lone star.

The water churns and flows backwards.

The walls of the bedroom disappear, my face is pulled back by the force, and together we are sucked through.

★

The three of us land with a thump at the top of Titch's street.

'You OK?' I ask Nus, and she nods and grins.

Titch stands up and looks up and down their street. 'Why do you think we're here?'

I shrug. No clue.

'Because of her,' Nusrat says excitedly. 'I recognize her from when I went to school.' And she points to the paper girl coming round the top of the street. 'Quick, pick me up!'

Titch carries Nus, and we scurry through a gate that has high hedges round it, and all three of us peer back. The paper girl takes a newspaper from her luminous yellow trolley, then opens the gate and steps out of view up the drive.

'Go!' Titch yells in my face. I protest by dangling my new pink butterfly crutches at them. Nus snorts. 'Aw, for goodness' sake,' grumbles Titch, and they peg it out of our hiding spot, dash to the trolley and nick a paper.

They're just turning into our spot again when the paper girl pops back out and clocks them.

Titch runs faster as the paper girl yells, and they chuck the paper at me as they scoop up Nus.

'Every hooman for themselves!' shouts Nus as she hurtles up the street in Titch's arms. I run after them towards Titch's house to deliver the paper to them, the wrong and very right house, with the advert my gran placed inside.

I zoom up the street on my crutches as the paper girl shouts after me.

I chuck the paper to Nus, and she posts it through Titch's letterbox. The moment it hits the doormat, the front door ripples and dissolves.

★

There's pressure in my ears and when they pop we're all hiding behind a red velvet curtain. At first I think I'm back onstage with Gran, and my heart does a little wibble at the choice I made.

Where are we? mouths Nus.

Titch grins at her. 'Mind your ears because in about thirty seconds there's going to be one heckuva noise.'

'You ready?' Titch asks me, and I nod. 'Jacket or stars?'

'Stars,' I say, and pull a matchstick out of my pocket.

'Three, two, one,' says Titch as they pull out their matchstick and, as soon as we hear the sound of hundreds of birds hitting glass and people screaming, we burst through the curtains and make a dash for the table, just as everyone looks the other way. I watch past-Titch point to where past-me should be looking, and then watch them wriggle away through the crowds to investigate.

Nus keeps watch through the curtains for the moment Grandad will call out to everyone and our moment of distraction will be over.

I draw the star tube, and Titch draws the jacket we've practised so many times this last week as Nus has timed us with her stopwatch.

'Hurry,' she whispers, and Titch and I grin as we shove the pint glasses back in the right spots and race towards Nus.

Titch beams at Jim and Bert as they fly past, and sneaks a fiver into Jim's wallet. They're too busy trying to work out what's going on to notice.

Titch hasn't forgotten the welcome to the club they gave them.

I reach Nus and give her a gentle high five as the curtain is raised, and we rise up with it, and the floor below turns to backwards-flowing water.

★

Falling, floating through nothing, this time we glide down to the river.

'Blimey,' says Titch.

'That's one mahoosive understatement,' says Nus.

I can't find the words to speak. This is incredible. Huge trees I don't recognize tower over us and shade us from the baking sun. We're on a flat plain, and the ground is jagged and cracked like it's hungry for more water.

The mighty River Cawl is just a tiny trickle. It will be thousands of years until it carves out the cliffs, and thousands more until we make our den HQ on its banks.

I can't believe what I'm seeing is real. Next to the few bushes dotted around are herds of duck-billed dinosaurs.

'They're a little bit different to our mallards,' whispers Titch in awe.

'Did we really have to come this far back in time?' I ask. My jaw drops as a herd of brontosaurus walk past us, nibbling at the leaves on the treetops. 'Couldn't we have just written ourselves a note?'

'In wobbly lettering?' asks Nus.

'I can't believe you, the Puzzler, didn't recognize your own blimmin' handwriting on the piece of slate!' I say to her.

Nus shrugs. 'Even a genius can have an off day.'

Titch snorts and we all laugh.

'If you're going to do summat,' says Titch as they pat a little armoured hedgehog thing by their feet, 'do it properly!'

There's a huge squawk above us, and I look up, for a tiny moment believing it might be Fig.

'Oh my stars,' I manage to whisper as a pterodactyl flies overhead.

I pull the purple chalk out of my pocket and hand it to Nus as we all make our way towards the slab of stone, the one – thousands and thousands of years from now – that two not-quite-friends will find on the riverbank, where three nearly-friends will throw a lump of fool's gold to make sure they find their way.

Epilogue

'I am *soooo* unbelievably bored,' I say to Titch, and scuff my feet in the mud at the base of the bandstand where we're sitting the next day.

'Nothing we do now is ever going to compare to seeing dinosaurs, is it?' says Titch forlornly. We have our phones in our hands and are chatting with Nus.

Dinosaur-less days are dull.

'Jinx!' we say and type. Titch and I link little fingers, and it makes my heart pull a tiny bit because that's what me and Gran do.

I left Gran curled up in the flat with Subeera, having

a kazoo-choir session with Mrs Marston and the skateboarder. The skateboarder is called Malcolm and was just waiting for us to finally properly say hello and invite him in. He brings Gran a bunch of flowers every day when he drops in to say hi and show her his moves along the hallway. Titch and I haven't dobbed him in, even though we know he nicks them from the flower beds behind the bandstand.

> Got to go. Mam says two hoomans
> are here to see me.

Titch widens their eyes at me and grins. 'What if it's future-us?' they gasp with glee.

I laugh and thump them. 'Or past-us!' I say.

Birds swirl overhead. Pigeons, starlings, spuggies. No crows. There haven't been any crows here since Ranveer brought us home from the beach.

I hear chatting and look over to the voices. Walking towards us are four girls I vaguely know from my form at school. They're the sort that seem to be naturally good at just hanging about. They're all wearing brightly coloured tracksuits. They wave at me, and I shyly wave back, then they walk over to us.

'Your gran would say they look like Teletubbies,' says Titch, and I nod, but even though it's funny I'm too nervous to laugh.

I get all shy and I don't know where to look. My fingers start to click even though I haven't asked them to.

Tina, the Queen of Hanging Around, says kindly to me, 'Hey, Mimi. You not going to introduce us to your friend?'

So I do. But I do a Grandad trick and stare at their noses, so it's like I'm properly looking at them when I'm not.

'This is Tina,' I tell Titch. Tina smiles. 'And Chanjeet and Hester and Miriam. All she, her. This is Titch,' I tell them, pointing at Titch in case they can't work out who I mean. 'They're my friend.'

Chanjeet smiles at me, then at Titch. 'Just call me Chanj. Nice hoodie.'

'Oh my God!' shrieks Hester. 'I was so going to say that before you!'

'Psychic jinx,' I say, and Tina and Chanj and Hester and Miriam stare at me, and I wish a crack would appear right now and swallow me up. But it doesn't. And then they all start to laugh.

Chanj and Hester link pinkies, just like I do with Gran. This time the thought makes me smile.

'What are you up to?' says Tina.

'Nothing,' I say. Which is true.

'What have you *been* up to?' asks Hester, trying to help me out.

I look at Titch and widen my eyes. *Where would we even begin?*

'Not much,' I say. 'Just hanging out.'

'Hanging out is *sooo* last year,' says Tina.

Miriam is holding her phone at bizarre angles, trying to take a pouty selfie. She nods.

'It got a bit dull,' says Tina.

'A *lot* dull,' says Chanj, and they all laugh.

'Budge up,' says Tina to Titch, and gives them a grin, and when Titch does, she sits down next to them. 'Do you two know anything about that purple building over there with the funny lettering on it? We've been trying to find out how to get in. Proper mystery, innit?'

I go really quiet.

Then Titch says, 'That mystery is *soooo* last year,' and I snort.

To cover up for it, I blurt out, 'We've got a den though.'

'Whoa, really?' says Hester. 'That is well cool.'

Then I feel awful because it was Titch's den first, and maybe I shouldn't have said anything, and I'm only just friends with them again and I don't want to do anything to spoil it, when Titch says, 'Maybe we could show you sometime?'

'Is it good for selfies?' asks Miriam.

'Plenty of natural light!' says Titch, and everyone laughs, and it feels really nice.

We can see Grandad walking towards us, and we all wave, and he waves back, and then Tina says they should be going, but she'll see me at school to get my number, and if Titch wants maybe they could have their number too? Titch nods. And then they go chattering back through the park like a bunch of tropical fluffy birds.

Our phones ping.

Hey.

'Ask Nus who the two hoomans were?' I say, and Titch types that too.

Did you think it was future-you two? BWAHAHAHA.

'Jinx!' we say.

Nus sends more:

> Two friends.
>
> Had funny names.
>
> One with a white streak in her hair.
>
> Wanted my help with some embroidery on a hankie.
>
> Think we've just found our next puzzle.

Titch replies with:

> MATERIAL FOR YOUR NEXT
> PODCAST EPISODE ;-)

Nus sends a smiley face and adds:

> *Our* next podcast. Need to rest.

We're about to say bye when our phones ping again.

Hold on. Mam's here with a box.
Says I need to open it at the same
time as you two.

Nus pings through a photo of a little cardboard box tied with string. There's a purple tag on it with her name on.

Titch and I look at each other and then at Grandad, who has made his way over to us. He hands us identical little boxes, with our names on the tags. He shrugs at us. 'No clue. Just doing what I've been told.'

Now?

Titch types NOW and we open our boxes together.

I untie the string and gently place it in my pocket along with the ribbon from my Guru jacket, a tube of stars, the pebble Titch gave me when we first met, and a conker. I take off the lid and so does Titch.

Inside is a silver necklace, the chain fine and sparkling as the light catches it. There's a silver circle hanging from it, and inside is a layer of glass. Inside that, as if suspended in the air, is a single dandelion seed.

Titch holds theirs up; it's identical to mine. 'Who are they from?' they ask me.

I fasten mine round my neck, and then look at the tag. 'It doesn't say. But I know who.'

'When do you think Gran and Fig did it?' asks Titch.

I shrug, imagining Gran wrapping them up and then giving the parcels to Fig and him wandering into the post office with them dangling from his beak, and the look on the faces of the people inside as he joined the queue for the counter. Or maybe Beryl was tasked by Gran with sending them to us, when the time was right. I think I'll ask her the next time I'm in Guru.

Then I decide I won't. I want to let Gran have one last mystery.

I kiss my finger and place it on the miniature dandelion bauble.

It's beautiful.

It really is.

Thanks, Gran, I whisper inside my head. Then I look up at the sky. *Thanks, Fig. Wherever you are.*

'Are you two ready for your lift to the river?' asks Grandad. 'You've got sticklebacks waiting.'

Titch and I nod and give each other a sloppy high five.

'Still haven't invented a handshake?' asks Grandad as he laughs at us.

'We're working on it,' I say.

'With Nus,' says Titch, and they grin at me.

'Howay then, Stickleback Catchers. I haven't got all day.'

'Can we *finally* go for lemon tops after?' I ask Grandad.

'And take one for Nus!' says Titch.

Grandad nods and walks towards the bowls club. I pick up my crutches, and me and Titch follow him to the car.

It's time for the sticklebacks to go home.

On Language

A Note from the Author

I've made a deliberate choice not to name the impairments and conditions the young people have. This is because for lots of disabled and neurodivergent people they spend a lot of time being medicalized, with doctors prodding and poking, and getting asked rubbish questions like: 'What's wrong with you?' The answer to that, I think, is: 'None of your beeswax, and absolutely nothing' – but that's not always easy to say. We get to choose when and if we disclose such things, not because someone is feeling a bit nosy.

I follow the social model of disability: not the charity model ('oh, poor you!'), and not the medical model (being defined by the long names that doctors use), but one that says disabled and neurodivergent people are brilliant exactly the way they are, and it's the world around them that needs to adapt and change. So that's how it is in this story. I hope that both disabled and non-disabled people, whether they have long complicated names for bits of them or not, will recognize some of themselves in these characters (I certainly do!)* as they take on the world exactly the way they are.

When you're an author you get to create your own world, and this is the world I want to live in. One that contains all sorts of hoomans, kindness and acceptance, access, a little bit of magic – and, most of all, love.

---

* The bits I recognize in myself are needing to do things in loops, being wobbly, and resting, and also that I'm an avid conker collector.

Acknowledgements

Everyone in the acknowledgements in *The Secret of Haven Point* – you're still ace, thank you! Please re-read that version; I'm saving paper.

Booksellers, librarians, bookshops, schools, teachers, pupils, bloggers, fellow lovely authors and readers – you have made the last year beyond extraordinary. I am really humbled and rather teary – thank you for all the support. Special thanks to Drake the Bookshop in Stockton, Waterstones in Darlington, the Rabbit Hole in Brigg, and the north-east trilogy that is Forum Books, the bound and the Accidental Bookshop. Also to Sarah, the legendary librarian at Polam Hall School, who, with Kim from Waterstones, is always coming up with new plans for a Darlo lass's books to conquer the world.

So much gratitude to Helen, my inclusivity reader.

Team Puffin! Cor, you're a bit good, like, aren't you? Thank you for holding my hand and turning this fledgling idea into something I'm so proud of, for making it beautiful. Jane, Nat, Ellie, Wendy, Michelle, PJ, Sophia, Alice, Anthony and Sarah – you are the dream team. Emma, my mentor and first champion – you made everything magical, thank you. Molly, my agent – you make this publishing malarky make sense (no easy task!), have my back at all times, and do the best email titles. Gillian and Valentina, I'm so grateful that you said yes to joining me on another adventure – I'm sure you must be able to hear my squeals of delight whenever I see your artwork (they're really loud).

For me, there is a tipping point when lots of swirling thoughts and scribbles finally come together and create the Big Idea. This story was no exception. Thank you, Gran and Grandad, for taking me bowling when I was little, and to all the fake aunties and uncles who looked after me and fed me ice cream – I wish you were all still with us to be able to read this. Thank you to my home town of Darlington, the mighty River Tees and Cocker Beck flowing through it for being the inspiration for Cawlington, the River Cawl and Wentback. I meddled with you far too much to allow you to keep your names! Special thanks to my walk to my studio through North Lodge Park, where there is a bowls club, a bandstand with star symbols, and the Darlington Bottling Company Ltd building. I still don't know how you get inside . . . Thank you to Mark, the skateboarder, for saying hello to me every single time I pass and complimenting me on my dungarees – you gave me the idea for an integral part of this story when I was stuck. Thank you to Beryl and Guru, an actual real-life person and place, and the heart of this town, who said yes to me popping them in this story. Thank you to the streams and becks and rivers that run through my town, and the boy in the Denes, over a decade ago, who first sparked this idea into life. The places in this book are real; the north east is brilliant; everyone should try a lemon top.

I was fortunate to be a lead artist with MIMA (Middlesbrough Institute of Modern Art) on the Celebrating Age project. It was an absolute privilege to work alongside amazing elders, many of whom are living with dementia. The gran in this book comes to visit the Club, and I know you would have given her such a warm welcome, as you did for me and everyone who shows up at your door; thank you, and your kazoo band is legendary. I'm super proud to be an associate artist with Blue Cabin, an incredible company that works alongside care-experienced young people, and has love at the heart of all the work they do. Thank you to the Oldies and the Young 'Uns, to Jenny, Dawn, Gloria, Lucy, Jane and Amy, and most of all to the incredible young people that I have the absolute fortune to spend time with.

Cake, Mads, Sophie, Alex, Mum, Dad, Mark and Harper Lee. I've run out of words and the ones I have left do not feel adequate. I love you. None of this is possible without you.

PS Mark, sorry for all the conkers, pebbles and feathers that are strewn around the house and keep accidentally going through the washing machine in my pockets. At least they finally came in handy.

About the Illustrators

VALENTINA TORO is a disabled illustrator and children's book writer from Colombia. She has written several children's books published in Latin America and has also worked as an illustrator for publishers around the world. What she likes most about making books is that, in them, she can imagine amazing worlds, like the one in this story.

GILLIAN GAMBLE loves adventures and wandering, rich colours and flights of imagination, people-watching on public transport, cold North Sea air, bobble hats, big questions she can't answer and lying outside looking up and wondering what it's all about. She is a self-taught artist who learned while her babies slept, as well as a multi-award-winning social entrepreneur responsible for starting several community enterprises and a trustee of Unltd, a charity that supports social entrepreneurs across the UK.

Driven by a motto she picked up as a child that 'life is big – be all you can be', Gillian strives to bring a sense of creativity and thoughtfulness to everything she does and to see the wonder in everything and everyone.

Have you read Lisette's debut novel, *The Secret of Haven Point*?

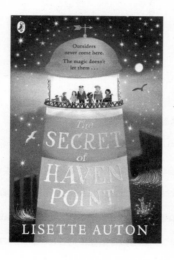

Turn the page for an extract . . .

'A charming tale of found families and mermaids,
with my favourite kind of hero at its heart'
Elle McNicoll, award-winning author of *A Kind of Spark*

Chapter One

Here are the facts:

1. My name is Alpha Lux. *Alpha* because it's the first letter of the Greek alphabet and I was Wreckling number one. *Lux* because the box I was found in had LUX SOAP FLAKES written all over it.
2. My face looks like a flame-grilled jellyfish.
3. I was raised by a mermaid.
4. I always tell the truth.

I'll give you a bit of time to let that sink in.
Ready?
Then let's begin . . .

Chapter Two

I was Haven Point's first Wreckling, but I certainly wasn't the last. There are forty-two of us now, not including the mermaids. When you're a Wreckling, you mainly spend your days squabbling, eating and planning adventures. Well, at least that's what my gang does. Oh, and Wrecklings also carry out *wreckings*, which is how we got our name.

These days we leave blankets in the Lux Soap Flakes box, and it's under the porch so no new Wrecklings have to get damp and cold like I did.

There was a full moon the night Cap'n found me. He thought I was a dead 'un, nowt but blisters and scrawn.

Back then he lived in Old Ben, the lighthouse, all

by himself. (The mermaids only started coming ashore after I arrived.)

Cap'n was outside because he's terrified to sleep on a full moon. He says it's the height of sea-magic and he worries that the waves in his dreams will steal him away. So imagine this: he's leaning on the rat-a-tat tree where the woodpecker lives, watching storm clouds roll across the horizon with the big sea-magic moon in the sky, Old Ben with his red and white stripes standing to attention behind Cap'n just like his shadow.

The full moon sets Cap'n's nerves on edge. It's like he can feel the blood pulsing through him in time with the waves. All his senses are heightened and shadows are making ordinary things look sinister and unreal. And then . . .

(This is where you get to meet me.)

. . . he hears the cats fighting. They sound like babies squalling, and Cap'n is fed up of them unsettling the kitten that lives in his beard. He sighs and gets the broom from the porch.

The whole world is made of shadows on a night like this. His boots crunch along the gravel and then *shloop* into the damp grass as he follows his ears, chuntering to himself as he goes.

There's a box by the wall and he thinks the bloomin' cats must have got themselves stuck in there. It's a really old box; it probably came from one of Cap'n's wreckings. (I'll tell you about them later.) And printed all over the top it says:

Lux Soap Flakes - cares for special things

I guess it did just that.

I love it when Cap'n tells me this next bit, cos he acts it out and does all the faces. He's really good at them.

Cap'n sees that the lid of the box has been closed in that way where the four flaps fold over each other. He doesn't wonder how the box got folded back up after the cats got in. Instead, he's on guard with his broom drawn like a sword because he knows furious cats are about to come hurtling out at him, and the kitten in his beard is mewing and scrabbling.

He holds his breath.

He pauses.

Then whips open the box, closes his eyes and prepares to be attacked.

Nothing happens.

He opens one eye.

He opens the other eye to see if it tells him what the first one did.

He sees me.

'Holy Neptune!' he whispers.

Then he drops the broom and goes helter-skelter skidding on the shloopy grass and rings the huge brass bell, which has a handwritten label above it that says:

EMERGENCY USE ONLY

I mean, I was there and I don't remember any of it. But it's a damn good story the way he tells it.